AMATEURS IN LOVE BOOK ONE

CRAVING *the* PLAYER

HANNAH COWAN

First Edition

Edited by: Faith Lane @faithlaneauthor

Cover Design by: Mary @booksandmoods

ISBN: 978-1-7777818-5-9

Reading Order

Even though all of my books can be read on their own, they all exist in the same world—regardless of series—so for reader clarity, I have included a recommended reading order to give you the ultimate experience possible.
This is also a timeline accurate list.

Lucky Hit (Oakley and Ava) Swift Hat Trick trilogy #1

Between Periods (5 POV Novella) Swift Hat-Trick trilogy #1.5

Blissful Hook (Tyler and Gracie) Swift Hat Trick trilogy #2

Overtime (Matt and Morgan Novella) Swift Hat Trick trilogy #2.5

Craving The Player (Braden and Sierra) Amateurs In Love series #1

Taming The Player (Braden and Sierra) Amateurs In Love series #2

Vital Blindside (Adam and Scarlett) Swift Hat Trick trilogy #3

Come Back To Bed — Sean Stemaly	3:15
Heartless — Diplo, Morgan Wallen, Julia Michaels	3:08
Just Friends — Virginia To Vegas	4:14
Think Of Me — Olivia Lunny	3:39
Sex — Eden	2:30
Side Effects — Carlie Hanson	2:54
Whoever Broke Your Heart — Murphy Elmore	3:04
Shh…Don't Say It — Fletcher	2:40
Like No One Does — Jake Scott	2:42
Beautiful Mistakes — Maroon 5, Megan Thee Stallion	3:16
Hard Boy — Frawley	3:39
Like This — Jake Scott	3:37
Maybe — Jake Scott	4:07
Shivers — Ed Sheeran	3:36
Hate u cuz I don't — Bea Miller	3:09
The Only Exception — Paramore	4:28

Dedicated to all of my ex-boyfriends. Thank you for making me feel unworthy and subpar. Because of you, I pushed myself to find what makes me happy, and have found my self-worth again.

Suck it, assholes.

1

Braden

SHARP NAILS TEAR THEIR WAY DOWN MY BACK, RIPPING through the sensitive skin and drawing blood. The blonde beneath me moans in my ear, begging me to pick up the pace.

We've been going at this for what feels like hours now. She's come more times than I can count, quite the opposite of myself. I've been unwantedly edging myself.

"Just like that!"

My frustration is obvious as I pull out of her in one swift movement and lean back on my legs, dick starting to sag.

"What are you doing?" she whines, lips jutting out in a juicy pout.

"Sorry. I just remembered that I have to go pick up my grandpa's friend's dog from the vet." My tone is dry and careless. I move off of the silk red sheets left in a disarray on her bed and toss the unused condom into the nearby trash can.

"You could say my name, you know." Her breathless voice only frustrates me more. In all honesty, I don't remember her name.

I try to block her out and focus on finding my clothes. I can just about plant a thank you kiss on the lamp in the corner of her room when I spot my button-up hanging from it. "And you expect me to believe that you have to pick up this dog in the middle of the night?"

She doesn't spare me an unconvincing frown as she wraps the blanket around her otherwise naked body—a wise decision on her part. It was her hot body that enticed me enough to come here in the first place, and as much fun as it is to stare at her smooth, olive skin, I already have a terrible case of blue balls. The thought makes me reach down and anxiously rub at my limp cock with a deep, aggravated sigh.

"Sorry, what?" I slide my arms through my shirt. My back burns when the material rubs across the new cuts in my skin.

"What is your deal?" she snaps.

I run a hand through my messy hair and pull my phone from the pocket of my jeans. As soon as I switch it on, I'm met with several texts asking about my whereabouts and disappearance.

"You're unbelievable!" she scoffs, pulling the blanket tighter around her. In a flurry, she rushes into the ensuite bathroom, slamming the door behind her.

Well, that makes things easier.

I pull my keys out of my pocket and the cold metal bites into my palm. The nauseating smell of her fruity perfume wafts throughout the house, making me rush to the front door even faster. I slide my sneakers on and fight back the urge to kick myself in the ass for letting my dick get me in trouble again.

I'm out the door and in the driver's seat of my car before my stomach has a chance to start swirling with disappointment.

―――――

"IF YOU KEEP DROPPING your arms like that, I'll gladly bruise up that pretty face, Clay."

Clayton takes another risky swing at my chest and I roll

my eyes at his poorly placed move. "C'mon, buddy. You gotta do better than that." I grab and twist his arm behind his back. I turn the six-foot ginger around and shove his face into the boxing bag in front of us.

Poor guy didn't stand a chance in hell with that sloppy throw.

"Your mouth twitches before every swing. That needs to stop. Anyone who studies you even in the slightest will know your tells. You'll never win like that. *Ever*." I move back a step and lift my arms into position before nodding for him to try again.

His eyes narrow as he bounces on his feet, observing me. Trying to learn *my* tells. As if I would put them on display for him. Less than a second later, his top lip lifts just the slightest bit, causing mine to lift in a grin.

In an instant I'm tucking myself under his right hook and swinging my left arm. I make contact with his abdomen, and the air is pushed from his lungs in a raspy wheeze. He clutches his stomach and curls over.

"Fuck you," he coughs.

"Damn, I guess I should have put my gloves on. My bad." I shrug.

"Remind me again why I can't have another trainer?" He asks me the question like he doesn't already know the answer while pushing himself upright again. After a few seconds, his grimace slowly evens back out into a scowl.

"Because nobody else wants your whiny ass," I snicker, walking toward my gym bag and pulling out my gloves. The gold stripes wrapping around the slick black material never fail to make my chest swell with pride. I worked day and night to afford these babies, and damn are they *ever* worth it.

"We both know that you just don't want to get rid of me."

"Yeah." I snort. "That's it."

Sliding my hands in my gloves, I clench my fingers and

tighten the Velcro strap. Patting both gloves together, I raise my brow and nod for him to try again.

The balls of my feet tap against the concrete floor as I bounce, keeping my eyes locked on my best friend. He's finally got his arms in the correct position, at least, but the tension in his shoulders worries me.

"Drop your shoulders!" I bark. "You're going to hurt yourself."

"I'm trying," he snaps but drops his shoulder slightly, most likely to humour me more than anything.

Without a second thought I send my fist toward him, but stop mid-throw when he drops his arms just enough to expose his face to me.

I warned him. Pushing my arm forward again, I hear a loud *smack*.

"What the fuck!" he shouts with eyes full of fire as he grabs his now bleeding nose. I bite back my laugh.

"It's not broken. Relax." I grin to myself and give my head a quick shake. "I told you that if you dropped your arms again, I would mess with your pretty face."

I turn away from him and reach into my gym bag, pulling out two towels. After I toss him the darker coloured one for his gushing nose, I keep the lighter one for myself. The sweat covering my bare torso is wiped away quickly before I discard the towel.

"What if you would have broken it?" he groans.

"Then you wouldn't have dropped your arms next time. Take the pain as a learning experience."

"You were coming for my stomach!"

"It looked like I was aiming for your stomach. You would have no idea if that were a trick or not. That's why you don't drop your arms," I say with unwavering confidence. I've trained to be a boxer nearly my entire life, learned almost everything there is to know about the sport. He needs to gain a bit of confidence in me. If my ego weren't the size of

Texas I would have been offended. "Anyways, pizza for dinner?"

"Sure," he replies, voice nasally from the pressure he's applying to his nose. His ability to go with the flow is one of the reasons we get along so well.

"Come on, if you get blood on the floor Dad will kill me." I lead the way to the showers.

"Maybe I'll leave a trail then."

I scowl.

Working for your dad has its benefits, but dealing with his rage when you break one of his rules is not one of them. No bloodshed is the most crucial rule in this gym. It has been since before I can remember. We Lowry men don't follow many rules, but the ones we do, we live by. As if by breaking a single one would throw the entire universe off kilter.

"If you want to go that far, I might as well get a couple more hits in. Soak the floor in your misery," I half-heartedly threaten.

He just scoffs, shaking his head. "I'd like to see you try."

"Yeah? Want to bet on how long you'd last in the ring with me?" I tilt my head and straighten my back so all six-foot-three of me tower over him.

Clay gulps but keeps his lips pressed together. "Whatever. Arrogant bastard."

I laugh. "Always full of compliments, Clay. So, stuffed or regular crust?"

———

"GRAB ME A BEER, WOULD YOU?" I shout as I drop back on the couch. My words are muffled as a slice of pepperoni stuffed-crust pizza is clenched between my teeth.

"Do I look like your damn mother?" Clayton calls back.

I shove my hand between the couch cushions and grab hold of the TV remote. My greasy fingers fiddle with the remote before finding the power button and the familiar sound of my favourite, hot as hell sports announcer fills the room.

"Pretty please can you bring me a beer?" I try again, snickering to myself when I hear the fridge door slam shut.

"Here."

I catch the cold can midair when he throws it toward me like a softball. I turn to face him and crack it open nice and slow. I take a long swig and rest my head back against the couch. "Thanks."

"Don't mention it," he grumbles and sits down beside me, holding out a paper plate. He wears a look that dares me not to use it, so I take it with a huff and set it down on my lap.

My attention drops to my phone when it vibrates, shaking the glass coffee table it's lying on. Reaching for it, I notice the several names spread across the screen.

I lean back and unlock the phone, grinning. A picture of a naked body fills the screen, and my eyes narrow. The girl's athletic, toned figure lies outstretched on what looks to be a bed, with a sheer, white, silky robe sagging off of her narrow shoulders. Her knees are bent, legs are spread wide open, the soft pink skin of her bare pussy glistening between them.

"What are you smirking at?" Clay asks. When I don't answer, he leans over my shoulder to look for himself. "Holy shit. Who is that?"

Locking my phone, I roll my eyes. "Fuck off and go find your own."

"I have my own." He sounds less than mildly confident in that statement.

"Then what are you waiting for?" I raise a brow, testing him before he flips me off and pushes off the couch. "Maybe if you got laid, you wouldn't be so damn uptight. You're acting like a twenty-seven-year-old virgin."

"Not everyone wants to be a 'fuck it and chuck it' kind of

guy until the day they die. We're not all that young anymore, dude."

Registering his words, I nearly blow chunks all over the living room. "I stopped ageing when I turned twenty-four, remember?"

"Right." He snorts.

The reminder of how old we are was unnecessary. It's not like I don't know how close I am to reaching my thirties. With Clay getting his shit together with most things, I'm reminded nearly every damn day of the week. The thought of becoming someone that needs to start meeting society's standards makes a knot form in my stomach the size of Texas and my blood run ice cold.

I feel proud of Clay for realizing what he wants in life goes farther than a good fuck and a cold beer afterward. But his path will never be mine. The whole idea of going to a job I hate five days a week before coming home to a wife and three identical kids waiting on the porch of a two-story suburban home makes me want to kneel and pray to be shipped off to another planet.

Nah, I'm happy with staying twenty-six forever. Society can kiss my pearly white ass for demanding a change

———

I'VE JUST WRAPPED a towel around my waist when Clayton pushes open the bathroom door, eyes droopy and dull as he shoves past me, stopping in front of the sink.

He follows the same routine as every night: wets his toothbrush with cold water, smears a thick line of spearmint toothpaste onto the rough bristles before shoving it into his mouth and brushing his teeth for precisely two minutes. I'm no shrink, but I would confidently diagnose Clay with a case of obsessive-compulsive disorder any day of the week.

We've been living together for two years now, and I'm still

trying to come to grasps with his overly cleanly, organized ways.

After exactly two minutes of scrubbing every square inch of his mouth, Clay spits into the sink and wipes a fresh towel across his lips. He doesn't tear his concentration from the small container of dental floss pinched between his fingers as he mumbles, "I forgot to tell you that there's some sort of concert tomorrow night at SP, and you need to be there."

I raise my brow. "There's a concert? At Sinners? Since when do they do that shit there?"

"Don't know. Ethan got tickets or something from one of the bouncers last week. There's one for both of us."

"Could be fun." I shrug and rub at the sting in my eyes, exhaustion stepping on me with its dirty shoe. I don't give the invitation much thought. Ethan is an eighteen-year-old boy stuck in the body of a twenty-six-year-old man. This isn't the first time that we've been *told* to go to out with him, and it won't be the last. I just nod my head and follow along. Night clubs aren't my venue of choice anymore, but a beer is a beer regardless of where you drink it.

Clayton gives me a nod but doesn't look away from the mirror.

"I'm going to bed. Don't forget that I need you ready to go to the gym at eight," I remind him before leaving the bathroom. I don't get anything more than a brief grunt in response, and I chuckle.

Our two-bedroom apartment—if you could call a full bedroom and a small den without a window two bedrooms—is so damn tiny that it only takes me a whole two seconds to walk down the hallway and reach my room.

I was lucky enough to earn my right to the actual bedroom by sucking back two more shots of tequila than Clay at a pub on Halloween the night before we moved into this place. I'm damn grateful for my stomach of steel, too, since there's no door or a lick of privacy leading to the den Clayton calls the Boom Room. But boom, it does not.

Where I might seem picky about the women I bed, Clayton damn near refuses anyone that doesn't meet his iron-set criteria to the absolute T. It's safe to say the Boom Room is filled with more tepid echo than anything else.

I don't bother turning on the light as I quickly swap out the towel for a pair of briefs that I find in a rare, clean basket of laundry and crawl into bed. When I get under the covers, I close my eyes and pray to God himself that I'll pass the fuck out soon.

2

Sierra

"I'M EXHAUSTED," I GROAN IN DEFEAT.

The three brown bags in my hands—each one filled with enough clothes and uncomfortable shoes to make my bank account and self-confidence beg for mercy—threaten to drop to the floor of the packed shopping mall. I can't say that I would complain if the ruby red high heels my sister forced me to buy ended up lost in the crowd of babbling shoppers, though.

"Tell me about it. At least you get to go home and relax now. I have a daughter just waiting to rip my head off for hiding her tablet before I left." My older sister, Clare, huffs while pulling open the heavy frosted glass door with the name *Courier Strip Mall* scrawled across the pane and leads us into the packed parking lot.

The autumn sun beams down on my exposed, pale shoulders. "At least Liz is cute." I offer her a quick sympathetic smile.

Raising a hand above my eyes, I squint to try and find her car.

"Of course, she is. She takes after me." She fishes out her

keys and hits the lock button twice. When the beeping rings out, we spot the shiny silver car.

Once we reach it, we shove our bags in the trunk. I slide into the front seat and cringe when my bare legs stick to the hot leather seats.

"I want a picture of you tomorrow morning before you go to work, Sierra. I'm so damn proud of you." Clare plops down in the driver's seat with a grin so wide I'm surprised that I don't see the corners of her mouth splitting open. "You got hired by one of the top marketing firms in the country! This is amazing."

My cheeks get warm as I wave her off. "It's a start."

"A start? Sierra, you spent a year working your ass off trying to market freaking dog food at your old job, just to end up even farther back than when you started. By the way, that dog food that in my honest to god opinion, shouldn't even be allowed to be labeled and sold as dog food in the first place. Their name speaks for itself. I mean, come on! *Poochie Goo Dog Food?* No way the ingredients are even legal. I say the job switch is happening at just the right time. I couldn't imagine what other companies Julia would have had you work with had you stayed." She finishes her speech with a long exhale and pulls out of the parking lot.

I fidget in my seat, shaking my legs and twiddling my thumbs to the point Clare reaches over to place a steady hand on them to get me to stop.

I've worked so hard to get this chance. To find a company that actually wants to show off my skills, not just shove a failure of a project in my lap that nobody else wanted so that I can fall to the back of the herd—alone and unnoticed.

Julia Stroll is a successful woman. I had hyped myself up to the point of near explosion the first day I met her, naïve with the idea that she would want to take me under her wing. You know, show me the ropes. Be my *mentor*. Or better yet, a *friend*. I hadn't had many of those after I graduated college. I spent far too many weekends with my nose buried in a textbook or watching Ted Talks to build any friendships that I would want to carry with me in the real world. But from the moment she laid eyes on me—those stone cold, vacant brown eyes—I knew that my perfect idea, my perfect *plan*, had already found its way into the shred pile.

Now here I am, three years and a briefcase full of less than admirable dog food and lice shampoo marketing experience later, about to be the new girl again.

"I'm a bit nervous, honestly," I admit.

"You'll be great. You've worked your ass off for this job. If Liz ever gets lice, I would use Itch Be Gone shampoo without a doubt." She bites the inside of her cheek to avoid laughing.

"Wow, you always know how to say the right thing. How did I get so lucky?"

"I wonder that myself." She smiles with satisfaction and flicks on her signal light before turning into my neighbourhood.

The continuous rows of green spruce trees bring a sense of familiarity to the air that I can almost smell and feel brush my skin. As we pass the beautifully bricked, colonial style houses lining the street, I can't help but feel an inch of jealousy climb up my spine.

After growing up sharing the only extra room in our childhood home with Clare, I've always dreamed about owning one that was a little larger than necessary. Not anything that would feel empty and cold on the days where my future children were at school and my imaginary husband was at work. But somewhere that we would never fully grow out of. A home big enough to host holiday dinners and my weekly book club meetings with all the neighbourhood mothers where we would get drunk off red wine and reminisce on the old days.

I had hoped that I would end up scoring large with one as soon as I finished school, but reality hit like a bitch when I realized I was aiming a bit high. Okay, way high.

Being fresh out of four years of college left me with nothing but a heaping pile of student debt, and a drinking problem that didn't seem too much like a problem at the time. The negative balance in my bank account kept my housing options pretty small once it was time to move out of dorms. I was lucky enough to find a decent-sized apartment within a few weeks of graduating, but my low budget pushed my living quarters way farther away than I had wanted from my old job, and even further from my new one.

The car comes to a slow stop outside of my small two-story apartment as Clare turns down the radio. "I'm serious about the picture, Sierra. I need to see how beautiful you look tomorrow."

I unbuckle my seatbelt. "I will. I promise." There's no way I would live it down if I forget to take the damn picture. Clare would guilt me for it long after I died. Hell, her parting words while leaning over my casket would be, *How could you forget the picture, Sierra? I would have had that picture to look back on today.*

I climb out of the car and with a final goodbye, shut the door and wave.

She rolls down the window. "Love you!"

"Love you too." I blow her a kiss and grab my bags before walking to my building.

———

As I'm placing the last plate into the dishrack, the intercom on my wall wails out a screeching cry. Wiping my wet hands on my cookie monster pajama shorts, I blow a stray piece of hair out of my face and head for the speaker by the front door.

"Open up. I got ice cream!" Sophie's voice pierces my ears. I shake my head and buzz her in.

When it comes to my best friend, I know that ice cream is code for some sort of drama involving her, or something that's about to involve her when she sticks her head in the middle of it.

A minute later, there's a string of knocks on the door.

"What kind of ice cream do you have? And remember, there's only one right answer!" I shout through the door.

"Cookie dough. Now let me in before someone snatches me and leaves you without a best friend. The crime rates lately have skyrocketed."

I unlock the door and step back just before all five-foot-nothing of her plows her way inside, heading straight for the kitchen. The grocery bag she brought is planted on the countertop as she pulls open the cupboard above the sink and turns around with two huge ceramic bowls in her hands.

"Three or four scoops?" she asks, her face hard with concentration as she digs through my utensil drawer for an ice cream scoop. Her perfectly waxed and tattooed eyebrows draw together as she focuses.

"Just two."

Her head turns to me so quickly that my eyes bulge. She cuts a hand through the air. "Three it is."

I move toward the counter and lean a hip against it. "So, are you going to tell me what's wrong or should I start guessing?"

"Nothing," she groans, shoving the scoop in the open tub of ice cream with a surprisingly terrifying amount of force.

"Right." I move around her to grab two spoons. "Then do you wanna tell me what the poor ice cream did to you before you got here?"

"You know Ethan Langton, right?" she asks with a weighted sigh, spinning on the heel of her still booted feet to face me.

"The guy that used to host all of the frat parties in college?"

The guy was a total tool. The only thing he had going for him was his washboard abs. But even then, the appeal faded

14

fast as soon as he opened that sexist mouth of his. Guys who think that a woman belongs in the kitchen in the 21st century have no right being so good looking.

"Unfortunately," she grumbles while grabbing her nearly overflowing bowl of ice cream and stomping across the apartment to my thrifted navy couch.

The four-seater, velvet couch is for better words, extremely out of style and butt ugly. But when you're twenty-six with absolutely nothing to your name but an outdated shirtless firefighter calendar and a pair of scuffed Louboutin's that you got as a present from your ex but are too stubborn to retire, you take what you can get.

"What about him has you so pissed off? We haven't even seen him in years." I grab my bowl and join her. It isn't until after I sink into the couch cushion that I notice the regretful look on her face. I swallow heavily as the realization dawns on me. "Oh. *Oh.* So, you slept together then? I mean, it isn't the end of the world. Right?"

"Isn't the end of the world? I slept with a man child."

Her head falls back and she grumbles a few sentences under her breath in Spanish. I hide my amused grin behind my hand. Sophie only rambles in Spanish when she's flustered, angry, or both. But both is *never* good. And from the flush on her cheeks and the way her back teeth are grinding together, I can only assume that she's definitely both.

Scooping a hefty amount of ice cream onto my spoon, I shove it in my mouth and sit quietly. I wish I could say this is out of character for Sophie, but the girl loves sex. No beating around the bush there. Guy, girl, she wouldn't turn down a tussle in bed with almost anyone. But Ethan Langton? That does surprise me. Overcompensating dickbags aren't usually her go-to, regardless of how deep the itch might be.

"When?" I ask after a few silent seconds.

"Two nights ago. It was a rare moment of weakness. There was a pool, and you've seen Ethan without his shirt."

"I have." I laugh quietly. "He's hot for sure."

"And boy, is he ever packing a rocket."

Crinkling my nose, I brush off her comment. "If it was so good, then why are you upset? Was he too quick on the trigger or something?"

"No! God no," she rushes, dropping her spoon in the melting glob of ice cream. "He wants to, like, go out. *On a date.*"

My brows jump up and questions fill my mouth like I'm playing a game of chubby bunny. But I sit in silence, waiting for her to elaborate. Only she doesn't say anything else. She puts the bowl of melted ice cream beside her and folds her hands together in her lap instead, looking anxiously around the apartment. With a nervous knot rooting in my belly, I try to fill the silence.

"So, are you just not into him then? I mean, a free dinner is a free dinner. Even if it is with a guy like Ethan, and *especially* if the sex was good."

"Maybe if it were dinner I would go. But he invited me to watch some band play at SP tomorrow night and you know how much I hate it there."

He invited her to a club? As a date? Yikes. What's that saying? Disappointed but not surprised?

"I didn't even know they let bands play there." I stretch my legs out in front of me and set my bowl beside Sophie's.

"That's beside the point, Sierra!" She slides a quick hand down her hair and squeezes her eyes shut. "I want to go, but I don't want to go alone. Who knows what would happen to me if I went into the bathroom without a partner."

"I think you're being a little paranoid, babe."

I, for one, haven't been to a club in years. But the memories I do have of the drunken nights spent with my arm laced through Sophie's, and a piece of paper over our drinks still burn in the back of my mind. Her parent's might have let her watch a few too many episodes of Dateline when she was an early teen. We did stay safe though, so I really shouldn't complain. Sophie was always one hell of a safety buddy.

"Why don't you come with me?" Her back straightens as she turns to me with wide eyes. I gulp. "Please?"

"I'm not third-wheeling for you at Sinners. Plus, I'll be way too tired after work."

Grabbing my bowl, I practically run to the kitchen, cursing under my breath when she chases after me, a long blonde ponytail slapping against her back.

"Please do this for me. I'll literally get down on my knees if I have to."

I drop my bowl in the sink and let out a sharp exhale. She won't stop until I agree. I know that for a fact. "You owe me for this. I'm serious."

Flailing arms slide around me, the smell of cotton candy overwhelming. "Yes, I do. You're the freaking best."

"I know. Now let go of me before I get a sugar rush from that damn perfume of yours."

3

Braden

HAVING MADE IT TWENTY-SIX TRIPS AROUND THE SUN HAS ITS benefits, regardless of how shit it might make me feel.

There are countless things that I've learned and collected in my head like a chipmunk storing nuts for the winter. And every once in a while, I make use of all of that information.

I've learned that if you want to be taken seriously in this competitive—sometimes unforgiving world—you have to carry yourself with an unwavering sense of confidence. Without confidence, how do you expect anyone to take you seriously? Without a sense of high-strung determination and power, attempting to skip a long line to get into a club you don't even want to be at would be nearly impossible. But with it . . . that's a whole different story.

"Big Dave, have you been working out?" My voice carries strong across the packed, brightly lit sidewalk as we walk toward the front doors of Sinners Paradise.

The at *least* three-hundred-pound protector of the neon gates turns away from the bloodshot-eyed teen in front of him, his lips lifting in a twitching grin. Clayton chuckles beside me when I raise my hand in a quick wave.

"I have, actually. You can tell?" Dave asks once we push our way in front of two women.

One of them has a waist long, platinum ponytail that reaches the top of her ass and if I had to bet, wouldn't even reach my shoulders with six-inch heels on. The other, a taller, dark-haired beauty grabs my attention by the balls and clasps a tiny fist around my throat, stealing my air. Her eyes are hard, narrowed on the dimple in my chin, and for some fucking reason, that has my blood burning with frustration, I wish that she would shift her gaze to mine.

With a shake of my head, I turn back around and force myself to refocus on the burly, unattractive security guard. "Of course. Those guns could end world wars, buddy."

There's an unnecessary flex of his arms when he puffs out his chest. I chew the inside of my cheek to keep from smiling.

"I'm still waiting for those boxing lessons." Dave says, moving the black rope aside that was keeping us from entering.

"Anytime. You know where to find me." I pat his round arms and nod to Clay for him to follow me inside.

"Are you seriously going to let them in before us?" I hear a snarky voice snap, the strength in the tone taking me by surprise.

Turning around, I lock eyes with a pair of narrowed ones —the colour of molten silver right before it's poured into a mold, glistening in the brass pot. They belong to the brunette I noticed when we first arrived.

She stands with a nearly overwhelming sense of confidence and poise, like she doesn't fear anybody or anything. Like we should all fear *her*. And maybe, if I was any less of an egotistical prick, I would have been terrified to piss her off even further, but that's not me.

Instead, I decide to lift a brow in a silent taunt before crossing my arms and snapping, "That a problem?"

19

Her narrowed eyes roll as she places her hands on one of her full hips. They're nice hips. Ones that I could grab and squeeze and knead in my palms until the skin was red and sore.

"Considering we've been out here waiting for over twenty minutes to get inside, yes. It is a problem."

"Sorry to break it to you, fighter, but that's not my problem," I say.

She laughs humourlessly, shaking her head. "How typical."

I cock my head. "What's that supposed to mean?"

"Leave it, Sierra," her blonde friend sighs.

Sierra, hey? I can already imagine that rolling off my tongue later while I'm fucking that attitude right out of her.

"Have fun inside, Sierra. I would say let's do this again, but I would rather light myself on fire."

Sierra doesn't get a chance to reply before Clay and I are heading inside. I can faintly hear her snap at Dave before we're sucked into the loud music thumping in the club.

I laugh under my breath at the memory of her snarky comments. That one doesn't lack fire, that's for sure.

———

"You made it!" Ethan slurs, stumbling over to our spot at the bar. As graceful as a baby deer, that one.

"I see you started without us." I stretch my neck so I can eye up the crowds grinding and drinking until they stumble, bumping into each other with grins that show they couldn't care less.

Most of these people won't even remember who they met or what songs they dirty danced to when they wake up. But that's what's fun about being young and careless, right? The lack of repercussions for our actions and mistakes. So why does the idea of tipping back shot after shot until I can't manage to walk three steps ahead of me without falling on my face not give me the same buzz as before?

Fuck, I really am getting old.

Ethan grins, naïve to life outside of places like these. "Do you have a drink already?" He's moving toward the bar before Clay and I have a chance to answer. "Two pornstars!" he shouts at the bartender.

"I forgot how annoying he is when he's sloshed!" Clay shouts, bumping my shoulder.

"Just when he's sloshed?" I snort. Clayton laughs.

"Here you go!" Ethan slides the red and blue-filled shot glass toward us with a sense of urgency. Some of the liquid sloshes over the top of the glass and sticks to the bar top.

"Thanks." I throw back the shot and fight back my gag when the horrendously sweet mixture slides down my throat, making my stomach whimper. Ethan is already making his way through the crowd when I push the empty glass back where he used to be.

"I'm going outside for a minute," Clay says, I nod, and he disappears in the crowd.

I settle my forearms on the bar and look around, quickly realizing that there's no way they're fitting a band in here.

Peering over a few heads, I search for anything that the band could even use as a stage but come up empty-handed. Unless they plan to shove a drum set in the middle of the dance floor, I think they're out of luck. Pushing myself away from the bar, I feel a small hand attempt to wrap around my bicep and squeeze.

My jeans pull tighter when I look down and catch an eyeful of a set of creamy tits spilling from a tube top. I place my hand back down on the bar and toss her a star-studded smile. The girl gives me a wicked smile in return. She pushes herself closer to me, sending the blood rushing straight to my groin when her tongue slowly slides along her bottom lip, her hooded eyes locked on mine the entire time.

"Hey, gorgeous," I say, hovering my hand over the bare skin of her lower back.

"Hey, Braden. Do you remember me?" she asks, a slight glimmer of hope lighting up her eyes. I frown.

"No." I sigh, long and hard. As much as I would love to have those tits smother my face all night, I'm not about to lie to get her in bed. That seems to be more Ethan's style than mine.

She stands silent for a moment as she processes my blunt answer. If she were smart, she would turn around and run straight for the hills. Remembering names isn't really my specialty, among other things.

"Fuck you," she spits, dropping her hand from my arm and stalking off.

I run the pad of my thumb over my bottom lip. *You almost did, sweetheart.*

With a dampened mood, I head for the little lit-up bathroom sign across the dance floor. I keep my back rigid as I move around the sweaty bodies, desperately avoiding the couple close to filming a damn porno beside me before I'm stumbling into the back of someone, an uncomfortable groan spilling between us as an elbow hits my spine.

I turn around to yell at whoever shoved me, only to see the back of a short guy as he pushes through the crowd, away from me.

What a damn pussy.

With a scowl, I start for the bathroom again, only to have something firm pushed into my crotch, moving in slow circles against me. Surprised, I drop my eyes to see a round ass grinding against me, matching the deep pulse of the song pounding around us without a care in the world.

Throwing all caution to the wind, I yank the girl closer to me, pressing my front to her back and letting my fingers dig into her flared hips. The smooth material of her black, strappy dress sticks to her body like a second skin, leaving nothing, yet far too much to my imagination as I let my eyes trail over the smooth, freckled skin of her shoulders.

I drop my head and brush the top of her ear with my nose. "You're bold, rubbing against me like we've known each other for years."

"Maybe we have," she replies breathlessly.

Reaching back, she scratches her nails up my arms before gripping onto my bicep and squeezing, pulling me tighter against her until there's no doubt in my mind that she can feel every pulsing inch of me pressed against her.

I move my hands to her exposed shoulders and trace the thin strap resting on her collarbone. She leans back against me and rests her head against my chest, swaying side to side with the music.

Her hair is soft, so fucking soft as I push it off her shoulder and bare her neck. A rich mix of cinnamon and orange penetrates my senses, making my mouth water with the need to drag my tongue over her pulse point and taste every inch of her. A thought that should seem ridiculous, considering I don't even know her name.

"I would have remembered a body like yours," I mumble and spin her around to face me. My breath catches in my throat when the same silver eyes from outside fall on me, this time half hidden by her droopy lids and thick eyelashes. I swallow my groan. "Or maybe I didn't."

Her eyes don't waver from surprise—not like mine. Instead, she presses her hands against my chest, fingers spread wide. I can't help but wonder if she recognizes me. If she does, I would assume from the attitude she had outside that she wouldn't be letting herself touch me or vice versa. But she is. And I would be lying if I said I wasn't hoping that she remembers exactly who I am.

As she keeps her palms flush to my stiff abdominal

muscles, I raise my brows, intrigued and unbearably captivated by the stunning siren in front of me.

Her gaze falls when her touch begins moving up my chest, and heat engulfs my groin as she watches her own movements. She scratches at my t-shirt with white-tipped nails, exploring my chest, moving her hands over my pecs and to my collarbone before eventually wrapping her hands around the back of my neck, fingers looping aggressively in my hair. Her eyes lift to meet mine again. She oozes confidence, and I can feel my underwear stick to the moisture collecting on the tip of my dick.

"I want to know how you got in so easy," she mumbles when I drop a hand to her ass. "Better yet, why didn't you take us in with you?"

I blink, surprised. "Your instant hatred toward me outside wasn't an obvious enough reason?"

She laughs. "Okay. Fair enough."

We continue to dance, but there's only one thing that I can think about. Sierra remembers who I am, and I've subconsciously made it my plan to give her a night that will ensure she never forgets it.

"What if I made it up to you?" I ask.

"How?"

I bend down and lean toward her. My words brush the top of her ear. "Let me take you home instead."

She shivers. "I thought I hated you."

"Hate sex is the best sex."

Sierra pulls back just enough for our eyes to catch. "Take me home then."

That's all I needed to hear. In a flurry, I grab her hand and pull her through the dance floor and out the front doors.

The chilly air nips at our skin, and I use it as an excuse to pull her tight to my side. I push us away from the bystanders still waiting in line to get in, and toward a yellow cab waiting along the curb. Throwing open the door, I let her climb in first before I slide in and pull her onto my lap, pelvis to pelvis.

"42 Clanmore Street," I shoot at the driver before grabbing the back of her neck and pulling her to me, pressing our lips together in a kiss I'm sure I'll still be feeling in the morning.

4

Braden

ALL I TASTE IS CHERRY COKE WHEN MY LIPS MEET HERS. THE addicting flavour has me snaking my tongue between her already parted lips and exploring her mouth.

Her need is as apparent as mine as her hands move over every inch of my chest, like she's trying to memorize the feeling of my skin under her touch the same way that I am with her. Her fingers slide under my shirt, meeting the bare skin with her nails as she drags them along every indent resting there.

My hand fists in her hair, wrapping the long brown strands around my knuckles as I pull her impossibly closer to me. I swallow the gentle moan that slips from her lips when I reach between us and lift her dress, letting my fingers trail up her inner thigh. I keep my touch soft, teasing.

I rest my head against the seat groan when I reach the hem of her panties, the only boundary left between me and the skin I will undoubtedly find swollen and wet.

My knuckle finds her slit, and I know it would be easy to fuck her right here, in the back of this cab, with how wet I find her. "Fuck, you're dripping."

She doesn't answer, only inches back to move her lips to

my neck, sucking, licking, kissing, *worshipping*. I desperately shove away her panties to the side and drag a finger up her sex. She sucks in a breath and her thighs clench around me momentarily before relaxing completely, leaving herself open for my touch. "Yes. *Yes*."

My eyes dare to roll back, the intense feeling I get from hearing her sounds of approval shoots through my veins like a reeling junkie who's just got his fix. I know instantly that I want more of those noises.

I spread her open with two fingers and she hisses from the sudden exposure before I'm sinking a long finger inside of her. *Holy fuck* she's tight, stretching around the intrusion. I press my palm to her swollen flesh and my finger slides deeper with a new sense of urgency.

Sierra lifts herself from my lap until just my first knuckle remains inside of her, and I take the chance to line up a second finger before she comes back down, taking them both this time. My palm slides against her pussy, wetter than before when she begins to rock against it, grinding her clit on my skin. Her face falls in my neck, opened mouthed, and warms the exposed skin with her laboured breaths.

"Is that good? Is this what you want?" I use my free hand to shove down the strap of her dress and free her left breast, grateful when I notice the lack of bra.

Not wanting the cab driver to catch a glimpse of what's mine for the night, I lean toward her chest and suck her pretty pink nipple into my mouth. Her gasp is barely audible, like her body doesn't want anyone to hear it but me. My cock aches, hard as stone as it presses painfully against the zipper of my jeans. I want inside of her. *Now*.

It's like she's running on the same frequency because the next thing I know, her palm is pressing down against me, eliciting a grunt of satisfaction from deep in my throat.

The cab comes to a sudden stop, jerking us forward as my

knuckle rubs against her clit, drawing out a soft cry from her before she jumps from my lap.

"Thank you for the ride!" she squeaks, eyes glazed over, avoiding looking at the driver as she shoves the door open and flies out of the cab.

With pussy-soaked fingers and a hard cock, I manage to pull out a wad of cash before setting it on the passenger seat and sliding out of the cab, not speaking a word to the silent driver.

Slamming the door shut, I turn around and pick up her waiting figure, sliding my hands under her ass and grinning into her hair when her long, toned legs wrap around my waist. Her grip is tight as she presses herself against me, not wasting any time before starting to play with the button of my jeans.

Her impatient touch has me nearly running up the sidewalk and tripping over myself when she slips a hand inside my boxers, grabbing onto my arousal eagerly.

She pulls back slightly when we reach the door but her small hand stays wrapped tightly around my dick. I look down at where she has me in a tight fist, pumping the thick shaft like she loves doing it.

"My cock looks good in your hand, baby."

I would take a picture if I didn't think it would creep her out. It looks like a fucking wet dream.

"It feels even better." Her thumb collects a bead of pre-cum and swirls it over the head. *Jesus Christ.*

I reach into my jeans and grab my keys before opening the apartment door. After slamming it shut behind us, I spin around and slam her back against the wall, cursing into the empty apartment when her grip on me tightens.

"Keep doing that and I'll fuck you right up against this wall," I threaten, dragging my parted lips down her neck and biting the delicate skin hard enough to ensure there will be a mark tomorrow.

"Is that a threat or a promise?" she asks.

No, I want you in my bed. Now.

I move us inside my bedroom, leaving the lights off as I throw her down on the bed. With her knees bent, she lets her legs fall open in front of me, and I lick my lips, desperate to taste her.

I rip off my shirt and throw it across the room before stalking toward her like a predator to prey, only stopping when my thighs hit the mattress. She takes me by surprise when she sits and starts to pull up her dress, keeping her eyes trained on me as it inches up her skin.

My lungs burn, and I realize I've been holding my breath, watching her strip for me.

My jaw slacks, blood burning as I take her in. I knew she was hot, but I didn't realize she was rocking such a dangerous body. A dipped waist met with full hips, thighs that I want to suffocate me, and an ass that any man would kill to feel in his palms. She's fucking gorgeous. And it's more than just her body. It's her narrow cheekbones, plump cheeks, and full lips. Her sharp jaw and round eyes. Fuck, I scored large tonight, that's for sure.

I grab her ankles and pull her to the edge of the bed, watching as her perfect, handful-size tits bounce with the movement. I slide my arms under her thighs and pull her even closer, until I can smell the sweet arousal and see the outline of her pussy through wet panties. With firm hands, I push her thighs apart. My mouth waters.

She pulls off her panties and exposes herself to me.

My cock throbs with need. I'm a starving man, out of control when I see her bare, swollen pussy without the restrictions of her silk underwear. With a groan, I dive between her thighs and run my tongue flat along her wet slit. Her hips buck up at the sudden contact, but I grip her legs and hold her in place, keeping her still.

"More," she pleads, voice shaking. Hearing her without

the spine-straightening confidence that I've quickly learned to expect only intensifies my need to satisfy her.

I want her to unravel in my bare hands. I want her to remember who made her come harder than she ever has long after she walks out my front door tomorrow morning.

"More? You want my tongue inside this tight cunt?"

I let my eyes move from the glistening pink flesh in front of me and work my way up her stomach, paying extra attention to the scar underneath her belly button where a piercing used to be and the large paw print tattoo underneath of her right breast. I chew on my bottom lip to suppress a groan when she palms the same tit, covering both her hardened nipple and tattoo.

My gaze falls to her face quickly, unable to stay focused on anything but her parted lips and eyes so heated I can almost feel them lighting a match to my insides, burning me alive from the inside out.

Dragging one hand to press flat against her hips, I use my other to spread her apart, and begin lapping at her arousal, moaning in the back of my throat at her soft sounds of approval that fall in the dark.

I plunge a finger inside of her before adding another right away with the knowledge of just how ready she is for me. They slip in easily and her eyes shut, chin lifting in the air and hips pushing up from the bed before I'm shoving them back down.

"Play with those nipples for me, Sierra. Need you to come."

My words are nothing short of a demand and she responds without a fight, twisting and pinching both of her tightened peaks between her fingers with a sigh of relief. I have no idea where the sudden need to be vocal is coming from, but I'll take it. Now isn't the time to question this shit.

I pick up my pace, slipping in a third finger and curling them, hitting the spot that has her gasping.

"Don't stop. *God*, I'm almost there."

I wrap my lips around her clit and suck hard enough that it releases with a pop before I punish her with a nip to her swollen flesh. She tries to kick out her legs, fingers gripping the sheets. My next words come out tight and harsh.

"It's Braden. Not God. Say it and I won't stop right now. Don't make me stop, baby. You're taking these fingers so good."

She has me hanging on by a fucking thread. I need to be inside of her, but I also have to know that I made this tight pussy come all over my fingers, soaking my hand while she screams my name.

Sierra tightens around me with each shuttered exhale, and when I suck on her clit for a second time, she stills before every muscle in her body tightens. She reaches her high with her chest rising and lip held between her teeth. I take everything she has to give me with a cocky grin on my lips before slipping my wet fingers into my mouth, staring into her pupil-blown gaze with my own as I suck them off.

I love the way her cheeks flush, as if me sucking her juices from my fingers is more intimate than me just eating her pussy like a starving man.

I crawl over her with the taste of her still on my tongue and reach into the side table, pulling out a condom and covering my cock with it before settling it between her legs. She's warm and wet against me as I rock against her center, feeling myself slip between her folds and my tip brushing her clit on every upstroke.

There's a beautiful flush on her cheeks, and her lashes flutter disbelief before I kiss her. She responds eagerly with a just as bruising kiss before nipping at my bottom lip and slipping her tongue in my mouth, commanding and leading me, using me for her own pleasure. It's so fucking sexy I begin to worry if I'll become a one pump chump once inside her. *I need to calm down.*

Fingers work their way into the hairs at the base of my scalp and yank hard enough to pull our lips apart and expose my neck to her wet, open-mouthed kisses. I need to reel her in. I need to take back the power before I lose it completely.

"You're going to be so tight, aren't you? You could barely take my one finger earlier. I'm going to stretch you out so good," I mumble.

Moving away from her lips, I shove my head in her neck. I begin to feast on the immediately addicting taste of her skin. Peaches and fucking sunshine. I've never compared a taste to goddamn sunshine before, but I would happily do it again because that's the only way to describe it. Warm, clear, *free*. She tastes like fucking sunshine. My hot breath fans out on her skin, bringing goosebumps to the surface.

"I need you inside of me *now*. Stop playing with me," she growls.

I laugh at her attempt at a glare but don't dare disagree. "Put my cock inside you then, *fighter*. Take what you need."

And she does. *Fuck*, she does. My jaw slacks when she guides me inside and then stops, sending me a look that says, *I'm not doing all the work, asshole*. With a brief shake of my head, I thrust the rest of the way inside and bite my tongue hard enough I taste blood when I feel her tighten around me like a damn vice.

"*Fuck yes*. Take every last inch."

Her nails scratch at my back. "Please, just fuck me."

More than satisfied with her plea, I pull out, thrusting back in again when I feel her become more adjusted to my size, building momentum every time my balls slap her ass, filling her to the hilt. I lean back on my knees and pull her toward me, entering her again with a guttural sound that I hardly recognize as coming from my own mouth.

Gripping her ankles, I push her legs up into the air and continue barreling into her, the sound of slapping skin echoing around us, intensifying the electricity zapping in the air every time our bodies meet. I can feel my high building—biting at my spine and forcing my thighs to clench tight. My stomach tightens, and I fumble with her clit, pressing down on it with the pad of my thumb and rotating, determined to get Sierra off before I fill this condom.

"Oh, my god!" she cries, eyes squeezed tightly. "Harder. I'm gonna come."

"That's a good girl. You take this cock so fucking good. Come for me, Sierra."

"*Yes!*" she screams, her pussy clamping down on me, holding me in place just as I feel my orgasm barrel into me.

My head falls back, and I thrust into her again before stopping, muscles quaking and my release filling the condom.

Sierra stays silent, both of us catching desperate breaths. I pull away and discard the used condom before coming back and seeing her lying on her stomach, arm tucked under my pillow, dead asleep.

I swallow down my laughter and mumble under my breath, "Goodnight, then, fighter."

5

Sierra

I'M PULLED OUT OF DREAMLAND ONLY TO HAVE BRIGHT
sunlight burn through my eyes, piercing into my skull. As if
the tequila headache wasn't enough, the nausea swirling in my
belly definitely is.

A thick ink-covered arm weighs down my chest as I try to
focus on the *now*, not the before when I was gulping back
alcohol like water after a marathon, and shaking my ass on
anyone within arm's reach.

Letting out a shaky sigh of regret, I trail my eyes up the
arm and try desperately to ignore the pulse between my legs
that thumps like a raced heartbeat when my heavy eyes fall on
the deep purple bruises covering Braden's throat. Damnitt,
Sierra. Hickeys? Are we *sixteen*?

The memories of last night come flooding in, making it
pound hard enough that I begin rubbing my temples in search
of relief.

Getting drunk was not a part of my plan last night. But
neither was coming home with a guy who reeks of broken
hearts and probably has a nauseating number of nudes in his
camera roll. I want to hate myself for being weak enough to
throw myself at by far the hottest guy I think I've ever seen,

but I'm far too prideful to look past the fact that I actually got him to sleep with me in the first place to follow through with the self-hatred.

I squeeze my eyes shut and try to come up with a plan.

There's no way that I'm staying here to deal with his no-doubt typical morning-after speech, so I guess that only leaves me with one viable option: disappear before he has a chance to rip my self-confidence to shreds.

The last thing I need to deal with is Braden's cocky, pussy wetting arrogance.

What happened last night, I know that that's not me. I'm not the type of woman who drops her panties for the hottest guy that comes up to her at a club. I'm normally too chicken-shit to do anything like that. But last night, I was that woman.

I was the one that other woman whisper about while watching her make a total fool out of herself by falling all over a guy who won't remember her in the morning. And as much as I would love to blame it on the heart-crunching pain I felt watching my ex-boyfriend push the girl he cheated on me with up against the back door of said club, I know that it goes far beyond that.

Braden jostles beside me, pushing the blankets down subconsciously and exposing the hauntingly mesmerizing eight pack to my sleepy eyes. I can almost feel his gentle touch running along my body before I mentally curse myself out. No. Just *no*.

Eying the room, I spot my dress lying across his dresser, my panties somehow looped around the bedroom door handle, and both shoes lying on opposite sides of the small room. He doesn't lack finesse, that's for sure. Or maybe that was all me. At this point, I can't be sure. I seemed to have become a different person last night. One with no inhibition or fears. Just a pair of wet panties and a one-track mind focused solely on the giant god of a man rubbing against me, and dancing along to a thumping beat without tripping over myself.

I want to shove my palm against my forehead at the memory of the arrogant dick parading around outside of the club like he owned the damn place before eyeing me up like a cat to a canary. My anger grows into a full-blown punching attack in my gut when I remember how riled up it made me to have that same man pressing his dick against my ass on the dance floor, and how quickly I had fallen under his lust trap.

Jesus, Sierra. I wasted no time in practically dry humping him on the way outside and letting him do all sorts of things to me in a cab. A *cab!* Heat crawls up my neck.

I use my free hand to peel Braden's fingers from my skin and inhale sharply when his arm topples toward the mattress. He doesn't stir any further, just mumbles something incoherent under his breath before burying his head further into his black pillow case.

I slip from underneath the covers and sigh as the heat that was once suffocating my body is replaced with a light, cold breeze flowing in from the slightly cracked window across the room. I collect my clothes and get dressed quickly, not attempting to hide my shame as I fist the straps of my shoes and open the door. Softly shutting the creaky wood behind me, I wait for the small click and drop my hand.

"Made it," I whisper, relieved.

The sound of a throat clearing has me jumping out of my skin.

"Ah, you must be the owner of the voice I had the pleasure of hearing all night long," a rough voice chides from behind me. There's not even a hint of annoyance in the statement, only utter amusement. I grow confused.

I spin around and gasp, a sweaty palm moving to rest against my throat. My shoes fall to the floor before bouncing a few feet away from me and stopping with a *clunk*. The smug look covering the man's impressively well-carved features is not enough to hide his shit attitude as he eyes me curiously. His low riding boxer shorts remain the only piece of clothing covering his tan skin as he crosses his arms and lifts a thick, confident brow.

Flustered, I quickly collect my shoes and stand up, pulling my dirty dress down as far as I can stretch it, not wanting to flash him. "Uh, yeah. I was just leaving." My words are rushed and almost . . . squeaky? I nearly sprint to the front door.

"You're not going to tell me your name at least? I think you owe me that after you kept me from receiving my proper beauty sleep. Now look at me, my looks are faded," he teases with an exaggerated pout. A large hand runs down his obvious six-pack. He's not as muscular as Braden, but I would have been attracted to him regardless. He's a handsome guy.

"Are you brothers or something?" I ask, not sure why I'm interested. Would it matter if they were?

"Hell no. Not in the ethical sense, at least. I'm Clayton, your bed buddy's better looking best friend."

"Clayton and Braden, clever." I snort. Half squatting, half bending, I put on my shoes.

"Definitely." His mouth quirks. "So, your name?"

"Why does it matter? You'll never see me again."

"Just curious." He shrugs, openly checking me out. I want to reach down and cover my breasts, knowing how open they are for viewing in this dress, but he looks away before I have the chance.

"My name's Sierra. Now can I leave?"

"Sierra, right. I heard that a few times last night."

I narrow my eyes and place my hand on the doorknob, squeezing. "You knew? Then why bother asking in the first place?"

"Double checking." He chuckles, a dimpled smile beaming back at me.

"Great," I groan. "Well, if there isn't anything else, I'll be leaving."

"See ya, sweetheart." He waves me off with a mock salute before I'm walking out the door.

I'm not sure I'm a big fan of this Clayton guy. But then again, I'm sure that I'm not a fan of Braden either.

———

"It was mortifying, Soph. You should have seen the arrogant look on his face when he saw me." I continue ranting to my best friend, wrapping my hair around my finger as I lean back in one of her patio chairs later that day.

"He sounds kind of hot." She takes a big sip of her lemonade, nearly finishing it off in one go.

"Sophie," I reprimand her.

"What? He was, wasn't he? You have to help me out here. Last night was one big cyclone of blurred figures for me."

"Well yeah," I scoff, incredulous. "Not as hot as Braden, though. Not by a long shot." An array of dirty thoughts—or more so memories—infiltrate my scattered brain before I quickly shake them away.

"Right, the guy you ran off on after he rattled your insides like no other guy has before." She shakes her head like a disappointed parent.

Brushing off her last few words, I bite my cheek. "You would have acted the same way. He's too hot, you know? Like the hot you can only read about."

Right," she drawls. "Silly me to think you would have stayed for at least one more orgasm before ditching."

Thoughts of what would have happened if I hadn't run out before Braden woke up have been festering all day. Would we have avoided the painful good morning and moved straight to slipping back under the sheets? Or would he have looked at me with regret and revulsion, questioning why I was still in his bed? I'm not sure the chance of *maybe* having his tongue between my thighs again would have been worth the risk of embarrassment.

"How did it go after I left you and Ethan alone, anyway? You haven't said anything." I change the subject with a newly formed twist in my belly and adjust my sunglasses to distract myself before I can dwell on it for too long.

"Before or after we came here?" she asks coyly.

"You came here?" I ask, startled. "And?"

"I don't kiss and tell." She fights back a grin and her neck flushes.

I send her a pointed look. One that says, *you're really going to pull that shit?* "Hypocrisy at its finest."

"You love me anyway."

"I do. And if you love me, you'll let me out of this damn sun before I turn into a lobster. You know how bad I burn."

My lips tug as I slide my sunglasses up into my hair and stand. I walk around her parent's oversized rectangular pool and pull open the glass patio door. Sophie's sandals slide across the patio tiles as she steps up behind me. A searing pain flames from my shoulder when she flicks my burning back, giggling maniacally before pushing past me.

"Sophie!" I shriek and chase after her, face tense with irritation. Her laughter reverberates through the house and weakens my resolve.

Damn her for falling into the vacant spot of best friend all those years ago. She's exhausting, but I don't think that I could imagine her any other way.

6

Braden

I peel my eyes open, my lips tipping in a lazy smile with the memories of last night. I stretch my arm across the cold sheets, scowling when I don't make contact with the warm body I was expecting. I search the room but come up short of anything but the searing feeling of disappointment.

And here I thought I was going to start my day with breakfast.

My eyes move around the room in search of the clothes that were ripped from Sierra's body last night. She could just be in the bathroom or something. Right? The gnawing in my stomach becomes more intense when I don't see her clothes. I groan, the sound a mixture of pure sexual frustration and . . . rejection? I push myself out of bed and pull on a pair of sweatpants from the dirty laundry bin.

I yank open my bedroom door and breathe in the rich smell of coffee before spotting Clayton draped over the couch. Dressed in only a pair of black boxer briefs, he covers his bare stomach with a bowl of Lucky Charms, milk splattered on his pecs.

"Sierra's not here," he sings while watching last night's Vancouver Warrior's hockey game on our shared flatscreen.

I don't watch a lot of hockey anymore. It unsettles me now more than anything. I guess giving up on one passion to pursue another does that to a person. I chose boxing over hockey and tried to never look back. Some days, I stumble and find myself reminiscing, though. Those are days that I like to forget, sunk deep inside of a woman who won't care if I remember her name in the morning. A woman who doesn't know the old me. The one that I've become accustomed to forgetting.

"What did you do to her?" I move toward him, feeling my skin start to beat with warmth. My harsh tone grasps his attention. He turns to look at me, more curious than afraid.

"Me? Nothing. You, on the other hand." He shakes his head disapprovingly. "She couldn't seem to get out of here fast enough. Are you having problems in the sack? It's okay if you are. I won't judge you."

The devilish grin tugging at his lips makes me think other-wise. "Fuck off." I glare at him, throwing up my middle finger. "Did she say why she was leaving?"

"Nope. But she did look quite upset." I lose his attention as soon as the Warrior's buzzer sounds, the signal that the opposing team scored a goal. "Stop sleeping, defence! What the fuck!"

Yeah. What the fuck? She was upset? After that mind-blowing sex? Yeah right. I might be an egotistical asshole, but I *know* when I satisfy a woman. And last night, she was more than satisfied.

"Her loss," I mutter. I'm not sure if I'm trying to convince myself or Clayton at this point.

I head toward the bathroom, passing my room on the way. I fight back the urge to take a can of Febreze to the whole fucking thing when the smell of her still lingers in the air, clinging on to every possible surface.

I mutter a curse. Just the memory of her sprawled out, exposed and eager for me, on *my* bed is enough to make my dick harden. I don't know if I should feel surprised or pissed that she left without saying goodbye. Maybe I should be relieved. Everything I remember from our conversation outside the club doesn't lead me to believe that she's my type at all. High strung, smart-mouthed women are more Clayton's style. Alcohol was probably the only reason why I found her tolerable last night.

The bathroom window provides more than enough light as I push open the damaged door, cringing when the top hinge threatens to give out. I manage to close it without losing it, and pull open one of the vanity drawers, digging for my toothbrush. When my gaze flickers to my reflection in the mirror, I spot a quick flash of red clinging to my back.

"Holy hell," I mutter, turning in the mirror. I squint and peek at the five long scratches racking down the entirety of my upper back, three of them deep enough to leave scabs on my shoulder blades. *Kitties got claws, that's for sure.*

With a shake of my head, I turn on the shower, more than ready to cleanse myself of last night's sins.

———

WITH A CLEAR HEAD, I step out of the shower, wrap a fluffy white towel around my waist, and leave the steam-filled bathroom.

"Bad time, Son?"

My head snaps to my dad, his brown eyes beaming under the cheap fluorescent lights hung above the kitchen table. He sits with perfect posture, shoulders held high and chin pointed to the sky. With shoulder length brown hair tied back in a loose bun, and a clean-shaven face, he looks way younger than forty-eight. I think it's gone to his head. He's far too confident for his own good. Even more so than me.

"I didn't know you were coming," I reply, too busy moving inside my room and ripping through one of my dresser drawers to look at the annoyed scowl I know he must be wearing.

"I tried calling a few times, but *clearly*," he clears his throat, "you were busy. I was in the area, anyway. Figured I'd just stop by to invite you to dinner in person."

"Come on, Dad. You came here so that I was forced to give you an answer as opposed to ignoring your calls and messages." I straighten my spine, standing stiff, shoulders straight and lifted like I'm preparing myself for a hit from behind.

"I told you not to call her that. She's not a fucking child." He lets out a long sigh, one that lets me know just how pissed off I've made him and how hard he's trying to reign in his anger. "I've let you avoid her long enough."

"Give me a break, Dad."

He waits until I join him in the kitchen before replying. "We're getting married. You can't stop that just because you don't like her."

I rip open the fridge and pull out a bottle of water with a dark laugh. "You're right. I don't like her. And I think you're making a mistake."

His huff is music to my ears. I drink the entire bottle and toss it into the trash.

"She's too young for you. I probably could have fucked her a time or two." I face him and shrug. The blonde swimwear model that can now label herself as his fiancée, is *my* age. What twenty-six-year-old woman wants to marry an old divorced guy with two kids the same age as her unless she has some hidden agenda? Some secret that she doesn't plan on spilling until she has whatever she wants? *Gets* whatever she wants.

See, my mother's new husband is exactly how I pictured—a wrinkly old investment banker/restaurant owner who tries embarrassingly hard to have a substantial part in my life, knowing that we will never be close, but still cares enough to try. That marriage is normal. This one, on the other hand, is *so* not.

How does he expect me to respect this woman? She has no more life experience than I do. Does she even want a family? What is her own family like? Do they support this marriage?

"Braden," he scolds before his jaw clamps shut, back teeth grinding.

I throw my hands up in surrender, leaning back against the counter. "I'll come to dinner, but I make no promises that I'll be able to behave myself."

"Thank you." He nods once, but his eyes remain narrowed and dark, moving around the room so he can avoid looking at me.

H didn't get the answer he wanted, but he's smart enough to take what he can get right now. I won't budge on my feelings so easily.

"It will be my absolute pleasure, Pops." I force a smile and push myself away from the counter. After he sucks in a long breath, he stands up and starts walking to the front door.

He only makes it a few feet away before he stops and turns to face me, looking me in the eyes this time. "Don't forget that I can still kick your ass if you fuck this up for me. You don't understand, and you don't have to. I'm a grown man. But I would appreciate your support. Whatever you think you can give me, I'll take it."

I feel immediately guilty at his confession. I'm a stubborn asshole, but I'm not a complete sack of shit. My relationship with my father is something that I appreciate more than anything. I would never forgive myself if I was the reason we lost that bond. So, I stomach my feelings and give him an inch, knowing Brooks Lowry isn't the guy to take a mile.

"I'll try. But that's all I'll promise."

His eyes lighten the slightest bit, no longer as dark and gloomy. Things have been tense between s recently, but I'll gladly be the one to clear the fog and let the sunshine back through.

"My house tomorrow night at six. Don't be late."

"Yes, sir." I salute him with two fingers, making him laugh as h''he leaves.

It's a loud laugh from deep in his belly. The kind that sounds like pure happiness. A laugh that I'm going to lock away and keep for later, knowing damn well I'm going to need to remember the sound of it tomorrow.

7

Sierra

I HATE DRESSES. THEY'RE ONLY GOOD FOR TWO THINGS. Drawing unwanted male attention to your body, and making you worry that you're going to flash your goods every time that you have to pick something up from the bottom shelf. The chafe currently living between my thighs would be enough to make me throw my stapler across my office in a fit of pained anger if my boss didn't happen to be standing in front of me. He's watching me oddly as I awkwardly shift my ass around on my leather office chair to avoid stripping off the top layer of skin.

"Are you alright?" Cole Travis, the head of marketing at my new job asks, the corner of his lips twitching.

"Yeah, of course." I clear my throat and attempt to sit up straight. The sharp-featured male lets a star-studded smile bless my eyes as he nods, seemingly happy with my reply. He toys with one of his gold cufflinks, drawing my eyes to the crisp, perfectly tailored navy-blue suit he's wearing. A blush pink tie is knotted perfectly at the base of his throat, sticking out against the white dress shirt beneath it. He looks wealthy. Wealthy enough to intimidate me.

"Have you chosen a project yet? I know I gave you quite a few options."

"Almost. I'm stuck between two right now." I smile back, clicking my pen repeatedly before I realize that I'm fidgeting and drop it on my desk, placing my palms on my thighs instead. Somewhere safe.

"I want to ask which two, but I think I'll wait and keep your decision a complete surprise." His eyes move around my surprisingly spacious office when he adds, "I'm excited to see what you accomplish here, Sierra. I don't believe you've ever been pushed to your full potential."

I take his words with a grain of salt, knowing better than most how quickly things can take a turn for the worst. Especially in a company like this. One where disappointment and one wrong move can ruin your career.

"Thank you for the opportunity, sir. So am I." Heat rushes up the back of my neck, and I drop my gaze to my open laptop, a bright, somewhat cliché quote beaming back at me.

A goal without a plan is just a wish.

"I'll check in with you in a few days. If you have any questions—anything at all, don't hesitate to ask." His kind tone is comforting as he gives me one final nod before slipping out the door. A dangerous amount of pride fills my chest as I finally let my grin breakthrough.

"Actually." Cole's voice startles me, causing me to jump slightly. I spot him peeking back through the doorway. "How about you take the afternoon off? It's a beautiful day."

"Are you sure?" I slip my bottom lip between my teeth. Is this some sort of test?

His unique turquoise-coloured eyes hold a playful glimmer as he shakes his head lightly. "I'm sure."

"Thank you, sir."

"Cole works," he replies, winking, before leaving my office —for real this time. Leaning back in my chair, I snatch my phone from my desk drawer and call my sister. She answers on the third ring.

"Sierra? Aren't you working?"

"That's why I'm calling! Now shut up and listen!"

"Okay, okay. Down girl."

"What do you say to margaritas and dancing tonight?" I can't hide my sudden excitement. Happiness warms my blood, and I buzz in my seat. It's been months since Clare and I have gone on a night out together.

"You had me at margarita," she replies excitedly.

"Perfect. Meet me at my house at seven."

Braden

My single-story family home sits on the other side of a newly patched road. It glares at me, mocking my level of nervousness as I continue stalling my arrival.

It's not like I'm not happy that the old man is finally happy again. It's the overwhelming and honestly, disturbing fact that he's marrying someone *I* could be marrying that freaks me out. Out of every other single woman in the world, he had to go and choose someone twenty years his junior. Figures.

I spot my brother's brooding figure in the living room window, his head shaking at something being said to him. It's still so weird using that term. *Brother.*

"Crap," I mutter when Tyler's head turns to the street, blowing my cover when our dad follows his gaze, eyeing me up. Throwing open my door with a louder than needed groan, I head to the house.

"Jerking off out there or something?" Tyler asks the second I walk inside and kick off my shoes.

"Fuck off."

"No can do, buddy. Lana made us a fancy dinner that we definitely don't want to miss." His annoyed expression matches mine to a T, not like I'm the least bit surprised. Tyler and I are similar enough that if you hadn't ever witnessed his grumpy "I hate the world" attitude and borderline anger issues, you would assume that we were twins. Of course, I'm the better-looking brother, but that's a discussion for another day.

"Did she? I can't wait."

"Drop the sarcasm, dip shits. She can hear you," Dad snaps, his voice menacingly low. Dropping down on the cushion beside Tyler, I lift my brows and clasp my hands behind my head.

"Where's your wife? How come she gets a pass on dinner?" My question is directed at Tyler, but I look to my dad as he leans against the large arch separating the kitchen from the living room, wearing an innocent expression. One that says, *Gracie is my favourite, that's why*.

"She's teaching a dance camp," Tyler says, smiling ever so slightly.

He's proud of his wife, no doubt. She opened her own dance studio last year, using it to help little kids whose parents can't afford regular dance lessons. She doesn't charge them anything. Not for their uniforms, shoes, or competitions. It's really something out of a fairytale for those excited new ballerinas. Something that Gracie's able to do because of the millions racking up in my brother's bank account from years spent playing professional hockey for the Vancouver Warriors. They're both so incredibly selfless that it makes me want to be better. *Do* better. Unfortunately for me, it's not that easy.

"I hope everyone's hungry!"

Oh, joy to the fucking world. Here she comes.

Three sets of eyes fall on Lana as she comes rushing into the living room, an apron wrapped around what looks to be a very tight red dress matched with a pair of terrifyingly tall heels—always dressing to impress, this one.

"Starving," Dad replies sweetly, slipping an arm around her waist. He looks hopelessly in love with her. It should make me happier to see him like this.

"Brooks!" She giggles when Dad's hand disappears behind her, grabbing her ass. Holding back my vomit, I turn to see Tyler doing the same. His hand moves to shield his eyes.

"Dad." I clear my throat. I can feel my eyes rolling when he ignores me and starts placing sloppy kisses on Lana's exposed shoulder. "Dad, the food's going to be cold," I say again, louder this time.

"Right!" Lana's the one to pull away first, finally taking notice of the people around her. "The kids must be starving, baby."

Her comment has my nostrils flaring. I'm *not* a kid.

"Right, right. Sorry." Dad chuckles nervously before waving us toward the kitchen.

"Thanks. For a minute there I thought I was going to empty the contents of my stomach on the floor," Tyler mumbles under his breath when we reluctantly start to follow Dad toward the kitchen.

"Next time it's on you."

There are no number of mental speeches I can recite in order to feel prepared for this dinner. No matter what I say, or how many fake smiles I wear, I'll never accept Lana as his wife. I don't know how, and I'm not sure I'll ever even want to.

"Deal," Tyler agrees.

"What the fuck?" I say under my breath when we reach the kitchen. "It smells like a teenage girl's bedroom in here."

At least ten vanilla scented candles stretch across the length of the new, sleek black table placed in the center of my dad's outdated, crowded kitchen. The dark wood looks like it can seat at least eight people, which is confusing in itself, considering that there are only five of us on a good day.

What limited walking space there used to be in this yellow-lit room has shrunk by more than half. Tyler and I are forced to walk shoulder to shoulder just to get to two empty chairs on the left side. We choose the ones farthest from the Stacey's mom wannabe so we don't have to listen to the love birds whisper dirty things to each other when we inevitably fall into tense moments of awkward silence.

Dad sits across from us with Lana on his right. He wears a broad smile while rubbing his stomach in big circles. "This looks delicious."

I can sense the double meaning in his words before I see his gaze moving up and down his fiancée's body with a nod of approval. It's something I would say if I were in his shoes. It takes a solid two minutes before he actually looks at the overly extravagant meal laid out across the yellow, tulip covered table runner.

"I made all your favourites!" Lana smiles wide, proud of herself.

Oh, I bet you did.

Cocking my brow, I trail my eyes over every dish, getting more confused by the second. Kale salad, salmon with tofu. Is that *quinoa?*

"When did you start eating rabbit food, Dad?"

His tight-lipped scowl doesn't pack the same punch it did when I was younger. I easily brush it off and speak again.

"If I had known that she was stuffing you full of green shit, I would have brought pizza." My lips lift slightly when I hear Tyler snicker before attempting to cover it with a cough.

"Braden," Dad snaps, steam nearly shooting from his ears.

I can't seem to shut myself up, though. Something about seeing someone make him eat like he isn't already as healthy as a fucking horse makes my insides churn. My dad has been a boxer for his entire life. He's probably healthier than I am. He doesn't need to be on a damn diet. Lana clearly doesn't understand how much we need to eat to keep up with the sport so that we don't wither away to nothing. Dad's probably just too nice to say anything.

"Yes, Father?" I sing, watching as he tightens his grip on the edge of the table, fingertips turning white.

"It's okay, Brooks," Mommy Dearest sighs. She places her hand on top of his in hopes of relaxing him. The rock on her ring finger that emptied out the entirety of my dad's savings account sparkles under the hanging light. If I have to sit here any longer, I might just end up eating my own fucking tongue for dinner. She looks at me. "I'm just trying to keep his cholesterol down."

"His *cholesterol?*" I nearly choke on my spit. My head spins in my dad's direction now, my eyes flaring with unspoken anger. "Do you have high cholesterol?"

He blinks a few times, mouth unmoving. His shoulders vibrate, most likely from shaking a long leg beneath the table. I lift my brows and clear my throat, growing impatient. "Do you, Dad?"

"No. But it's always good to take precau—"

I stop him mid-sentence. "Well then. I'm glad that that's settled. But as much as I would love to eat *whatever* is in front of us, I actually think that I left my fridge open." I click my tongue, planting a disappointed smile on my face. It's clear nobody buys the quickly thought up excuse, but I honestly could care less. "Clayton would kill me if I let his yogurt spoil. You know how he is, right, Dad? Just crazy about that yogurt."

"Don't you dare leave me here alone," Tyler threatens in a low voice, turning to watch me stand up from my chair.

"Sorry, Ty." I mean it. "I didn't sign up for this."

"Neither did I!" he replies, voice raising an octave.

"Braden Christopher Lowry," Dad growls, standing up, his chair sliding across the tile before smacking against the wall with a decent amount of force. "Sit back down. *Now.*"

"Don't use your '*dad voice*' on me." I laugh, brushing away

52

his red-faced anger like it's nothing. "It doesn't work anymore."

It's not hard to imagine the lengthy list of colourful words he's thinking about yelling at me from across the table as I roughly push my chair in and lift my glass of water, finishing it in a single gulp. He chooses to keep them all to himself, for Lana, I suppose.

"It was lovely to see you, Lana. Maybe pizza next time, though?"

Her glossy lips open like she's going to say something before she nods her head instead, not muttering a single word.

"Awesome. I'll leave you guys to it then." I shoot my dad a dimpled grin before walking away from them, not stopping until I feel the cool breeze on my skin.

————

I'VE ONCE AGAIN FOUND myself stuck in the shittiest bar in town, a dewy long-neck bottle cool against my warm palm.

I don't wander my way over to Jim's for the expensive beer or the rude bikers smoking their joints in the back-corner booths—but for the silence. It's an odd place to go in search of silence, but that's exactly what I find here every single time.

Jim's is far from a busy place, which means I can come here to think without anyone breathing down my neck asking me if I'm okay. If I need to *talk.* I'm positive that I don't have half as much shit going on in my life as most of these other fuckers trying to drown their feelings with overpriced whiskey, but we all have one remarkably simple personality trait in common.

We're all selfish, unapologetic pricks in need of some place to relax. Everyone here has a story, one that they don't ever plan on sharing with anyone.

Maybe they lost everything in a divorce because they were too prideful to apologize after every fight with their ex. Maybe they're losing at some sort of internal battle that could have easily been won by a few trips to a therapist. Or, just maybe, they could be struggling with the realization that their life means nothing past boxing matches and pussy, yet not have the want or fire under their ass to do anything more. Wait, that one's just me.

Nobody cares what your story is once you cross the threshold and breathe in the old wood smell that paints the air of Jim's. You're just another faceless figure here. Just how I like it.

"Want another?" A familiar voice asks. I simply nod and meet Jade's vacant stare with my own.

Jade is one of the only two bartenders in this dump. She's a single mom recovering from years of cocaine addiction while working every night at a place full of *other* addicts. Ones who are either in the middle of recovering, pretending to be recovering from something, or boldly refusing to recover. I feel for her, I really do.

"How's your baby girl?" I slide my empty bottle of beer across the counter before grabbing the new one, raising it to my lips and taking a long swig. Jade slings a small white towel over her shoulder before cracking open her own beer and copying my movements.

"Excited to be starting preschool next month," she replies with a small, rare smile that I only see when she's talking about her daughter, Samantha.

I return the smile before taking another sip. "And her dad?"

The skinny prick used to show up here every night, blown out of his mind and just itching for a fight. Most of the guys, myself included, used to love giving him a reason to throw his fists around so Jade didn't have to be on the receiving end once she got home. Finally, after a hard long year of seeing her show up to work covered in more colours than a colour wheel, she kicked him to the curb.

"Hasn't shown up since. You don't have to keep worrying, Braden," she teases, but I can see the appreciation pass through her green eyes.

I shrug. "As long as you and Smartie are safe."

Her smile is genuine—warm even, as she sighs and pulls the towel off of her shoulder, opting to wipe the counter. Our conversation ends when I see her turn her attention to the shadow walking up to the bar, stopping a few feet away from me.

"Could I get two Margaritas?"

"Sure," Jade replies, the amusement in her tone puts a smirk on my lips. I don't miss the barely there noise of disbelief she makes while moving down the bar to mix the drinks.

Turning to look at the oblivious woman beside me, the one who ordered a girly mixed drink in a bar full of old men and doped up bikers, I shake my head.

"I think you stumbled into the wrong place, Barbie."

With her fancy designer bag, platinum blonde hair, and glossy pink lips, the girl looks like she was meant to be at Sinner's, not this hole in the wall dumpster fire.

"My name's not Barbie, asshat," she shoots back with an angry scoff. There's a look in her eyes that I can't exactly pinpoint. A look that says, *I think I know you, but I can't be too sure.* It confuses yet intrigues me.

I push my now empty beer bottle away from me before resting my elbows on the bar and leaning forward, testing her. "And my name's not asshat, but you already knew that."

"Right," she hums in agreement. "It's Braden." She avoids any further eye contact, staring forward at the wall of glass bottles so that I have trouble catching the slight twitch in the corner of her mouth.

"Do I know you?" I ask tightly. When I was younger, I would have taken her knowledge of me as a compliment. But now, with a famous half-brother and a newfound love for privacy, I'm not that guy anymore.

"Not really."

My face tightens as I zone in on her proud expression. What the fuck does that mean?

"Here you go. I'm sorry that it took so long. We don't usually carry the mix up front," Jade mutters, joining us again, this time with two green slushie filled glasses.

"That's okay. Thank you." The blonde shoots her a look of appreciation, wrapping her small hands around the two glasses, and glaring at me before walking away with a strong sway of her hips.

"Margarita's, huh," Jade mumbles to herself, shaking her head in disbelief. She rounds the bar and walks to an empty table, starting to wipe it down.

I keep my eyes locked on the back of the blonde, watching her maneuver around the empty tables before stopping in front of an occupied one. She sets the first drink down in front of a brunette facing the opposite direction before placing the other down in front of an empty seat.

The blonde is wearing a wicked grin when she sits, now facing my direction. She says something to her friend seconds before the brunette whips around, her wild eyes searching the bar before stopping on mine.

I feel my jaw unhinge when our eyes meet. *Sierra?*

8

Sierra

"HAVE YOU BEEN HERE BEFORE?" I ASK, DRAGGING MY EYES across the wooden sign that dangles awkwardly from above the door of this supposed Jim's bar.

"A time or two." Sophie replies casually, like it's not out of the ordinary for her to stumble upon places like this. I suppose it isn't. Sophie's always been the fearless leader between the two of us, not afraid of anything or anyone.

My best friend has a natural type of confidence, the kind that doesn't waver regardless of the situation. I'm the opposite. I wear a false sense of bravery like my favourite oversized sweatshirt: *constantly*. It's become second nature to me. I must be a glutton for punishment because there's really no time to be shy in my world. Let alone my type of work.

Sophie and I stand out in this neighbourhood. We look out of place with our expensive heels and glossy blown out hair. And when a man stumbles out of the bar dressed in a pair of oil-splattered coveralls, his hand finding the wall for balance, it only serves as a reminder of that. The putrid smell of vomit blows off of him in the wind and in our direction.

I spin to face the street, my stomach swirling. I slide my hand into the right pocket of my wool coat and wrap my fingers around a pen, clicking down on the end over and over again as if on instinct.

When my stomach settles, I spin back around. Sophie is trapped inside her own bubble of excitement as she completely bypasses the drunk now collapsed by the door, and takes a step forward, yanking open the door.

I stay rooted in place and listen to the creaky hinges with a judgmental brow raised to the sky. When I make no immediate move to follow her inside, my best friend wraps a dainty hand around my forearm and pulls me in with an unbelievably firm grip.

The musky smell hits me like a brick wall when we cross the threshold, making my nose crinkle. I attempt to find an empty table through the thick layer of cigarette smoke in the air. "When I told you that Clare ditched me, I was expecting you to take me somewhere a little less . . . dirty," I grumble while squeezing my body through a small gap between two occupied tables.

I sound judgmental, and I know that I'm being exactly that. But I don't do well in new places unless I'm five tequila shots deep.

"Well, suck it up, buttercup. I'm tired of the same old, same old. Live a little, Sierra."

It's not hard to see where she's coming from and wish that I could swallow my own worries in order to make her happy. But it isn't as easy for me to "live a little" as it is for her.

"Okay. But why here of all places? Those guys are literally smoking joints back there."

She stops us in front of a bar height, two-person table, and tosses her purse down on the top beside the words *suck a dick* that have been etched into the wood. Following my stare, she looks at the group of intimidating bikers before giggling like a schoolgirl.

"When's the last time that you smoked pot? It's been a

couple of years at least." She's grinning now, sitting on her chair as I do the same with mine.

"Back in freshman year." I fold my arms and leanin back.

God, we were wild in college. *I* was wild. Back when everything was as simple as waking up for an afternoon class and then stumbling back home wasted out of your mind the following morning. Weekdays blurred into weekends when I was living on cloud-nine, naive to the world and drunk ¾ of the time. But life is a nasty vengeful bitch just waiting for her chance to push you off a cliff and watch you drown in a world of responsibilities and credit card debt once you hold that diploma in your hand.

"Those were the days," she sighs.

"Being a grown-up *could* be worse. My new boss seems super nice. Especially considering he walked in on me having an internal freak out and didn't say anything about it. Even told me to call him Cole." Pushing a stray piece of hair out of my eyes, I watch her eyes double in size.

"Is that his first name?"

"Well yeah."

"Yikes."

"Yikes? Why yikes?" I rush.

"He wants to bang you, babe," she replies, her tone too casual for my liking. This is not the time to be *casual*.

"This is *so* not a joke, Soph. Maybe he's just the laid back, down to earth type. It's pretty common for employers to tell their employees to call them by their first name, right?"

"Maybe," she starts carefully. "But you're too hot for it just to be a casual thing. I would watch out, S. He might go cray-cray on you."

"Noted," I mumble, dropping my gaze to the cracks running along the wooden table. It looks like somebody attempted to fill them with a brown crayon.

"Want a drink? I do. Be right back!" Sophie is out of her seat and rushing past me before I can reply. As I watch her natural curls bounce with each step she takes, I find myself tugging at my straight strands, too thin to stay in a curl for longer than five minutes tops.

When we were teenagers, Sophie would spend an hour every other morning curling my hair for school. She was and still is, the only one that could get it to cooperate.

A few minutes later, a massive round glass is set down in front of me, the familiar slush of a margarita bringing out my smile.

"Thank you." I wrap my lips around the thin straw and close my eyes, nearly moaning when the sweet flavour hits my tongue. I peek open my right eye when I hear Sophie throw herself in her seat. There's a wicked smile tugging at her lips, and I shake my head before she has a chance to speak.

"What?" I ask, growing more confused by the second when I notice her eyes ping-ponging behind me.

"So, you remember that guy from the other night, right? The one with the hot roommate and the huge di—"

"Yeah, I remember him, Sophie," I interrupt. She knows that I haven't forgotten about him. How could I? I spent far too long in the bath last night because of him and the memory of his tongue between my legs.

"Well, he's sort of sitting at the bar right now."

"What?" My stomach drops to the floor, heat rushing up my neck. I nearly choke on air when I spin around in my seat and meet a pair of bold amber brown eyes waiting for me. I'm embarrassingly breathless when he grins, a set of adorable dimples resting on both of his cheeks.

Braden slowly raises a glass bottle to his parted lips and takes a longer than needed drink before setting it back down gently. He starts to trail his eyes down my figure, catching on the deep V in the tight maroon dress. My heart thrashes in my chest.

The intensity in his stare heats my skin. I know what he's doing, staring at me like he wants nothing more than to bend me over this table and have his way with me, and fuck do I wish that I don't crave the same thing.

A twitch in his right eyebrow pulls me back to reality, or close enough to it. Blinking, I watch him pull out his wallet and place a stack of cash down on the bar. He stands up and heads in the direction of the restroom, not sparing me another glance.

With my pulse in my ears, I spin back around. There's an ache between my legs that I have a feeling won't be disappearing anytime soon.

"You're going to follow him, aren't you?" Sophie asks coyly, nodding to the hallway.

"Should I?" *No, I shouldn't.* Right?

Sophie rolls her eyes dramatically before waving toward the restrooms. "Yes, you idiot. Go!"

I can't find the words to reply as my head subconsciously moves up and down. "I'll meet you at home? Or maybe not?"

My margarita remains barely touched as I collect my purse from the back of my chair and beeline it to the bathrooms, not bothering to give Sophie anything more than a quick wave goodbye.

I have no idea what I'm doing, going to meet a guy in the bathrooms for a quick fuck, but all I know is that if I don't, I can't help but feel like I'll regret it forever.

———

MY PULSE QUICKENS with each step I take.

By the time I turn down the hallway, I come to an abrupt stop. I ache to feel the cool metal of the pen in my jacket pocket as my anxiety flashes like a caution sign with the words *turn around* written above it in thick neon letters.

I can always turn around, I remind myself. I don't *have* to do this. But I *want* to. So damn bad it makes my knees shake.

The mere thought of Braden thinking that he's won something here—that I'm just like every other female he's lusted over, the ones that run after him, panties around her ankles, thighs slick from her excitement—makes me want to kneel over and vomit. The last thing a guy like Braden needs is another sexual win. But would it be a win? Or would it be something more along the lines of an agreement? A win for both sides. I get another mind-numbing orgasm and he gets to add another tic to his win column.

I shake my head profusely, annoyed with myself for even entertaining this idea. But it's too late to turn around now. *It's time to be a big girl, Sierra.* Take what you want and stop questioning yourself. Relax.

With that mental pep talk, I start for the bathroom again. The hallway rounds, and I take as many deep breaths as I can before I make the final stretch. I turn the corner and freeze.

"Took you long enough."

Braden's pink lips are tilted in a grin, his back against the wall, arms crossed and biceps stretching the tight sleeves of his t-shirt.

"I wasn't sure if I was going to come." *A lie.*

"You wanna know something?" He doesn't wait for me to respond before pushing away from the wall and taking two large steps toward me. "It hurt my feelings when you ditched me the other morning. I had big, *big* plans for you."

I can't help but drop my gaze to the noticeable bulge pressing against the zipper of his jeans, remembering exactly how it felt to have his cock throbbing inside of me.

Gulping, I reply, "I just figured that I would beat you to it."

"You figured wrong." He closes the distance between us, making my lips part in surprise. His breath is hot on my neck, causing the hairs on my arms to rise. "I guess you'll just have to make it up to me now."

I gasp when my back hits the wall, his body moving to shield mine as he places his palms on either side of me, boxing me in. He leans forward, his nose rubbing against mine, the smell of him surrounding me. The mixture of leather, spice, and pure masculine energy makes my mouth water, craving to have it as a permanent stain on my skin.

"Somebody could walk down here any minute," I whisper, my eyes falling to his mouth, watching his tongue swipe across his plump bottom limp.

I know that nobody would see me, not with this man covering my tiny body with his giant one, moulding them together into one. And honestly, I'm not sure if I even care if anybody could. Not anymore. My words are a cop out. A lame one at that.

"Don't go shy on me now, baby. We both know you're anything but."

The words spark something dormant from deep inside my chest, something that flares into a ball of fire, pushing me to make my next move.

I waste no time in grabbing the back of his neck and pulling him to me, pressing my lips to his. My eyes roll back at the feeling that lights up my veins, pulsing through my body at his rough touch.

His hands are everywhere, yet nowhere close to where I crave them to be. He nips at my bottom lip, forcing my mouth to open for him before his tongue is trailing along mine, moving in ways that make my core ache with need. God, the things he can do with that tongue—

"Hold on tight," he murmurs before grabbing my thighs and lifting me. I wrap them tightly around his waist.

The breathy groan that escapes his lips when I press myself against the bulge in his tight jeans is enough to send me straight to hell.

I reach between us and grab him through the scratchy material, sliding my palm along the hard outline of his cock and squeezing.

"That's it, fighter. It's nice to see you again," he rumbles, his long lashes fluttering.

"Is it?" My nails scratch at the skin above his underwear, making him shiver before I'm popping open the button of his jeans.

Suddenly, he's moving us while looking over my shoulder to guide us toward what I hope is the bathroom. His lips close over the sensitive skin of my neck, sucking, biting, tasting, leaving a trail of marks behind. My back hits a solid surface for the second time in the past few minutes as he shoves open the door and flips the lock.

The dirty tile countertop is covered in God knows what, making me cringe when Braden stops in front of it. I gawk up at him as he debates whether or not to drop me on top of it.

With a scowl, I say, "I'm not placing my bare ass on that."

I release his cock and wiggle against him until he loosens his grip enough for me to set my feet on the ground. He watches me place my palm firmly on his chest, his eyebrows raised and something carnal in his eyes.

"We'll have to find another way," I mumble, staring at the bulge in his jeans with an eagerness that surprises me. My clit throbs, tired of waiting.

He inspects my body with dark primal eyes, and it makes me feel more confident than I think I ever have. The way he's staring at me, almost like he's taking mental pictures of what every inch of me looks like in this moment—my skin flushed and body eager—and keeping the images for later, is both intimidating and sexy at the same time.

His heated gaze gives me the push I need to raise my fingers to the thin straps of my dress and gently slide them down my shoulders, letting it pool at my feet.

I know the decision to skip a bra tonight was the right one when Braden's eyes widen, his surprise evident in his stuttered breathing. It doesn't last long, though. I knew it wouldn't.

He narrows his eyes and stalks toward me with purpose. It

only takes him two steps to reach me, and when he does, his eyes are so dark with built up sexual tension that I want to jump him right there.

"No bra? Why am I not surprised?" he asks. His huge hands push against my bare chest, squeezing the two breasts with a grateful sigh that shoots like liquid fire up my spine.

Spreading his fingers, he slides them across my nipples while looking up to watch my lips part with a slight whimper. He gives a sharp tug to my left nipple before shaping my body with his calloused palms. My back arches, a deep-rooted want so apparent in my actions as I push against him eagerly, *desperately*.

He slides his fingers under the band of my lace underwear before dropping to his knees in front of me. Warm, wet lips press against my chest, covering every inch of available skin in sloppy, open-mouthed kisses. When his mouth closes around my nipple, sucking and licking the hard bud, I reach behind me and fumble with sweaty palms to grab onto the countertop, desperate to keep myself steady.

"Fuck, you're so responsive."

Braden's voice vibrates against my skin before crawling inside my chest, burying itself deep. He starts sliding his mouth down my stomach, getting closer to the pulse between my thighs.

"I'm always like this. You're not anything special," I rasp.

His fingers continue to dance along the top of my underwear, teasing me to the point a growl of pure frustration builds in my throat. I refuse to give him that level of satisfaction. If I had more strength in my arms, I would reach down and force him to stop teasing me.

"Oh yeah? I'd like to know the names of every other man that's made you this wet this fast before."

Fucking prick.

"That could take all night. There's just been so man—"

I gasp when he finally moves a finger to the center of my

panties. He smirks when he feels the wetness waiting there for him, soaking through the thin material and covering his finger. My breathing shallows out when he peels away the only thing keeping him away from where I ache, desperate for release.

I'm surprised to feel a heavy knot form in my belly when he rids me of my panties. I don't know why I've become so damn nervous watching him narrow his gaze on me the way he is—like a man starved of food for too long—after everything that we've already done together, but I am.

The sudden urge to reach down and shove him away is overwhelming, but the need to have him spread my legs and dive in face first is even stronger.

My jaw drops, a sigh falling in the air when he answers my silent prayers and swipes his tongue along my slit. He places a hand on my stomach, steadying me as my grip on the counter loosens, muscles and bones quaking.

Squeezing my eyes shut, I feel him push my legs further apart and swirl his finger in my arousal before sliding it deep. His deep chuckle is wrongfully sexy, running over my skin like warm honey and leaving a trail of goosebumps behind before his mouth is back between my legs.

The toe-curling pleasure his mouth brings has me curling my fingers in his hair, pulling him closer to me. His eyes meet mine when he slips a second and third finger in and flicks at my swollen clit.

My head falls back when the tightness in my belly starts to grow. He closes his lips around my clit when he senses how close I am, sucking and biting while keeping his fingers snug inside me, moving them in ungodly ways. His eyes stay connected to mine the entire time I fall apart, watching with laser focus as I sob in satisfaction.

"Good girl," he groans against me, twisting his fingers a final time before I'm whimpering a strangled version of his name and clenching my thighs tightly around his head.

The idea that I could strangle him right here and now is

an interesting one, but I let my legs go limp. I'm too selfish to skip out on another orgasm.

He pulls his fingers out and stands up, quickly stripping out of his jeans and boxers. I feel my mouth water as I watch his thick cock slap against the rippled muscles of his abdomen. How he even fits that monster in those tight boxers is beyond me.

"Face the mirror and bend over," he commands with a growl that sends a throb to my already soaking pussy.

I force myself to nod and do as he says, sliding my hair over my shoulder when I hear the tearing of a condom wrapper.

Looking forward, I place my palms on the edge of the counter and watch him eagerly through the lipstick-covered mirror. I catch sight of my reflection and shudder.

I'm the perfect picture of helplessly aroused and danger-ously eager.

He slides the condom on swiftly, expertly. There's a smirk on his lips when his attention falls on me again, taking notice of the fact that I've actually followed his instructions. I see his heavy approval in his eyes, and revel in the fact I've pleased him before I look forward and clear my throat, shaking the image from my mind. *No. Not happening.*

I'm relieved when he grabs my hips with steady, commanding hands and tears me from my thoughts. He uses his left hand to slide up my back before pushing me down so the cold counter presses against my heavy breasts. The sudden action takes me by surprises, and I gasp, more turned on than I expected by the feeling of my hard nipples rubbing against the cold surface. Suddenly the state of cleanliness in the bath-room carries no weight.

Braden gives me no warning before I feel the tip of his cock push into me, easing its way inside, slow and steady as I clench tightly, trying to accommodate all of him. His size makes me sigh, waves upon waves of pleasure tinged with the pain of being stretched so wide swirling together into a feeling of euphoria. It's a feeling that I could see myself getting used to, regardless of the fact that I know I shouldn't be thinking like that. Especially right now.

I sneak a look at him over my shoulder and find myself consumed with the look on his face, unable to look away. His lip is between his teeth, head hanging back, neck limp. The scar etched through the middle of his right eyebrow is emphasized when both brows pull together in a way that has me pulsing around him. The sight of unmistakable pleasure spreading across his face has my grip on the counter tightening.

He slides the rest of the way in and groans, "I forgot how tight you are."

My breath comes out of me in a rush when he pulls all the way out before slamming back into me. His thrusts become rough, unforgiving, and I cry out, begging him for more. I need him to keep going, to keep fucking me until I beg him to stop, unable to take anymore.

He curses under his breath and grabs my hips, squeezing them to the point of bruising.

"Don't stop," I whimper. "Don't fucking stop."

Braden shakes his head once. "Just keep taking it like that . . . *fuck yes.*"

His movements don't falter as he reaches forward and grabs hold of my hair, wrapping it once around his knuckles and yanking me back toward him. His front presses against my back, warm skin slick with sweat connecting with every thrust of his hips.

Our eyes meet in the mirror, the sight so erotic my knees threaten to buckle. I can feel his hot breath on my shoulder, neck, then ear as he mumbles, "I need you to keep quiet for me now, Sierra."

Nodding quickly, I reach back and squeeze his forearm, letting my nails dig into his skin. My tongue slides between my teeth as I hold back a loud cry. I feel my legs give out from under me when my orgasm sends my body into a fit of trembles. White-hot pleasure shoots up my spine, sizzling my nerves, fraying them. I cry out when he reaches around me and plays with my clit, rubbing it until my high falls, leaving me breathless and jelly-like.

Braden lets go of my hair and I fall forward on my hands. He grabs my waist, holding me up, not stopping his unforgiving thrusts as he does so.

"I'm almost there," he grunts, eyes squeezed shut.

My strength starts to come back a few seconds later, and I manage to stand on my own, throwing myself back to meet every single one of his thrusts. Fingernails dig into my skin at the same time he throws his head back, releasing a deep guttural groan while filling the condom.

I can't seem to look away from him, too entrapped by the complete satisfaction and relief etched in his tightened features. His sharp jaw is rigid, teeth grinding so hard I'm surprised I can't hear the sound.

His movements slow to a stop as he places his hands down beside mine and rests his forehead against the middle of my back.

Braden's words are slurred whispers. "So, are you going to run away from me again? Or have I convinced you that it's no use?"

9

Braden

I'M PLEASANTLY SURPRISED WHEN I WAKE UP TO HOT BREATH fanning across my chest.

An explosive tingling sensation shoots up my right arm when I attempt to pull the numb limb from under Sierra's body before giving up with a quiet groan. For such a small person, she creates way too much damn heat.

As if hearing the silent insult, Sierra mumbles incoherent words in her sleep, her voice light and delicate—the complete opposite of the brash one that I've become so accustomed to. She nuzzles her face into my neck, and my chest rumbles with a silent laugh.

I let myself relax again and soak up the sight of the naked body curled around mine. Circular bruises peek out from under her messy hair, decorating the smooth skin of her neck with hues of purple. The possessive marks bring the memories of last night back full throttle, and my cock thickens.

After leaving the bar and hailing another cab—no emotionally scarred drivers this time—we stumbled inside my apartment where I bent her over the back of the couch and thrusted into her. It wasn't long until we were christening every surface we could find, and then stumbling into the bedroom where she rode me until we both passed out.

Each memory from the night before creates a heavier need to wake her up with a morning fuck, regardless of the ache in my muscles and her ridiculous rule.

No morning sex.

I have no idea how, or *why* I agreed to such a stupid rule, but now that I think about it, it was definitely the booze. It's always the fucking booze.

I look up at the ceiling and use my free hand to push my shaggy hair out of my eyes, the strands damp with sweat. Dropping my eyes, I watch Sierra's dainty hand stretch across my abdomen, her manicured nails scratching at the toned muscles. It feels good, relaxing even. She pulls herself closer to me with a sigh.

The movement causes the thin black sheet to move down her torso, exposing her bare chest and hardening nipples. The bared skin taunts me, silently beckoning me forward. I swallow the growing lump in my throat.

I've never been a big fan of waking up beside someone, especially not somebody that only my penis is overly acquainted with, but if waking up to a body as gorgeous as this one is what I've been missing out on, then fuck have I been an idiot.

Sure, there are some women who seem to get the wrong impression after coming home with me, waking up tucked into my side, freshly fucked and hungry. They assume that maybe I'll wake up and realize they're my soulmate, my *person*, as Clay would call it. But the mirage usually fades quickly. It's a hit to the pride being told that he's just not that into you.

"You're the worst pillow ever. You fidget too much." Sierra pushes herself off of me before letting her head fall onto her unused pillow with an exaggerated huff. Tangled but glossy caramel brown hair spreads out around her, smelly strongly of mangos and a bit of her floral perfume.

"Maybe that's because I'm not a pillow." I chuckle lowly.

She grabs a handful of the blanket and tucks it under her chin. "Whatever."

"Someone's a grouch in the morning."

I force myself out of bed and stretch my arms above my head, knowing damn well my dick is rock hard, nearly pulsing with how worked up I've found myself this morning. Sierra attempts to keep her eyes to herself but fails miserably.

Her gaze is narrowed, eyes hot as she trails them down the tight ridges of my stomach before focusing on the thick length right in front of her. I watch her lips part, still swollen from last night, and crave the feel of them around me again.

I want my hands in her hair as I fuck her mouth until she gags, forcing her to take as much of me as she can, spit dribbling from the corners of her mouth. My palm twitches, desperate to wrap around my shaft and give it a pump or two, suddenly claimed by the thought of her.

"Are you going to move or stand there all day?" she asks smugly, her legs now crossed in front of her.

I blink twice, and realize I've been staring at her mouth for a creepy amount of time. "It's too early for your snark, Sierra."

I clear my throat and pull on a pair of boxers. "There should be something for you to wear in the bin by the bed unless you want to put your dress back on."

Without giving her a second look, I leave her to get dressed. When I get to the living room, I spot two sock-covered feet dangling from the couch and grin, feeling my blood cool to a normal temperature. I move quietly around the sofa and give each foot a hard yank. I burst into a fit of laughter when Clayton jumps into the air, terrified and about two second away from snapping.

Hating jump-scares: another one of Clayton's many quirks.

"Morning," I snicker, falling back in a fluffy maroon

armchair across from him. Clay folds his arms and turns the volume up on the TV. He tries to tune me out, but I only speak louder. "Sleep well last night?"

"You're a prick," he replies.

"Oh, I'm sorry. Did we keep you up or something?"

He stands up from the couch and grabs his empty coffee cup from the coffee table. He stomps off to the kitchen and disposes of it in the sink.

Sierra comes walking out of my bedroom a few seconds later, coughing uncomfortably. Her eyes hold a hint of suspicion and curiosity as they flick between Clay and me.

I notice Clayton's jaw slacken when he sucks in a breath, eyes feasting on the image of her. She's decided on wearing one of my old hockey shirts and a pair of rolled up sweatpants. The white shirt is ripped and stained from years of wear and tear. It swallows her whole. It's definitely not what I would have expected her to grab, but I won't complain. She looks fucking hot in it.

"It should be a sin to look that good in the morning," Clay says in approval, taking the words right from my mouth.

She swallows nervously, and drops her eyes to the floor, clearly uncomfortable with the sudden attention from the both of us. Something hot and stiff flicks my spine when she starts biting her thumb nail, an anxious habit I've noticed Lana doing a few times when we first met.

I pin Clayton with a sharp look, regardless of the fact that he isn't, nor doesn't want to pay me any attention.

"Uh, thanks." Her cheeks are flushed as she stares at her toes.

I'm not sure if she's offended by his comment or just not used to receiving them. Either way, I'm immediately not a fan of the way she's shut down, her insides nearly completely bare and in clear view. The confidence and sass that I've begun to associate with this woman is gone, leaving only a nervous girl behind.

I'm about to walk toward her when her walls come back up. With a fake smile and a roll of her eyes, she says to me, "I forgot my phone in your room."

Before I have a chance to tell her to drop the act, she's inside my bedroom, shutting the door softly behind her.

Turning to Clay, I hiss, "Way to go, asshole."

"Me?" he reels. "I was just being honest. You're the one who left a naked model in your bed alone. You were probably the one that offended her. At this rate, it won't be long before she comes crawling to me looking for a real man."

"Trust me. You couldn't handle a woman like Sierra." I sink into the armchair.

The last time Clay tried to score with a girl at Sierra's level was about two years ago, and he was beaten to a pulp by said girl's boyfriend not even twenty minutes afterward. He claims that the blowjob he got in the bathroom was worth it, though, regardless of the fact it was the beginning of a serious life change.

He hasn't pined over anyone since then. I assume he's just not interested in fighting over anyone anymore. It would be ridiculous of me to bug him for that.

It's not only guys that like to play games. We just get the brunt of the blame for it.

"I'm starting to think that neither of you can handle me."

I turn to my bedroom door and see Sierra. She's back to her confident self, standing in front of us with a hand on her hip and an easy-going smile. She looks just as sexy as she did last night, with the addition of some wild sex-hair that I'm not surprised to find still resting on her shoulders. It's going to take a lot more than a hairbrush to get those knots out.

"You wanna find out?" Clay asks, now in the kitchen. His tone is far too hopeful in my opinion.

Sierra tilts her head in mock consideration. "No, I don't think so."

My laugh tears through the room. Sierra seems less than

impressed by the both of us as she sighs in what I assume is disbelief, and heads for the front door. My sides start to ache when I reach up and wipe a hand down my face, clearing the laugh induced tears from my skin.

"Buddy, I think it's time you retire your game. It's rustier than the bathroom showerhead," I say.

Clayton's head snaps in my direction, and he shoots me a less-than-subtle warning look. Feigning innocence, I purse my lips and blow him a kiss.

"If you two are done, I want to talk to Braden," Sierra says, staring at Clayton, watching as he nods along with her every word. "Alone," she adds when he continues to smile at her.

"Right." He nods before rushing off to his room. Sierra lets out a thankful sigh once he's gone, turning to look at me.

"Alone at last," I say.

Waving me off with a lazy swish of her hand, she mumbles, "I left my number on your bed."

Surprise floods through me. I'm not sure what I was expecting this morning, but I definitely did not expect it to be this easy. I would have bet my winnings from my next boxing match that I would have had to sneak my number in her phone and call myself to get her number.

"Duly noted, babe."

"Don't call me babe," she snaps. "And please keep this to yourself. Your friend creeps me out."

Blowing out a light laugh, I nod. "So. No strings. Just sex then, yeah?"

She blinks once before saying, "Yeah, just sex."

10

Sierra

"JUST SEX?" SOPHIE SPUTTERS, SPITTING CHEWED UP LETTUCE from her salad across my desk. It lands on a picture frame of me, Clare and Liz from our trip to the zoo last month

Liz sits on my shoulders, wearing a wide smile with two missing teeth and a pair of light-washed, blue jean overalls with bronze buttons. Clare stands beside us, struggling to hold three melting ice cream cones in her hands. It was scorching hot that day. I think I'm still finding skin to peel from the nasty sunburn I got.

It's been a week since I last saw both Braden and Sophie. Work has held me by the tits, keeping me busy to the point of near exhaustion. I don't have much energy left by the time I get home at night to do more than microwave a frozen meal and crawl into bed. My phone remains chalked full of unread texts and unanswered calls. It's a wonder I've even managed to shower and throw on makeup every day.

Sophie wipes her mouth with a napkin that was previously folded on her lap. "Just sex with a guy like that? No way in hell. I'm calling it now, S. It won't work."

"You only think that because you don't even know the guy.

He's a total douche-bag." I stab my plastic fork into my salad container and bring a bunch of leafy greens to my lips.

I never knew how much I would love being able to eat my lunch in an actual office instead of outside or jammed inside of a small lunchroom until now. And from Sophie's laid-back posture, I can tell that she approves as well.

"A sexy douche-bag," she mumbles, still staring at me with an unconvinced glimmer in her blue eyes.

"Doesn't matter. I'm not looking for anything more than sex. You know that."

Still not believing me, Sophie scoops up the rest of her salad before shoving it in her mouth and tossing the empty container in the trash can by the door.

"Whafefer," she mumbles with her mouth still full. After swallowing her food, she continues, "All I'm saying is that you might want to be careful if you're so against catching feelings. A guy like Braden won't hesitate to dump you out on the street like it's garbage day once you're no longer all shiny and new."

"I know." I nod. "You don't have to worry about me."

"Uh, yes, I do. You're my best friend, Sierra. I worry about you more than anyone."

Slapping a hand above my left breast, I let out an exaggerated sigh, my eyelashes fluttering. "I love you too."

"Anyways," she sings. "I saw Maeve the other day."

I freeze instantly, blood draining from my face. The mood between us shifts, and I hate myself for allowing just the sound of her name to have such a negative impact on me.

"Oh? Did you two talk?" *Please say no.*

"She saw me before I could turn around." Sophie visibly cringes from the look on my face. I'm not surprised, I don't even need to look in the mirror to know that I must look like a kid who just had their lollipop snatched from their mouth.

"Great."

I push away from my desk and begin busying myself with the lunch wrappers covering the top of it. The slight tremble in my hands only fuels my temper as I drop the empty salad container into the trash can and shove it down harder than necessary. Once, twice, three times. I let my repressed anger break free each time I shove the container further and further into the garbage bin. I close my eyes, letting out a shallow breath before righting myself and turning around.

"She seems a little off," she says slowly, guilt dripping from every word. Her forehead is wrinkled and she avoids my stare. I feel instantly selfish for reacting the way I did, seeing how upset it's made her, but I can't find it in myself to apologize. Neither of us have done anything wrong. Maeve is the one to blame for all of this.

Catching one of my oldest friends having sex with my boyfriend of four years will never not sting. And six months later, I'm still not over it. I'm not sure if I should be by now, but I'm definitely not. I still miss them both so much that I hate them even more for it. They don't deserve to be missed. They deserve to live a very miserable life together. They should be missing *me*.

"I don't care." The lie burns my throat. "She seemed fine when Logan was shoving her up against the wall of Sinners the other night. Actually, she seemed pretty fucking great."

Okay yeah, I'm bitter. I have a right to be.

"What?" Sophie gasps. "She definitely didn't mention that."

"And you're surprised, why? She lied to us for months, Soph." I lean back against the wall with my arms crossed, trying desperately to ignore the pain beginning to grow between my eyes.

"I know. I just thought that she could have changed, you know? If she had gone back to how she used to be, maybe we could have been a group again."

I place my hand on her slouched shoulder. "I hoped for the same thing. But she broke my heart, Sophie. I trusted her with my life and she used that against me for who even knows how long."

She nods before leaning her head back against my stomach. The memories of that night never seem to fade or lose their colour. They stay clear and vibrant, like a freshly painted canvas.

I got home from work and heard him calling out *her* name from *our* bedroom. I remember the spiked up, messy head of blonde hair peeking out from beneath our heavy white comforter. Her short black dress was strung carelessly across the back of my office chair. The sound my wine glass made as it fell from my hands, shattering against the hardwood floor. I can feel the burn in my throat from when my choked sob flew across the room, the two bodies jumping anxiously from the bed.

"Sierra?" Sophie calls, watching me curiously. I force a smile and fall back in the now, shoving the memories to the back of my mind.

Moving my gaze to the sunflower shaped clock hung from the wall behind my desk, I say, "Lunch goes by too fast." I laugh awkwardly. "I'll call you later?" Or, in other words, can you please leave?

"Right." She coughs, standing up from her chair. "Have a good rest of your day, babe. Talk later."

I round my desk and place my palms down on the smooth wood, nodding firmly. An array of emotions flicker across Sophie's face before she settles on a forced smile. She raises her hand in a small wave and pulls open my door, walking through it silently.

As soon as she's gone, I close the door and a choked sob is ripped from my throat. I move a shaky hand to my chest bone and struggle to suck in a shuttered breath. Balling my hands into fists, I clench my jaw, angered by my lack of strength. *Keep it together, Sierra.*

They never deserved you. They mean nothing to you anymore. You can do better. You *will* do better.

I repeat the mantra over and over again until I've made myself believe it. Even for just right now.

———

As I SLIDE a thick stack of clasped papers into my briefcase, a knock on the door startles me. My eyes—tired and somewhat blurry from the sting of my drying contacts—fall on Cole's broad shoulders as he leans in the doorway, the epitome of confidence and bold male energy. I think it's easy to admit that he intimidates me nearly as much as Braden does.

A heat festers in my chest at the thought of Braden. Nearly six-and-a-half feet of towering *man* and sexual prowess wrapped in a mess of arrogant words, fearlessness, and a whole ton of experience. I'm not sure how anyone could help not being intimidated by all of that. I wouldn't doubt that even someone like Cole would find Braden's presence unnerving.

"Heading out?" Cole asks with an easy smile that makes my nerves somewhat settle.

"Yes, sir. I have a box of toaster waffles calling my name." I laugh lightly, sliding the straps of my purse up my arms until they rest on my shoulder.

"As great as those sound, I actually came to invite you to join myself and a few other co-workers at the Italian restaurant down the street. Best fettuccine in the city, hands down." His million-dollar smile does little to calm the growing uncertainty that fills my stomach at the thought of having such a casual meeting with my bosses.

With my luck, I'll crumble under the pressure and end up stuttering a ridiculous attempt at a joke that will end up labeling me as the awkward girl for the rest of my career here. Not the worst label, but not exactly one I'm aiming for.

"Thank you for the offer, bu—"

"We don't bite, I promise. It'll be fun," he tries again, this time placing his palms together in front of him. The gesture looks like a silent plea, and my resolve weakens.

I'm not sure whether it would look worse for me to decline all together, or risk making a nervous fool of myself. Not wanting to upset the people who hold my entire career in their hands, I agree.

"Okay. When should I be there?"

He grins. "We can head over now, actually. Everyone is already on their way. I offered to ask you myself. It's only a five-minute walk."

Oh. "Okay." I inwardly cringe at my simple reply before squeezing the strap of my purse with a tight grip and waiting for Cole to lead the way out of my office.

When we both step into the empty hallway, I close my office door and turn back to see him waiting for me. The troublesome nagging in my head becomes quite a nuisance as I feel my palms begin to sweat. Sending him a reassuring look I don't believe myself, I follow him to the elevator.

"So, Sierra. How do you like it here? Any complaints?" he asks when we reach the shiny silver doors. I reach forward to push the down button before stepping back and casually wiping my palms on my skirt.

"It's been great. Everyone's super nice."

"Glad to hear it. Sometimes the pressure gets to be too much for some of our new hires. I think they expect it to be an easy job."

I nod along with his words. I can see where that idea would come from. Back when I first told my parents I was planning to spend four years getting a marketing degree, they were a little underwhelmed. Although, I think it stems from them wanting me to follow in their footsteps and want to "save the world" or so my father would say.

My parents both spent decades of their lives on humanitarian missions in third world countries. A job that I'm positive they love more than Clare and me. It's also a job that has been the root of several family disputes over the years. It's easy for them to look down on us for not wanting to do better for the world, putting ourselves and our own careers first. Because of that, we don't spend a lot of time together. We never have. The only difference now is that Clare and I are grown up, meaning there's nothing to force us into seeing our parents like there was when we all lived in the same house.

Nobody puts the effort in, and our family remains distant. I'm sure that's how it will always be. I can't see that changing for anything.

My parents fear what they don't understand. And they don't want to learn any different.

The elevator doors slide open with a quiet ding and we walk inside. I feel tense, rattled from my thoughts. I'm frustrated with myself for letting my parents get to me, but will myself to let it go when Cole settles beside me, the elevator doors closing.

"I'm really thankful for this opportunity. I don't plan on wasting it," I say, confident in every word I speak.

He meets my gaze. "That's what I like to hear. We're lucky to have such a hard worker on our team."

My lips tug up. I stare at my closed-toe black heels and try to relax. It would seem that all of my hard work is finally going to pay off.

Let's hope that I don't fuck it up.

11

Sierra

I WISH THAT THE PIT IN MY STOMACH HAD SHRIVELLED UP AND died the minute we walked inside of our destination—the fancy Italian restaurant a few blocks away from the office—Paninaro's, I think it's called. However, I still feel like I could hurl over at any given moment.

The pungent smell of parmesan cheese and breadsticks burning my nostrils doesn't overly help the situation, either. The salad I had for lunch churns and churns, forming a tsunami of lettuce and tomatoes in my belly.

I jump, startled when a warm palm touches my lower back. The contact is unwanted and unnecessary. I freeze as if on instinct, and struggle to keep my hands from shaking and clamming up.

"In the corner booth," Cole mumbles, his voice husky and much closer than it used to be. I can feel his breath on the shell of my ear.

My blood runs cold as I struggle to swallow past the boulder in my throat. Forcing my lips to tilt up in a sorry excuse of a smile, I give a brief nod.

Looking ahead, I focus on two tall, well-figured receptionists—the ones I've become accustomed to finding giggling together in the break room every morning, holding tall plastic cups full of some sort of frothy liquid. Tonight, they'll sit in a sleek black booth directly in front of me.

Across from them sits the CEO of Brenton Marketing, Clark Brenton. He wears an easy-going smile, his sharp features completely relaxed. It's easy to tell, even from a distance, that he's extremely confident and self-assured. And I'm sure having two stunning women sitting just a few feet away, completely enamoured by his chiseled jawline and unique aqua-coloured eyes helps with that as well. The two women look about ready to do anything this guy asks of them with a pleasant smile and an excited "yes, sir."

"Hey, Clark." Cole greets his boss like you would an old friend when we reach the large booth, his loud voice—firm yet somehow lazy—grabbing the table's attention. "Ladies." He grins at them both. I'm sure his white teeth sparkle beneath the warm lighting.

The two women turn to stare at us—or me, rather—eyebrows raised with silent judgment. I lift my hand and wave when I feel my anxiety near its peak. They're expecting me to introduce myself, but I can't seem to speak, still too focused on the heat radiating from the hand glued to my back.

Two sets of perfectly lined eyes stare at me with a sort of vacancy that urges me to drop my hand back down. My cheeks flush a deep red, feeling a rush of rejection shoot through me.

"Hi," I squeak.

Frustration like I've never known nips at my spine. My career is the one place, the one *thing* that doesn't make me nervous or anxious. I'm damn good at what I do. I can stand in front of an auditorium full of executives and spectating companies and not blink an eye—because I *love* my job. But I'm acting like an idiot right now in front of two of my bosses all because I'm a little flustered by a simple hand on my back? How embarrassing.

"Hi." I hear the woman on the inside mutter, partially under her breath. "It's Sienna, right?""

Ouch. That one burns more than I would have expected.

"Sierra," I correct her.

"Sure." She nods absentmindedly and turns back to her orange drink.

I know that I shouldn't take offence to her apparent lack of interest in me, but I've never been good at dealing with women outside of my field.

"It's Tiffany and Lauren, right?" I ask, forcing my shoulders back in an attempt to try and keep my composure. I bet they're planning ways to get me fired as I stand here. My mere presence is probably a stain on their entire week.

The girl sitting on the outside of the booth—Tiffany, I think—huffs dramatically and rolls her round mahogany-coloured eyes. "Yeah, that's us. Are you going to sit down now? We were waiting for you two to finally get here to order. I'm starving."

The need to shove my face in a brown bag and hyperventilate is starting to make me dizzy.

"Sorry," I mumble quietly, and slide myself into the empty seat beside Tiffany, grateful for the space from Cole. She doesn't bother giving me any more room on the bench.

Pulling down the edge of my navy skirt, I try to ignore the snickers beside me when Cole slides in the booth across from us. He's not hanging half-off the edge of his seat like I am, though.

"I'm sorry for making you guys wait. I left my wallet at the office and didn't notice until we were almost here. I made us turn back to get it," Cole says, and I meet his gaze, blinking, uncertain as to why he just covered for me.

He didn't forget his wallet. Honestly, I didn't even know we were late in the first place. I usually stay at the office later than everybody else in order to get ahead of my workload for the next day. Still, I wasn't even planning on coming to this stupid dinner. How was I supposed to know that Cole was going to drag me here?

"Oh, it's okay!" Lauren pipes up without hesitation.

"I ordered you a beer, man. Hope that's okay," Clark says, pushing a full glass of frothy brown liquid in front of Cole. Cole responds with a grateful smile before wrapping his fingers around the dew-covered glass. Clark turns to me now. "We didn't know what you would want, Sierra. But the waitress should be back soon."

Great, thanks.

"Alright." I nod and look away from the table to the wall across the restaurant where the bold washroom sign rests. It's not a unique getaway by any means, but it's a getaway nonetheless. I slip off the bench without a second thought.

"Where are you going?" Cole asks, concern washing out his features as he stares at the hands I have clenched tightly around my purse.

"Washroom. I'll have water if the waitress gets here before I'm back."

I don't give him a chance to reply before I'm taking off toward the bathroom, hoping like hell that it's unoccupied. I don't particularly want, nor need, an audience when I hit my mental wall.

I allow myself the luxury of sucking in a shallow breath, hoping it will somewhat calm me when I successfully maneuver around the crowded tables, only bumping into the backs of a small handful of chairs on my way.

Pulling open the women's room door, I beeline it for an empty stall. I push myself through an open one at the end of the line and shut the door behind me, twisting the lock with shaky fingers. Turning around, I let my back hit the metal and squeeze my eyes closed. My palms press against my eyes until I see static.

I don't know what I was expecting, showing up to a dinner I knew I wasn't really invited to, but this certainly wasn't it. It's clear nobody but Cole wants me here, and honestly, I'm still confused as to why he invited me in the first place. I have no relation to these people, there is no work relationship or friendship outside of the office. There isn't even one *inside* the office.

Tiffany works for Clark, I think, but I have no idea who Lauren works for. The only times I've ever seen her are when she's gossiping with Tiffany in the break room. Unless I'm missing something painfully obvious, I find it odd that those two would have been asked to come tonight as well.

I stay rooted in my place for a few much-needed minutes before the fog in my brain manages to subside enough for me to form a clear thought again.

Fixing my posture, I unlock and open the stall. My heels clink against the floor as I walk to the long, marble counter, stopping in front of one of the four sinks. I turn on the tap and collect some cold water in my hands before splashing my warm cheeks.

With the pink fading from my face, I spare a glance at the stalls and find them all unoccupied, which leaves me in the safe confines of this judgement-free zone for a few seconds longer. The cold-water clings to my cheeks as I stare back at my flushed complexion.

The uneven splotches of light brown freckles cover my pale skin, spreading over my small nose, across my cheeks, and down to my small chin. My silver eyes watch my every move, the obvious judgment in them only sparking my growing annoyance with myself.

I could have been in my fluffy pink robe, sprawled out on the couch watching reality show reruns right now. But no, here I am, hiding in the freaking bathroom because I'm too socially awkward to sit through a single dinner with a few colleagues. *Typical* Sierra.

With a final groan, I push my dark hair out of my face with slightly-damp hands and reach for a paper towel to wipe myself down. After throwing away it away and preparing myself with one final pep talk, I move to the door and whip it open.

I nearly trip over my own two feet when a familiar masculine voice settles along my skin, worming its way into my chest. Stopping dead in my tracks only a few steps from the door, I slowly spin around.

"I knew it was you who rushed past me out there. I could never forget that ass."

12

Braden

"So, fill me in. Considering that you've been too preoccupied to make time for your old withering mother these past few weeks, I can only assume you've been busy to the absolute tits."

My mother wears a deep-set scowl that makes me laugh. It's the same scowl I've been on the receiving end of far too many times. Ever since I turned old enough to speak or walk, really.

"You're not old nor withering, Mom. Stop being dramatic." I twirl a glob of spaghetti around my fork before shoving it in my mouth. After a hefty swallow, I moan, "Damn, Antonio. Give my compliments to the chef. This is fucking delicious, as always."

My step-dad sends me a warm, appreciative smile and dips his head. Paninaro's has been in Antonio's family for generations, opened up by his great, great grandfather a few years after he migrated to Canada from a small town in Italy. I don't know much more than that. The relationship that I have with my step-dad is slim, only built out of necessity and the respect he's earned from treating my mom so well.

"You're welcome to come here anytime, Braden," Antonio

89

says. *"Quello che è mio è tuo."* *What's mine is yours.* I know he means it, and for a flicker of time I feel guilty for not building a closer father-son relationship with the guy. He tries really hard. That has to count for something.

I serve the table a tight-lipped smile. *"Grazie."*

Antonio would never say it, but he appreciates the fact that I've tried to learn his language. I can see it in the way his green-speckled eyes shine as they stare at me after every Italian word I speak. Sometimes I'm rather ass at it, but I try nonetheless.

"How's your father and his child bride?" Mom asks the question so casually, her wine glasses tipped back as she takes a small sip, eyebrow lifted. The red liquid sloshes the sides of the glass when she sets it back down on the table cloth. I try to string together a response, but fail.

"Jesus Christ, woman," Antonio whispers, shaking his head and reaching over to place his hand on hers. "You can not call her a child bride. It is rude."

"Is that not what she is, Tony? She is our son's age. It's inappropriate!"

I stare at her, lips slightly parted, unsure of what to say.

My parents got divorced when I was young. The entire thing was messy and rough for everyone, but it was nothing compared to the arguments they've encountered since Dad's been with Lana. Mom doesn't do well with change, and if my shock and confusion was anything like what my mother felt, then I would say her reaction was and is completely warranted.

It's not that we both don't want him to be happy. My father was my fucking role model growing up—my super hero, even. He deserves happiness more than anyone I know. But is this the way to get it? Are we keeping him from being happy? Is he just going through a phase? His version of a mid-life crisis? Fuck. I don't want to think about it anymore.

"You should talk to him about it, Mom. He's still waiting

to hear back from you about your wedding RSVP," I say between mouthfuls.

Mom opens her mouth to speak, and from the passion in her stare, I can tell words are being thrown my way. But I'm no longer paying attention. I'm focused elsewhere now, on a figure wrapped in a deep navy skirt and loose blouse, moving with near-lightning speed toward the bathrooms, wound up like a coiled spring.

She seems completely unaware of her surroundings, mind set only on fleeing whatever has her spine straight as a steel rod and hands fisted. I tune out my step-dad's concerned tone as he says my name a few times, trying to grab my attention again, asking if I'm okay. It's not until Sierra disappears behind my mother's back—completely out of my view—that I retrace her steps.

My brows collide, pulling tightly together. I know I'm glaring mildly at the two women residing at the table Sierra scurried from. By the look of relief they both share, they couldn't be happier to see Sierra bee-lining it to the washroom. However, I feel my eyes narrow into a more cold, intimidating glare when I notice the rest of the group.

Sitting across from the women are two businessmen types —the kind of men who spend more money on custom tailored suits and name brand watches than they do on what kind of luxury car they drive. The first one, let's call him *Bert*, sits on the inside of the booth, watching the breasts of the blonde across from him rise and fall with each breath she takes. There's something carnal in the way he eyes her. Something that makes my gut twist. He's clearly a boss or somebody who holds some sort of power over her. I can tell by the way she's watching him: cautious and nervous but trying to play it off with a coy, flirtatious smile.

I've seen Jade wear that same look every time Jim Sullivan walks into his bar. It pisses me off seeing it now, just as much as it does then.

I relax the fingers that I don't remember fisting, and move my stare to the second guy at the table—*Ernie.*

He wears confidence nearly as well as I do. Relaxed shoulders, one arm extended, forearm resting on the table so he can show off his expensive watch. The light from the ceiling lamp above the table reflects off of the tiny diamonds embedded around the face of the watch, making each one in what appears to be a thousand, dance around the room. His jaw is covered in a brown scruff—like he hasn't bothered shaving for a few days.

I decide without a sliver of doubt that I don't like him.

"Excuse me," I mutter, pushing away from the table, ignoring my mom's questions as I follow Sierra. I bump the shoulder of one of the waiters as he rounds the corner and nod apologetically at him before I come to a stop beside the ladies room door. I fight back the need to whip open the door and stomp inside to see her with an ineligible grumble. I'm not her boyfriend. She's more than capable of dealing with her own shit, I know that.

I'm about to leave in an effort to save my pride when I smell Sierra's perfume. The smell of fresh cut flowers and vanilla brings out my smile. I turn to her when she steps through the door and covers her shock-ridden, parted lips with her hand.

The tight material of her knee-length skirt emphasizes every single one of her delicious curves—the ones I hope are still covered in the bruises the shape of my fingertips—as she leans back on her right foot with a sense of forced confidence.

She might think that she's pulling off her little "I'm too confident to be shaken by anything" act that fooled her table, but it won't work on me. I may not know her all that well yet, but I've begun to pay attention to the little mannerisms she tries to hide.

I find myself speaking before I can stop myself. "I knew it

was you who rushed past me out there. I could never forget that ass."

"Braden," she sighs, exasperated. "Why am I not surprised to see you here? Trapping women in public bathrooms seems to be your thing."

"They are when it comes to you." My mouth curves up.

It's purely coincidence, really. I wouldn't have guessed that I would run into her at my family's restaurant of all places. Barely anyone I know ever comes here. I like it that way.

"Did you need something? I have to go back out there." Her voice wobbles slightly as she speaks and looks past my shoulder at the table barely visible around the corner.

I follow her gaze and bite back my laugh when I see Ernie cough and reach down to the front of his slacks to adjust his dick, palming it slightly. He's watching the girl beside the blonde suck from a paper straw, clearly hoping she'll suck something else after dinner.

"I think they're fine without you." I laugh, turning back to her, letting my shoulder brush her neck. I feel her shiver. "Who are those people anyway? Don't tell me you work for a sex ring and that's your pimp. I'm way too broke to start paying you."

I want to knee myself in the balls as soon as I've finished speaking. Yeah, that was definitely the wrong thing to say. Her scoff is immediate, cheeks flushing red as she slaps my chest— *hard*. "Do I look like a prostitute to you, asshole?"

Accepting the invitation to openly check her out, I don't hesitate. I slip my eyes up and down her body. She's tall— taller than most women I go for, but I couldn't imagine Sierra being any shorter. I like that the top of her head meets my chin when I whisper dirty things in her ear, and that I don't have to bend down so far to kiss her.

Her legs are long, which helps them fit perfectly on my shoulders, her heels able to dig effortlessly into my sides while I'm eating her out. Why the hell would I want to change that?

The more that I look at her, the more I find myself liking what I see. That thought alone is enough to break the intensity of my stare and force me to take a cautious step back, away from her.

Unable to keep my foot out of my mouth, I tell her, "No, you don't. But you do fuck like one."

Her eyes flare, steam practically shooting from her ears and I know that I'm about to get my ass handed to me on a silver platter.

"Fuck you, Braden. You're unbelievable." She doesn't spare me a second look before she's attempting to move around me.

Sidestepping, I stretch my arm out in front of her. She stops in her tracks, staring at me with an icy glare. "Get out of my way before I rip your balls off and shove each one down your throat. Don't think that I won't leave you here while you choke on them either. I wouldn't even think twice about it."

Her threat has the opposite effect of what she was hoping for. I'm hard as a fucking rock, utterly turned on by her aggression. "I'm confused, Sierra. I thought you liked my balls. Especially when they're hitting your chin while my cock is half-way down your throat."

She glowers at my arm just long enough for the skin to break out in goosebumps before moving her stare to my face. I find myself locked in the middle of a staring match. But I won't be the one to back down first. My pride doesn't like the idea of losing when it comes to *anything*, let alone something so minuscule.

"Half-way down my throat?" she scoffs, never breaking eye contact. "You give yourself *way* too much credit."

"There's the Sierra I met outside Sinners. You're sexy when you're pissed."

She raises a defiant eyebrow and with her chin tipped, leans in just enough that her breath brushes my lips. "Just when I'm pissed?"

I swallow the remaining distance between us and relish in the heat her body exudes pushed up against mine. My eyebrow twitches with a silent dare. I wait for her to make the first move. Not because I have an issue with being the one to shove her back against the wall, but because I would fucking love for her to be the one in control, demanding and taking what she wants from me.

"No," I reply, my voice becoming raspy and strained from the unreleased tension building between us. "You're one of the sexiest women I've ever seen. No matter what you say or do."

I drag my palm down the wall and slowly move it to the side of her arm. Goosebumps rise on the smooth skin beneath my fingertips. She swallows, bobbing her head slightly before she's grabbing the back of my neck and pulling me toward her.

Her lips are on mine instantly. It's an urgent, dirty, needy kiss that has me groaning into her mouth with a feeling of relief and utter desire to have more of her. She swallows the sound, our tongues now tangled and my blood pumping in my ears to an off tempo beat.

Her palms move to my chest, lying flat and firm before she's pushing me, my back slamming against the wall. I smile against her lips when she slides her fingers under the fabric of my shirt and drags them up my skin, touching as much of me as she can, as if she forgot the feel of my body. The air between us crackles, charged with pure sexual frustration. I want to take her right here, right now. But I'm aware of where we are and who we came here with. It's not the time or place, regardless of how bad my cock wants to slip inside her hot walls and fuck her until she can't stand straight.

Deciding that I might as well take as much as I can while she's here, I release her mouth and thread my fingers in her hair, moving it away from her face. A string of muttered words fall between us at the sheer sight of her right now.

Lust drunk and frazzled, her eyes are half-lidded, pupils blown. I clench my fingers in her silky hair and take her mouth, rough and hungry. There's nothing gentle about the way I kiss her, like I'm trying to somehow own her lips and the way they return the favour just as feverously. I kiss her like nobody else is here, like we're alone in the bathroom or inside of my apartment and she does the same, convincing me that it's not just a one-sided feeling.

There's an unnatural amount of chemistry between us, and I plan on taking full advantage of it before it sizzles out and disappears.

Without breaking the kiss, I spin us around and box her in, letting myself completely consume her space like she has mine. She gasps, head falling back against the wall when I move my thigh between her legs and untangle my hands from her hair, planting them on her hips.

I use my grip to pull her toward me, my thigh becoming engulfed by the heat between her legs. She's soaked, I can feel her beneath my jeans.

"It's taking everything in me not to fuck you right here, Sierra. I want you riding my fingers, coating my hand in your cum before you take every last inch of my cock inside you until you come again. I don't want you to be able to walk without feeling the ache between your legs that I created. Let me take you home."

It's a need disguised as a plea, one that I hope she buys into before I spend the rest of my day jerking off under cold water to the image of her and everything that I plan on doing with and to her.

She has me in knots, impossible to untangle.

I feel the frustration and disappointment build to a near point of explosion when her eyes widen, suddenly alert, no longer fogged over. A deep flush washes out her light freckles when she shoves me away and frantically readjusts the bottom of her dress where it had ridden up. She doesn't look at me once while collecting herself with a silent urgency, and it pisses me the fuck off.

"Shit. Shit, shit, *shit*." She presses two fingers to her swollen lips, looking as embarrassed as a teenage boy caught by his mom watching porn for the first time. "No. No way. We're in a hallway. Oh my God." Hands clasp on the top of her head and she begins to pace.

I push my hair back and lick my lips, the taste of her mouth still on them. "Relax. Nobody saw anything." *Who cares if they did?*

"You don't know that. Anyone could have walked by." She frantically tries to flatten her hair. "Cole—my boss could have seen! You need to stay away from me. I don't think straight when you get close to me. I'm not myself around you."

I try not to take her words as compliments, but I'll admit I don't quite see the problem with what she's saying.

"Boss, huh? He probably would have liked to see it. The guy looks like he only knows how to be on the bottom. I'm sure he could have taken some notes."

"This isn't a joke, Braden. Just forget about it. I have to go."

I don't make any effort to stop her when she brushes past me. She wouldn't have stayed regardless, and I'm not about to make a fool of myself by attempting to convince her. "Try to keep it in your pants for the rest of the night, yeah?" My tease falls flat.

"Don't call me. This was a mistake," she mutters before walking away and joining her table again. My jaw ticks with anger at her sudden departure, but I ignore her parting words.

I will be calling her. Preferably sooner rather than later. She can count on that.

13

Sierra

Fuck Braden and his ability to yank me around by a set of puppet strings.

Every single ounce of my self-control is yanked from my grasp the minute he opens his mouth, leaving me with nothing more than crushed dignity and wet panties. It's embarrassing —down right scarring for my self-esteem.

He's dangerous. An all too tempting distraction that I can't afford right now. Or *ever*. The air between us becomes so charged with sexual want and attraction that I can't manage to keep any sort of boundary up. When I try, he just kicks it over, smiling that arrogant grin the entire time.

When I was with Logan, there was always an attraction there. But it never sizzled in the air, danced on my skin, or expanded in my chest until I couldn't damn well breathe. We were together for what feels like forever, having met when I was only eighteen and he was twenty-one. It was a few years before we moved from friends to being in a romantic relationship, but it was a sudden change. I always assumed that we had a strong sexual connection, a shared lust for one another, but now, I'm positive that we never did. What we had was comfort and trust—a shared responsibility to take care of each other's sexual needs and wants. How utterly disappointing.

I can feel Braden's heated gaze on my back as I walk back to my table. My bottom lip slips between my teeth as I sway my hips more dramatically, knowing full well he was already rock hard when I left him standing there. He deserves to be teased. After all, he did accuse me of being a prostitute.

Lauren is the first one to notice me when I reach the table.

"Oh, Cole. Sienna came back," she cheers sarcastically, toying with the lipstick coated straw between her long fingernails.

Cole's eyes meet mine when he spins around. "We were just about to send a search party after you." He laughs. "Everything okay?"

"Yeah, just a long line." *A very, very long one.*

I cock a brow at the two girls when they don't move to make room for me and mumble under their breath instead. The snickers they both make in response to my growing anger only results in the snapping of my last strand of patience as I shake my head.

"Okay. What the hell is you—"

"Baby? What are you doing here?"

I whip around to stare at Braden as he walks up beside me and confidently slips his arm around my waist, pulling me flush up against his side. He's so tall that I have to tilt my head to meet his stare as he settles beside me, palming my hip with splayed fingers. His lips stretch in a boyish grin that draws me close. My arm hooks around his torso, squeezing him with a silent thank you.

When someone clears their throat, I blink twice before following the noise. Cole stares at the large hand splayed across my hip, but doesn't seem to buy into the touch. I find myself leaning slightly into Braden.

"Is this the boss that you were telling me about? It's so great to meet you, Colt," Braden speaks up again.

"It's Cole," Cole corrects him when he finally tears his eyes from my body and dares to take his chances eyeing up Braden. "And who are you? I don't think Sierra has ever mentioned you."

The arrogance in his tone rubs my skin like a fresh sheet of sandpaper.

"I'm the boyfriend."

"You're *her* boyfriend? For real?" I hear Tiffany mock, the humour in her tone punching at my bruised ego, leaving behind a dull ache.

"Yeah? What about it?" Braden asks in a low, threatening voice, not missing the obvious insult.

I want nothing more than to jump over the restricting mental ropes holding me back from tearing this bitch a new asshole. But these are my coworkers. I can't do anything that could ultimately hurt my career. I've worked too hard to throw it all away over a few rude comments.

The taste of blood rings in my mouth before I notice that I've been biting down on my tongue. I need to get out of here. With a shaking hand, I tug on Braden's belt loop. His breath fans across the top of my head as I peek up at him and meet his concerned stare with a pleading one. *Please take the hint.*

The top of my head is cold again as Braden looks away, clearing his throat. "You guys wouldn't mind if I took Sierra home, would you? My mom's actually expecting us for dinner."

I send a forced smile to the group and fiddle with the strap of my purse. Catching the glare Tiffany's shooting at me from across the table, I let my teeth latch back onto my tongue.

"Yeah, no problem," Cole clears his throat. "See you tomorrow." The last words are spit through a clenched jaw as he watches Braden plant a kiss on my head.

"Yeah. See you all tomorrow."

I feel Braden's hand slide into mine, our fingers interlocking as he looks down at me curiously, a softness in his eyes that I haven't seen before. It looks a lot like pity, but it feels the opposite.

"So nice to meet you, Colt. Have a good one."

Pushing out a breath, I tug on Braden's arm and start leading us through the restaurant, focused on the exit. Neither of us speak a word until we get outside. The sun peeks through the clouds, shining in my eyes and fresh air fills my lungs.

The hand once held in Braden's slaps against my thigh as he drops it and steps back. His brows are scrunched between his eyes as he avoids eye contact, opting to stare down at the concrete instead. The silence continues to grow, acting like a barrier between us that I'm extremely grateful for.

Wanting nothing more than to get away from here and end this little charade, I say, "Thank you. You didn't have to do that."

He straightens his back and looks at me again. The softness I saw back in the restaurant is long gone, replaced only by a familiar, vacant stare. "No worries. You looked uncomfortable."

"That obvious?" I laugh lightly, unable to keep it to myself.

"Like I said, don't worry about it. You shouldn't let people talk to you like that." His eyes dart around the parking lot. He looks like he wants to be *anywhere* but here. With me. "My mom's actually still inside, so . . ."

"Right." I nod. "I need to go anyway. My car's still at work."

"Yeah. I heard it's going to rain. Might want to hurry." He shoves his hands in his pockets, shoulders tight.

I nod again. "I guess I'll see you around, then?"

"Yeah. I'll see you around." He turns and walks back inside seconds before I feel the first raindrop splatter across my forehead.

I think that sounded an awful lot like goodbye.

14

Braden

Rain pelts down from the dark sky, soaking into the material of my t-shirt, making it cling to my skin. The temperature seems to drop with the press of a button. I shiver, soaked through and through.

"Seriously? What next? Being struck by lightning? Stepping into an ankle deep puddle and losing my shoe?" Sierra shouts from behind me, the anger in her words so prevalent that I begin to feel guilty for leaving her standing there alone and upset.

I'm annoyed with the way I'm acting, but I need to walk away. I need to leave her behind me and brush off the feeling of protectiveness that's now burrowing itself in my chest. It's a new, uncomfortable feeling that I know right away I don't like, nor have any reason to be contemplating in the first place.

Then I think about her boss and the way he watched her when she got back to their table—like she was a forbidden fruit he couldn't wait to take a nice juicy bite out of. Yet he didn't stand up for her—

not once—when she was being belittled right in front of him.

It pissed me the fuck off, and I knew that I had to do

something. Sierra puts on a hefty image of perfection and bravery in front of others, but she's not made out of impenetrable armour. Nobody is.

Regardless of what I know I *should* do, I stand here in the rain anyway, watching her shake like a fucking leaf in the middle of a busy parking lot and wondering how I'm supposed to put distance between us when she's standing so defeated, soaked from head to toe and stranded without a damn car.

I'm not exactly the good guy, but I'm not the bad guy either.

Sighing, I spin around on my heels and choke back a laugh. With drenched brown locks sticking to her pink cheeks, head thrown back and eyelids fluttered shut, Sierra looks beautiful—peaceful even. I don't bother fighting back my grin as I push my sopping hair away from my face and watch her, the view uninterrupted.

She drops her head now, staring at her open-toed shoes. Her head shakes, fists clenching and unclenching at her sides. The tension in her shoulders keeps her body rigid as she kicks at a cement barricade and groans in pain.

She looks like she wants to light the world on fire and watch it burn to ash. It's a sight that has me on the balls of my feet, anxious to be by her side so we can do it together.

"You want a ride?" The offer slips out before I can stop myself.

Five minutes ago, I was ready to leave her out here alone and delete her number before I ended up walking off the edge of a cliff, falling face first into an abyss of the unknown. Now I'm offering her a ride home?

Sierra's pretty pink lips part when she spins around, relief washing over her, tense shoulders dropping. If she were offended by my offer, she doesn't show it. "Uh, yeah. Sure. If you don't mind."

I reach into my pocket and dangle my car keys in the air

with a brief nod to let her know that it's not a big deal. "It's the red one."

I head for my car but stop after a couple of steps, suddenly frozen in place, watching as her eyes begin to shine and her bottom lip trembles ever so slightly.

An ache grows in my chest as I keep myself from going to comfort her. I've never found myself in this position before—being somebody that might be able to bring comfort to someone else. It terrifies me.

Despite that, I call her name.

She doesn't respond, just wraps her arms around herself and shivers. I close the distance between us and wrap my arm around her, tucking her into my chest with a heavy sigh. "You're going to get sick."

Sierra exhales a shuddered breath while leaning into me, but keeps her arms by her sides. I try not to think too much of it and focus on the way her breathing begins to steady instead, each puff of hot air creating a burning sensation on my frozen chest.

Her touch is electric, sparking under the water running off our bodies. The tingle it leaves on my skin makes it hard to focus—hard to remember where and who we are. It's addicting. It enthralls me and makes my brain fuzzy.

When I think she's a bit more relaxed, I try again to lead us to my car, desperate to both get out of the rain before we come down with hypothermia.

"Wait. Not yet." She pulls away until we're a few inches apart and presses her hands to my pecs, fingers splayed out.

She wears a look of embarrassment that has my jaw tightening, a growl of frustration vibrating in my chest. It was the same embarrassment I saw when she reached her table inside, and having her look at me the same way has my fists clenching until my palms burn.

"I'm sorry if I embarrassed you back there. I should have been able to handle them myself," she whispers, her voice thick with emotion, sounding utterly defeated. Her thumbs rub my wet shirt over and over before she grips it in a fist.

Furrowing my eyebrows, I shake my head. "You shouldn't have had to handle them in the first place. And I meant what I said before. It wasn't a big deal."

"It was a big deal to me."

It was?

She nods, letting her eyes drop to my mouth. Her reaction has me realizing that I said my words out loud.

I don't have time to kick myself in the ass about it before she's pressing her lips gently against mine. I blink a few times before kissing her back, tasting her tears and fighting back the urge to go inside and throw my fist around. I busy myself touching her instead, using her body to calm and steady me. I grab her face in my hands and try to warm her skin by rubbing my thumbs across her sharp cheekbones.

We need to get to the car. I know that I need to get us warm, but when I move my hands to her hips and pull her flush against me, I don't think my legs would move even if I tried.

A set of furious shivers rack through my body, but I'm not sure if it's from the cold anymore.

The rain continues pounding down around us and our clothes are soaked, yet neither of us care. The only thing I care about right now is how good her chest feels pressed up against mine and how badly she makes me want to be inside of her. Whether it be in a public bathroom, my bed, or outside in the pouring rain, I can't get enough of her. I could spend all day with my mouth against hers.

Her lips part as she pulls away, yet manages to stay close enough to brush her nose against mine. "Can you bring me home now?"

I don't need to be asked twice.

———

Sierra flicks her bedroom light on before slowly turning to me—wearing a coy, almost shy smile—and pushing off her wet skirt. She lets the fabric fall to the ground with a thump, so wet it must weigh a few pounds. Her eyes shine with a playfulness that has my lips twitching.

My mouth waters at the sight of her naked body. My cock hardens in my jeans, feeling near painful with how tight they've become. Her blouse is so wet it's see-through, and her breasts spill from the top of her cream-coloured laced bra behind it.

I swallow the space between us and pull off her blouse before reaching behind her, unclasping and throwing her bra away. Without preamble, I grab her hips and pull her to stand in front of me as I sit on the edge of her bed. Leaning forward, I catch her nipple in my mouth, sucking and biting at the rosy bud.

"Yes," she sighs in approval.

Her eyes widen with both shock and a hot flash of need when I reach up and collar her throat, squeezing lightly.

"Eyes on me." It's an order, not a request, and it doesn't take long for her to understand, nodding once. "Good girl."

I want to watch her writhe from the feel of my tongue lashing at her nipples as they ache with need and her skin burns from the rough brush of my stubbled jaw. Every primal instinct is begging me to take us both to the floor and slide inside of her.

I'm desperate to feel her hot pussy gripping my shaft like its very own lifeline, but I won't. I want to take my time with her. She needs to remember exactly what it feels like to have me buried balls deep inside of her in case she ever thinks of letting anybody else between these smooth thighs.

Sierra bucks her hips and her fingers find purchase in my hair, tugging on it hard enough that my scalp aches. I drag my open mouth to her other breast before repeating my actions on that nipple, tasting, sucking and biting down on it, soaking in each whimper that slips from her lips.

I release her throat and my hands begin to shape her body, stopping briefly on her ass as I begin to knead it in my palms. My touch drags to her front, teasing the inside of her thighs.

She whispers my name and I groan, pulling away from her chest to decorate her smooth skin with anxious, greedy, open-mouthed kisses. My tongue dances just above the band of her underwear, still holding her glazed stare before I rip the thong down her thighs and yank her forward until she straddles my left thigh.

She gasps, surprised by the move but recovers quickly when I grip her hips and drag her toward me, making her clit rub against my leg. Her hands find my shoulders as she steadies herself before dragging her bare pussy toward my knee and back again, beginning to ride my leg, using me to get herself off.

I keep my hands steady but relaxed on her waist, letting her be in complete control. My cock presses against my zipper, hard to the point of utter discomfort, but I don't make any moves to get myself off. Watching Sierra fall apart on my leg is too fucking sexy to interrupt.

"That's right, baby," I praise, watching her teeth sink into her bottom lip, wishing it was me feasting on her mouth. "Make that pussy come. Soak my leg before I fuck you."

Her chin tilts, and I can't find it in me to force her to keep her eyes open when they flutter shut again, her movements becoming ragged, less controlled.

The pressure on my shoulders increases when she uses me for balance, too focused on getting herself to the edge of that cliff to stay upright. She's getting close when I bury my face in her neck, nipping at the skin below her ear, slashing it with my tongue.

The peaks of her chest brush against me when she arches her back and whimpers, "Please. I need you to touch me."

"Where?" I say the words against her neck and she shudders, leaning into me further. I pinch her nipple between my fingertips. She cries out. "Is that enough? Or do you want both?" I pinch her other one and pull just as hard before twisting them both in between two fingers.

She doesn't reply, only increases her movements until her breath hitches and her spine straightens, forcing her to lean away from me.

"Fuck, Braden. Yes, *yes*. I'm coming." The words come out gargled, in broken pieces. Her hands slip from my shoulders, and I move to catch her before she falls to the floor. I can't help but attack her neck again, as she rides out her orgasm on my thigh.

When her body goes slack against mine, I grin wickedly. Moving my hand between her thighs, I drag a finger along her drenched slit and groan. With her cum coating my fingers, I slip them in my mouth and suck them clean while she watches with heavy, lidded eyes.

"*Fuck*, you taste good," I groan.

There's an insatiable fire in her eyes as she watches me, digesting my words. Knowing she's so turned on by the simple act, even after coming so hard just minutes earlier, has my shaft twitching in my pants, pleading to spring free of its tight confinement.

I pull my fingers from my mouth and wind them in the hairs at the base of her neck, tilting her head and kissing her, letting her taste herself on my lips. Flicking my tongue at her mouth, she parts her lips for me, letting our tongues glide alongside one another, tasting and sipping and memorizing. Without breaking away, I grab her by the waist and stand, hoisting her up. She tightens her legs around me as I spin around and lay her on the center of the bed, crawling on top of her.

I pin her in place with my hips, grinding my cock against

her hot pussy and growling, "I need you so bad, Sierra. I fucking ache to be inside of you."

She bites down on her bottom lip, and her eyes flutter shut. Before I can do it myself, she spreads her legs and pulls me closer, whimpering when my zipper brushes her swollen clit.

I back off the bed long enough to shove off my jeans and briefs. My cock is hard and heavy between my legs as I move above her, nearly losing it from just the heat radiating between her legs when I press against her. I slip a finger between her wet, pink flesh, and rub a knuckle across her sensitive nerves before rolling it between my fingers. Sierra arches her back, pressing hard against me.

My heart thumps hard and fast against my chest. I wouldn't be surprised if she could feel it. I haven't been this turned on in my entire life. The need to touch and hear her makes my blood pound in my ears to a near deafening point. I desperately want it to stop, to let me relax and go back to the way it used to be, when sex was a simple means to an end. It couldn't feel farther from that now.

When we're together I fuck for *her*, not me. I want to fuck her to the point my name will be the only one that ever leaves her lips again. Not because she'll miss me, but because she won't be able to think about another cock stretching her hot cunt the way mine has.

Every time she's kissed, I want her to think about how right my dick feels in her mouth and down her throat.

When another man brushes a hair out of her face, I want her to remember the burn of me wrapping it around my fist and yanking her close while devouring her throat like a starved animal.

The thoughts won't leave my head. Won't give me any reprieve. They just keep knocking around in my skull, torturing me until I give them what they want.

But I won't give them what they want. I know I won't.

Sierra is not mine. I seem to have forgotten that she is just a fuck buddy and can be replaced without a second thought.

As if needing to prove a point to myself, I grip my shaft and thrust completely inside of her, keeping my eyes locked on her tits as they jolt from the sudden movement. She gasps, hands searching my body for something to grab and steady herself with. I pull out almost completely before plunging back in.

Again, and again.

She feels hot, tight, and like something I could become addicted to if I let myself fall down that hole. My thrusts are savage, unrelenting. There's nothing personal about the way I fuck her. Like she's nothing more than a willing body. The nostalgia of it washes over me and has my molars grinding.

"Braden!" she cries when my thumb slides across her clit. She fists my hair in an attempt to grab my attention but I refuse to give it to her.

Don't look at her. Fuck her like a stranger.

She claws at me harder, more impatiently with every slap of skin. So, I grab her thigh to move it around my hip and slide even further inside that tight vice, hitting the spot that has her seeing stars in hopes that the increase of pleasure will distract her.

It doesn't. Fuck me, it only makes *my* resolve flounder.

Her pussy quivers around me, and I know she's about to come. The pressure at the base of my spine says I won't be far behind her.

Throwing her other leg over my hip, I fuck her harder. My balls slap her ass and sweat beads between my brows and on my chest.

"I need you to come for me, Sierra. I need you to coat this cock in your cum," I groan through clenched teeth, fighting to keep from taking her mouth and stealing her moans as they barrel into me.

"Look at me," she growls, reaching toward me and scratching at my chest. "I'm not just some faceless fuck."

I almost freeze when she calls me out, completely aware of exactly what I've been doing. I ignore her.

Grinding my teeth some more, I sweep up some of her wetness and rub circles around her swollen clit. It's a jackass thing to do—using her own body against her—but I don't let myself feel guilty for it when she tightens up like a spring and her walls clamp down around me, pulsing as I come right along with her.

"Fuck. Yes." My thrusts become messy, and my vision becomes black around the edges as she milks every last drop of cum from me. A smug smile threatens to pull at my mouth before I swallow hard and blink twice, settling back down on earth.

Neither of us say anything as I pull out and get off the bed. My thighs burn, and my muscles stay tense, pissing me the fuck off.

With a tick in my jaw, I pull my damp clothes back on, keeping my back to her. It isn't until I pull out my phone to check the time that she speaks up.

"You're a real piece of work. You know that, right?"

Her words strike a nerve, and my hands form fists at my sides. I have to focus on keeping my composure and not turning around to look at her. I'm not sure what I would find if I did.

She doesn't sound hurt or offended. Just angry and frustrated. But I don't risk it, even when continuing to ignore her has my stomach churning.

I know that she *is* right. I know that she didn't deserve to be fucked like that—like she didn't matter. Yet I did it anyway. She can hate me all she wants, but I know it was the right thing to do, regardless of how cruel it was.

"Oh, and you're lucky I'm on birth control, dickbag," she

adds, each word laced with venom. I feel the colour drain from my face, and my shoulders instantly sag with guilt.

I've never once had sex without a condom. I'm sure there are quite a few in my wallet right now, too. I just didn't fucking think about it in the moment. I'm such a total prick.

I clear my throat and grip my phone so tight I fear it'll snap in half. "Good. That's good."

She scoffs before I hear her get off the bed and the ensuite door slam shut, the lock clicking soon after.

Taking her storming off as exactly what it is—a dismissal —I run a hand through my hair and yank until my scalp burns. The shower starts, and I shove my phone in my pocket before leaving her house with a giant ball of regret in my stomach.

15

Sierra

Running sweaty palms down my leather skirt, I try to convince myself that saying yes to this family dinner isn't going to come back to bite me in the ass. I'm nearly one-hundred percent positive that it will, but I refuse to leave my apartment wired with nerves and nausea.

It's just my parents. How bad could it really be? I nearly snort when I realize just how stupid that question is.

They've been taking some time off work to travel this past year—as if parading from country to country for work the past twenty doesn't count as travelling—and are only *now*, six months later, taking a break to visit their two daughters and granddaughter.

It's so disgustingly typical of them to think that visiting us is some sort of gift that we should worship at their feet for. Like we should be grateful and not so damn stubborn with our feelings of neglect.

I can still hear my mother's clipped tone in my ear from when she called and *told* me that we were having dinner together the night they got back into town. If I had just paid closer attention to the caller-id when she called that morning, at the asscrack of dawn, I could have avoided the entire thing and blamed it on work or something. But since I was too exhausted and worn-out from the complete pity fuck I received the night before, I picked up the phone and was greeted with the raspy, snippy voice that belongs solely to my mother before I had the chance to warn myself.

"We already made the reservation for Sunday night, Sierra. Don't argue with me, it's the least you can do for us. I'm too old to argue. You know this," she said, as if fifty-five is the new ninety.

I simply responded by asking where the reservation was, and immediately had to fight the need to hiss like an offended cat when she responded with, "The restaurant connected to our hotel. The fancy one. Remember? They have the best fish."

I've always hated fish, but I told her I would be there and hung up before I couldn't bite my tongue any longer.

My parents always stay at the same hotel when they visit. Considering they sold our childhood home the minute Clare got pregnant and moved out, there really isn't another option.

I'll never forgive them for leaving me no choice but to move in with my sister while they went and traveled the world, responsibility free.

A hotel is their only option in Vancouver. And for some reason that I really don't care enough about to know, the hotel restaurant is the only place that they will eat. It probably has something to do with the sticks that have somehow climbed further and further up their asses with every trip they take for work, and how it's made them too good to eat anywhere with less than a five star rating, but who knows. Definitely not me. I haven't known anything about them for quite some time now.

The door buzzer makes me jump, yanking me from my thoughts as I take one last look in the mirror, nod in approval, and grab my purse.

Fidgeting with the high-collar of my button-up peach blouse, I undo the top button and pull the shirt away from my hot neck as I head out. I fan the material and sigh when a cool breeze sticks to the sweat there. If Clare's already down there waiting, I must have been stuck in my own thoughts for far longer than I thought.

With that in mind, I say a quick prayer under my breath and head downstairs with my wool coat under my arm and a grim smile on my face.

———

"MOMMA," Liz sings from the backseat. She's snuggled into her booster seat with her favourite stuffed giraffe in her fists, not bothered by the lack of light in the car. It's only seven o'clock, but it's already fairly dark outside thanks to the change in seasons.

"Yeah, baby?" There's a slight waver in Clare's voice, most likely from nerves, but I don't mention it. She's already on edge enough as it is.

Our parents have only seen Elizabeth, their *granddaughter*, a total of three times since she was born. She just turned seven this past July.

Their lack of involvement hurts Clare, but they just don't see it. They don't care. I feel awful for my sister, having watched her raise a daughter all on her own after being divorced when she was twenty-three, so young and alone. I know that I was there for her and Liz, but it's not the same. She needed her mom, and she wasn't there for her. It wasn't fair to anyone.

"I don't wanna see Nana and PopPop." There's a finality to her otherwise gentle voice that makes me wince. *Tell me about it, kid.* "Why do we have to? Do they 'member me?"

Clare sits silent for a moment, her tongue pressed to her cheek. I can only imagine the things she wants to say but knows that she can't. Kids are like sponges. They absorb literally *everything*. Not like we both wouldn't love for Liz to let a few of our thoughts slip during dinner. Just not tonight. A scene is the last thing any of us want.

"Because they're family. And we always make time for family, Bug."

I turn to Clare and smile even though she doesn't take her eyes off of the road. I wait for another question to come, but Liz seems satisfied with that answer for the moment.

After another ten minutes in silence, with only the radio playing in the background, we arrive outside of the hotel restaurant.

There's a chill that slides over me when we head for the doors, one that makes my skin prickle and my stomach clench with fear like someone's reached their hand inside and squeezed. I swallow slowly and shove my hands inside the deep pockets of my coat, fiddling with whatever I can find.

The automatic doors slide open when Liz skips a few steps ahead of us, arms flapping in the air. She looks the epitome of carefree and naïve.

It makes me jealous.

When we're young, we're always so eager to grow up. All we think being a grown-up means is no longer having a bedtime and being able to eat junk food whenever we want. It's not until we actually do grow up that we realize just how badly we miss our youth, and how we took it for granted.

We would do anything to go back to the days of no responsibilities and worriless nights. But we can't, because like our youth, they're long fucking gone and there's a slim to none chance that they will ever come back.

We pass by a busy stainless-steel bar cluttered with a few suit-wearing intimidating men perched on leather stools, and the glowing shelves lined with generous arrays of expensive alcohol behind it before we stop in front of a hostess table. The energy in the restaurant is familiar from the various times we've dined here, yet I still can't seem to get a reading on what makes it buzz with a sense of comfort the way it does. Maybe it's the bright, yet somehow not blinding lights that dangle from the high ceilings, or the classical music that plays at just the right volume. Who knows.

Slim fingers grasp my exposed wrist when we stop and wait for the hostess to show us to our parents. My eyes slide to the left and find Clare's waiting gaze. The panic in her wide stare makes my mouth dry like I just sucked on a cotton ball.

"Don't freak out," she says mighty slowly, watching me like I've suddenly become a ticking time bomb that she's terrified of setting off. "ButitlooksliketheybroughtLogan."

I double blink. "Say again?"

"It looks like they brought Logan, S. I would recognize that sleazy smirk any day. You told them what happened right? That you're not together anymore? *Shit.* Of course, you did. It's been months."

I stop listening after she says his name, the sound of blood thumping in my ears too loud to focus on anything else. My stomach burns as what feels like acid rips holes through my insides.

I swallow past the bile in my throat and follow Clare's stare to the table off to the side of the restaurant, half-hidden behind a massive fish tank filled to the max with exotic looking fish.

"Did you know he was coming?" I think I mumble, fully aware that my tongue feels incredibly numb. It's not until I wipe the back of my hand across my forehead, testing it for sweat, that I realize that both my hands are shaking. *Pull it together, Sierra.*

My breath catches in my throat when we're noticed and a masculine hand lifts in the air, two fingers creating a "come here" motion when we continue to stand in place.

I can feel Liz's confusion and worry when she uses a small palm to grip my lower thigh, squeezing to try and get my attention. With a fleeting smile, I manage to calm her slightly, her hand not moving, but squeezing much lighter.

The two long fingers continue to wave us over, but my feet refuse to move, glued to the fucking floor like the bottoms of my heels have melted and stuck to it.

I close my eyes and imagine a *Bugs Bunny* worthy X marked below Logan's seat. When I don't hear an anvil fall from the sky and crush the cheating sack of shit into smithereens, I open them again, disappointed. I shake the thoughts away and with a quick inhale, square my shoulders and steel my features.

I tell myself that I can look at him. That my knees won't give out on me and leave me a blubbering pile of embarrassment on the floor.

There's nothing that he can do now that will hurt you anymore than what he already has. I repeat that sentence over and over again until I'm at least half positive that I won't lose my fucking head. He's nothing more than an ugly reminder of why men suck, and why I'm perfectly content with being single until the day I die. He's the past, regardless of how apparent it is that he wishes he still had a place in my present.

Logan Newcrest is like a stray cat—you leave out a bowl of tuna for it one too many times and it keeps coming back for more, no matter how often you kick the scraggly thing away.

Only in my case, I've given my stray cat one too many chances at redemption and now he won't piss off until he gets another.

Feeling a bit more secure in myself, I meet his stare with one full of ice. His lips tip in an amused, nauseating smile.

"Let's get this over with, guys," I say, turning over my hand and grabbing Clare's.

Clare gives my hand a reassuring squeeze that says everything she doesn't. I appreciate that she doesn't say anything. Doesn't ask me if I'm sure, or if I'm positive. There's a quiet voice in my head that tells me I might not have been able to do it if she had.

I'm the one to lead us to our table, needing to take control wherever I possibly can. When we round the fish tank and take in the full view of our table, I don't let myself show even a sliver of the anger I feel pouring from every pore in my body.

My mother, all five-feet of her, jumps up from her chair at the far end of the table and claps like the restaurant isn't full and that it's just us at home. Her antics used to embarrass me when I was younger, but not anymore. You get used to it.

"Elizabeth! You look so gorgeous, sweetheart," Dina Caster says in awe of her granddaughter.

She swiftly ignores Clare and me, and stares down at the tiny girl that moves to hide behind Clare's leg, eyeing the older woman—who might as well be a stranger to her—like she doesn't know why she's talking to her.

"You remember us, don't you, Lizzy girl?"

My father, Leonard, grins that wide, carefree grin that used to wrap around me like a warm hug when I was Liz's age. It doesn't have the same effect on my niece, however. She moves further behind my sister and grips onto her thighs like she'll sink through the floor if she doesn't have something steady to hold onto.

"Mom. Dad." Clare dips her head at the two of them before turning to crouch in front of Liz, gripping her shoulders lightly. "Say hi to Nana and PopPop, baby."

My mother clicks her tongue rudely and walks to Clare's side when Liz doesn't immediately do as she's told, attempting to brush her aside to get to her terrified granddaughter. "Don't be rude, Elizabeth. Say hello to your grandpa and me."

"Mother," I hiss, wishing for a second that shoving an old lady, let alone your own mother, wasn't frowned upon. "She probably doesn't remember you. Did you really think that she would? It's been what? Three years?"

"Hello, Sierra," she sighs, eye-lids sweeping shut for a moment as if my mere existence exhausts her. She doesn't even bother looking at me when she turns to the elephant at the table. "Are you not going to say hello to Logan? It was so thoughtful for him to agree to come tonight. He is such a busy man nowadays with his company taking off! You must be so proud of him."

Hearing my own mother speak of my ex-boyfriend's accomplishments with a sense of pride that I've never heard from her in regards to my own, only makes my skin burn hotter.

I stare at her without blinking, keeping my features lazy, bored. "Why is he here, Mom? You know full well we're no longer together. I remember telling you why, as well."

It's Logan that speaks next after clearing his throat way louder than necessary. "I'm right here, S. Speak to me. You know I only bite if you want me to."

I spare him a fleeting glance and clamp down on my tongue. If his arrogant, tasteless words weren't bad enough, his choice of outfit accessories is.

The navy and pale pink striped tie that I got him last Christmas is knotted snugly at the base of his throat and lays flat over a crisp, white button-up shirt, while a gold Rolex—the one I saved for for a solid year and gifted him on his birthday—is fitted below the custom cuff-links on his left wrist.

I snort, unable to hold it in. "You couldn't be an even bigger prick if you tried, Logan."

My mother scoffs at my comment while my father lightly shushes her.

"Let's just sit down, shall we?" he suggests desperately.

A set of tired, mahogany brown eyes flicker between Logan and me, yet Leonard Caster says nothing in my defence. Like always, he's too terrified of his wife to ever dare speak out against her.

It's still a wonder to me how he can stay married to my mom—happily, at that—when they're such opposites. Whereas my mother doesn't mind making her presence known in a crowded room, Dad would rather slip under an invisibility cloak to avoid even a single set of curious eyes.

I can almost feel his embarrassment from the scene that this wife has caused, but knowing he probably didn't agree with her inviting my ex-boyfriend, yet still went along with it is enough to keep my sympathy for him at bay.

He will always be the same timid-mouthed man I've known my whole life.

Swallowing hard, I stiffly dip my chin and take the empty seat beside my niece when I notice that everybody else has already sat down. I sigh in relief when I see Clare sitting beside Logan, shooting me a wink when she catches me looking. And when I spare Logan a quick flick of my eyes, I smile at his scowl of disapproval.

Clare and Sierra : 1

Cheating Bastard : 0

16

Braden

"YOU DIDN'T WANT TO CHANGE FIRST? I LOOK LIKE A FUCKING slob beside you." I don't bother looking at my brother when I speak. I'm too busy watching the perfectly squared ice cubes melt in my glass of whiskey.

The Vancouver Warriors just won their home opener—barely, but who cares—and Tyler, being the winning goal-scorer of the game, called to invite me out with the small group of players that wanted to celebrate the win in the public eye. I instinctively wanted to say no, not because I don't love drinking fancy fucking booze in the company of my brother, but because being around so many professional hockey players makes my insides burn.

I miss the damn sport, and knowing that I could have been playing alongside my own brother, not necessarily on the same team, but in general, yet chose a completely different career path, fills me the smallest nip of regret.

I keep reminding myself that I did it for Dad, and that there was no guarantee I would have been drafted into the pro's anyway, but not knowing at all, that shit *sucks*. It eats at me some days, but boxing is in my blood. It's a passion of mine that I could never give up.

I'm so damn proud of Tyler for not allowing his own inner demons to stop him from accomplishing what he's always wanted, and for becoming a staple name in hockey.

That doesn't mean I'm not a bit jealous, though. Every time I turn on a game and see my brother and his brother-in-law, Oakley Hutton, and one of my college hockey teammates and good friend, lighting up the rink together with so much skill, power, and confidence, I can't help but imagine myself right there beside them. Just like the good old days.

"We both know that if I went home after the game, Gracie wouldn't have let me back out," Tyler says with a snort. His smile spreads around his clear glass as he takes a sip of his drink. The humour in his dark eyes makes my chest rumble with a laugh.

"Right." I tap the side of my glass with my finger and hum. "How has she been lately? The nausea still kicking her ass?"

My brother's wife is three months pregnant now, and has been dealing with some gnarly morning sickness the entire time. If I remember correctly, I think she had to get prescription pills from her doctor when it got so bad that she couldn't even get out of bed most days. It was hard for her not to be able to work, but every time she even attempted it, it wasn't long before she was calling Tyler from the bathroom, begging him to come take her home.

A long, frustrated grunt fills the space between us as Tyler's empty glass is shoved toward the bartender. "Yeah. It's getting better but it's killing *me*, man. She looks so fucking miserable all the time and there's nothing that I can do to help."

I want to give him a reassuring hug, but settle on squeezing his shoulder knowing full well he's not the biggest fan of receiving comfort from anyone other than his wife. "How much longer until it eases? Or will it not go away?"

"Doctor says it should go away in a few weeks. Hopefully it'll just be a first trimester thing."

I nod. "Well for all of our sakes, I hope so too. I don't know how much more of your bitching I can take before my ears begin to bleed, Ty."

"Fuck off," he grumbles, even though the corner of his mouth twitches, begging to lift into a grin. "What's up with you? I haven't seen you since you bailed at dinner."

"Not much."

It's only a half-lie. I haven't done much of anything since I left Sierra's house last week. I haven't texted her, and she hasn't texted me. Things have gone back to normal. That is if my new normal has become not being able to get even the slightest hard-on unless I'm flicking through memories of what Sierra's pussy tastes like.

I haven't been able to get it up for anyone, at fucking *all*, the past few days. I even spent my Saturday night in a dark hallway at Sinners with my pants down at my ankles and a hot mouth wrapped around my soft cock, unable to get hard. The big breasted brunette was offended, not like I could blame her, and left me bracing myself against the wall alone with my dick hanging between my legs like a limp noodle. I didn't even give myself time to be embarrassed that my cock had become so utterly useless before I left, got in my car, and began slamming my hands on my steering wheel until the anger passed.

"What's the scowl for them? Someone key your car or something?"

"Nobody fucking keyed my car. Nothing's up."

Tyler turns his bar stool until he faces me, right arm planted on the bar top, knees spread wide in his expensive, custom black dress pants and the top two buttons of his white dress shirt unbuttoned. His black hair—buzzed on the sides, longer in the middle—is messy as hell, like he hasn't touched it since he took his hockey helmet off after the game. Knowing him, he probably hasn't. He has a brow kicked up as he watches me, eyes doubtful, making it clear that he doesn't believe a damn word I've said.

"I saw Clayton the other day when I stopped by the gym," he says while signaling the bartender to refill his glass. My stomach drops.

That little shithead.

Tyler's drink is refilled quickly, and he takes a sip before facing me again. "He mentioned a girl. Sierra, I think her name was? Said you were seeing her or something like that. I told him he had to be lying because there's no way my brother had a steady girl and didn't tell me."

I lift my shoulder in a lazy shrug, trying to play it off like the topic of Sierra doesn't affect me. Tyler would never let me live it down if I told him just how much it did actually affect me.

"We were fucking around for a while. It's done now." There's the smallest hint of a smile on his face that has me tonguing my cheek. "I'm serious. I haven't seen her in a week."

"And how has that been?"

The grip on my drink tightens. I swallow hard. "Fine. What are you? A shrink now?"

"Fine?" he echoes, head tilted while he belts out a rough laugh. "You sure about that? You don't sound real sure."

Pushing away from the bar, not wanting to deal with getting the third degree any longer than I have to, I get up, drink still in my hand. Tipping my glass, I gulp down the last few sips before slapping it down on the bar and shoving my hands in the pockets of my jeans. "Going to the bathroom," I mutter and stalk off until his bursting laughter fades into nothing.

I'm rounding an excessively gigantic fish tank when I stop, my chest beginning to constrict. My nostrils flare and my back molars grind together as I take in the scene playing out a few feet in front of me.

Sierra.

Sierra.

Sierra.

The need to kick something dangles on the edge of feeling almost numbing when my cock grows hard, pressing against the zipper of my jeans. There she sits, all perfect posture and self-aware. Straight faced and confident. Pale peach lips, sharp cheekbones, strong jaw.

She doesn't smile, pout, or frown. Her full lips remain in a straight line, completely still, like she's promised herself a giant margarita if she doesn't so much as budge them with a strong exhale.

The peach blouse she wears is the same shade as her lips, making them pop that much more. It frustrates me that I can't figure out exactly what she's thinking behind those blank silver eyes and long, thick black lashes.

She's put up a wall, it's easy to tell. One that she doesn't plan on letting anybody at her table have the chance at sneaking past. I can't help but stare as she briefly narrows her sights on the slightly hunched over man sitting across from her. The same one that I can see clear as fucking day dragging his foot up her leg from beneath the tablecloth before it disappears from view.

He's fucking ballsy.

I've never wanted to rip a limb from someone's body more than I do right now. I stand rigid, glaring daggers at the back of the guy as he slips his hand beneath the table and bends forward.

I blow out a hot gush of air when Sierra flinches and turns toward the young girl sitting beside her.

So she flinches when he tries to touch her, yet invites him for dinner with the other people at the table that I assume are her family? Confusion clouds my judgment, making it harder to stay calm.

My lips curl inward at the thought that she's been out, able to fuck around with other people, while I now have a hard-on for the first time since being inside of *her*. It's infuriating. Absolutely maddening. A spiked pit grows in my stomach that feels a hell of a lot like jealousy.

Every muscle, bone, and fiber in my body wants me to stalk over there and toss the prick from his seat until he's not even in the same building as Sierra. From the fitted suit jacket and shiny black dress shoes that look like they've never been worn before tonight, I know he's here to impress. And that's the last damn thing I want to let him do, for reasons that I will deny over and over and over again until they burn to ash.

I don't want him to see the way her eyes burn with something primal and unapologetic before she tosses out a sassy comment, or how her bottom lip pulls slightly to the right side when she's nervous.

They're completely selfish thoughts. Ones I have no right thinking about. Maybe that's what pisses me off the most.

17

Sienna

VOICES AROUND ME MESH INTO A SYMPHONY OF UTTER MISERY.

My heels click clack on the sidewalk as I move toward Clare's vehicle like my ass is on fire. A deep, dominant voice rambles on and on about something with my father, growing louder and louder by the second. I know Logan is trying to catch up with me, but I only move faster.

My hackles are still raised. I'm beyond frustrated with the way Logan touched me during dinner like he had a right to do so. What started off as simple, yet unwelcomed brushes of his foot along my calf soon became firm squeezes of my knee under the table regardless of how far I had tried to pull myself away from his wandering hands.

I've never been one to love the attention that comes with causing a scene in public. Add in a very impressionable child to the mix, and I knew that there was no way that I could get away with backhanding the son of a bitch without risking teaching my niece that that is an appropriate way to act.

I can't even remember the last time I was so livid my hands shook and my chest constricted like a python had coiled itself around my ribs, planning on making me its dinner.

Logan was supposed to stay rotting in a cemetery filled

with all of the other figures of my past that had hurt me in some way over the years. I've been working so damn hard at moving on with my life, to not see reminders of him in every bottle of rum in my cupboard or picture of London on the wall of my home office.

But of course, it was my own mother that had to pour gasoline all over everything that I've accomplished before sending it all up in flames. I'm not sure why I'm even remotely surprised.

My most prominent childhood memory of her is from Christmas morning when I was ten. Clare had promised me that she would no doubt be winning the Best Sister In History award with the Christmas gift she bought me.

Turns out, Clare had saved up all of her babysitting money from the past two summers so that she could buy me the dollhouse that I had been begging our parents for for the past three Christmases. My big sister hadn't even managed to wrap it in Christmas paper yet before my mother had forced her to return it, claiming that her and Dad had already bought me one while accusing Clare of trying to act like my mother when I already had one that loved me just enough.

I wasn't even surprised when I woke up Christmas morning to find a small, rectangular shaped wrapped box waiting for me under the tree instead.

"You are never too young to start journaling, Sierra," Mom said with a familiar scowl after I had unwrapped a leather-skinned journal and everyone watched my face fall flatter than a pancake.

It was never mentioned again, not because Mom felt like she did anything wrong, but because her pride couldn't take another beating from her eldest daughter.

Nothing stopped Clare from continuing to buy me gift after gift each year, though. She just learned how to hide them. And once I started making money to buy her gifts, we started celebrating Christmas together. *Alone.* Just the two of us.

Even looking back on it today, I know that I wouldn't wish to change a single thing about it. Our mother would never own up to it, but she is responsible for the tight, unbreakable bond that her daughters share.

My fingers barely touch the door handle on the SUV before Logan shouts, "Sierra! Wait up!"

I suck in a breath through my nose before letting it out my mouth. Ignoring my better judgment, I turn my head to find him waiting a few steps behind me. My parents aren't behind him, most likely already in their car, leaving without a good-bye. I can hear Clare on the other side of the vehicle, buckling in Liz.

Logan's hands—the ones I remember being so smooth, not an imperfection in sight, the kind that belong to a man who hasn't known a lick of manual labour in his life—lay wiggling at his sides, like he isn't sure what to do with them.

I can't figure out if it's regret that has his mouth drooping or frustration from the night not going exactly how he wanted it to. Either way, not my problem.

"I want to go home, Logan. You shouldn't have come tonight. You know that, right?"

His foot lifts off the pavement before planting itself back down again. "I missed you. I don't regret coming."

I nearly laugh. "I'm not sure you know what regret feels like."

"Can you stop throwing cheap shots? You've already shut me out. Don't you think I've suffered enough?"

My jaw unhinges. Anger like I've never known sizzles under my skin, frying every nerve ending in my body that would have otherwise helped me continue to the bigger person and get inside the car.

"You've. Suffered. *Enough?*" Each word comes out in a

sharp burst, my hands opening and closing at my sides when they begin to shake.

Logan throws his hands into the air, exasperated. He's annoyed. With *me*!

"How's Maeve, by the way? Does she know that you've spent your night with me and my family? Not sure she'd like that very much." This time I meant to throw a cheap shot.

He shrugs it off anyway, replying like he never even heard me. "I don't know what you want me to say, Sierra. You already kicked me out and blocked my number when I said I was sorry! You know it didn't mean anything. It was an accident."

"An accident? I didn't know it was possible for a penis to fall inside of a vagina *accidentally* but look at that. You learn something every day!"

Logan groans with a roll of his eyes. "Here we go again. I'm not sure why I keep trying. You're always so damn dramatic."

You're always so dramatic.

Dramatic.

I'm dramatic.

The weight of his words doesn't fail to fall on my wounded pride, making it burn like lemon juice squirted into an open wound. I feel squashed down by the unrealistic expectations of everyone around me to the point of pure exhaustion. I feel tired. Tired of having to continue to prove myself time and time again. Of feeling like nothing I do is ever good enough for anybody else. Of never living up to the expectations of my parents.

Any strength to continue this fight floats away, leaving me deflated. My shoulders sag forward and my eyelids begin to droop. Thankfully, my sister, wherever she is, decides that this conversation is over when I don't say another word.

"Get the hell out of here, Logan," she says, voice way too calm and controlled. Slim fingers slip around my wrist and lead me into the car, the door already open. I don't remember her opening it.

Clare gingerly helps me slip onto the seat while I serve her a look that says "I can do it myself." She simply shrugs me off and pulls the seatbelt enough that I can grab it easily and click it into place.

Clearing my throat, I slap on a barely there smile and nod once. She sighs but takes a step back, closing my door and getting in the driver's seat.

No words are said as she starts the engine and pulls out of the lot, merging onto the street. The radio plays quietly, just loud enough to help fill the void of a conversation that I don't want to have.

My head falls against the window, and my eyes have only begun to flutter shut when my phone vibrates in my purse. I debate whether or not to pull it out and look, worried that it might be Logan deciding that the conversation was in fact, not over. But I decide to reach into my purse and pull it out regardless, not wanting to start hiding from my past now.

My stomach lurches when I see the text lighting up the screen.

Braden: Come over. I need to see you.

Tapping my finger on the screen, I chew on my bottom lip, wanting to immediately say no, but stopping myself before I do.

Go over to Braden's house? To what? Get another pity fuck?

There's no hidden reason as to why he wants me to go see him. There would only be one reason for going over . . . and I know that it would help get my mind off of everything that's been dredged up tonight, pity fuck or not.

Ah. Fuck it.

Sierra: On my way.

No turning back now. "Change of plans, Clare. I'm not going home."

Braden flops down on the bed beside me with a satisfied sigh, wearing a wicked grin that has me questioning my sanity. Our eyes meet, his somehow glowing in the darkness of his bedroom.

The overhanging feeling of confusion that blanketed my shoulders when I arrived earlier—watching Braden eye met up with a less guarded, more attentive expression compared to the last time we were together—has been lifted, replaced with one of satisfaction.

There are questions I want to ask, and things I want to say. But they can wait for a time where my heart isn't racing and the delicious throb between my legs has disappeared.

"Shit, Sierra. I think you've ruined me for anyone else."

He's nearly beaming, his expression so calm and collected, so at peace, while I struggle to hide the surprise from mine. Sometimes it's impossible to understand this man.

He seems to sort through and understand his emotions like it's the easiest concept in the world.

I flip on my side and prop myself up on my elbow, eyeing the dimple in Braden's left cheek. "How do you do that?"

He turns his head. "Do what?"

"Act so calm. You don't try to keep how you feel to yourself. I don't know how to do that."

There's a small part of me that questions whether or not entertaining small talk in bed with this attractive, rough-around-the-edges man will only get me in trouble down the road, but the bigger part of me says to go with it. So, I do.

He seems to gnaw on my confession, two bushy, chestnut-brown eyebrows knitting together in thought. The scar that runs through his left brow has to be pretty old as it's nothing more than a thin white line now. Before I know it, I'm tracing the scarred flesh with my finger, feeling the smooth skin surrounded by rough short hairs and wondering how he got it.

Did he get in a fight when he was younger? Or was he a rowdy little boy who smacked his head on anything and everything? If he was, I hope he's at least apologized to his mom.

My finger stills its movements when he, whether consciously or subconsciously, leans into my touch, pressing his cheek into my palm and hums a deep, raspy sound of satisfaction that I store away for later.

After a few quiet seconds, he speaks. "There are certain things that I do keep to myself. Tons of things, actually."

My elbow gives out, and I rest my shoulder on the bed, stretching out my legs with a yawn. The long hairs on his calf rub the top of my foot as I move it back and forth along the cold sheet. "Could have fooled me."

He winces subtly before fumbling over two otherwise simple words.

"I'm sorry." His warm palm grips the meaty part of my thigh, a few inches above my knee, and hooks it over his hip. "For what happened last time. If I'm being honest, I didn't think you would answer my text earlier, let alone actually come."

I blow out a breath. "Yeah, you were a complete asshole. I almost told you to go to hell. Maybe I should have."

"You should have. I deserve it."

He does. Just because I couldn't help wanting to scratch an itch that only Braden seems to be able to soothe recently doesn't necessarily mean that all is forgiven and forgotten. How he treated me the last time we were together felt like I was receiving a punishment for a crime I didn't commit.

It was completely unfair. I wasn't sure whether to be offended, hurt, or confused as I stood in the shower, under the scalding water, praying that when I got out and walked back into my room, Braden was long gone, never to be seen again.

A muscle ticks in his cheek, under the skin of my fingertips. I trace the sharp lines of his jaw, from the tip of his earlobe to the bottom of his chin.

The air is thick as I draw it into my lungs and say, "I'm guessing your explanation for the other night falls in the category of things that you keep to yourself, huh?"

He turns his face into my palm and kisses it once, twice, and a third time before letting out a shaky exhale. His chocolate-eyes are warm yet guarded as he watches me with an obvious curiosity, like he's trying desperately to dissect my thoughts.

"Do you want an explanation from me, Sierra?"

"If I said yes, would you give me one?" I counter.

"Yeah, I think I would."

Oh. Surprise has my mouth running before I can stop it. "That's okay, I'm over it now."

I offer Braden a weak smile before rolling onto my back, my head colliding with a thick pillow. A pillow that smells more like him than he does. It sticks to my skin and swirls in my belly. *God.* Really?

I hop out of bed and make a rush out of the room,, desperate for some space to get myself together.

It's once I'm nearly out of the room that he tells me, "You're invading my life, Sierra. I was just trying to keep you out. But clearly, it didn't work."

———

THE STREET outside my apartment is dark and empty, void of human life. The time by the car radio shows that it's just past midnight, so I'm not surprised.

My hands are clasped and tucked between my thighs so that I don't fidget with them. The silence in the small car is deafening. It feels wrong. I feel out of place.

It wasn't the right move to stay the night with Braden, not when his admission shook me so thoroughly. I needed space to clear my head, then more than ever.

So, not even ten minutes after I stumbled back into

Braden's bedroom, I asked—or begged, I guess—for him to drive me home.

He didn't argue when I asked, didn't beg me to stay the night, and I was grateful for his understanding, even though my request could have been seen as alarming. It wasn't until he led me out of his apartment building, a strong hand resting on my lower back, that I realized he might know me a bit better than I had originally thought. And that didn't scare me as much as I expected it to.

The fact I'm *not* more scared, is what scares me the most. How ironic.

"Thanks for the ride," I murmur.

His fingers tighten slightly around the steering wheel and he nods, still looking out the windshield. I'm sure that either one of us would be able to hear a pin drop in the backseat right about now.

After a strong swallow, I offer him a tight smile and unclasp my hands so that I can pull open the car door. But the minute they lay flat on my thighs, he's collecting them in his large, strong ones, squeezing like he doesn't exactly know what to do with them now.

His thumbs rub along the top of my hands, and my eyes flutter shut for a second. When I open them again, I find Braden watching me with a look that I recognize instantly. *Vulnerability.*

"I need to walk you inside, okay?" he asks firmly. I open my mouth to agree but he cuts me off before I start. "Don't bother arguing with me either. I just want to make sure you get inside safely."

I shake my head and laugh lightly, feeling the sound bubbling in my chest and ears. "Okay. Walk me inside."

He looks taken aback by my easy acceptance, but brushes it off with a grin. After a final squeeze of my hands, he lets them both go and we step outside.

Braden meets me on the sidewalk and like earlier, places a

firm hand on the small of my back, guiding me to the building.

When we reach the doors, he reaches in front of me to pull it open, holding it with a strong arm until I've walked inside. I have to use my fist to stifle my laugh when I catch him ducking his head to make it through the doorway.

Sometimes, I forget that he's taller than any guy that I've ever been with. All thick thighs and corded calves. He makes my five-nine height look embarrassing.

Once I've unlocked the second door and we've walked up the stairs to my second-floor apartment, I feel all the happiness from only a second prior fizzle out of me, annoyance taking its place.

18

Braden

I SEE HIM BEFORE SIERRA DOES.

The guy stands a few doors down from her apartment, clearly not sure which one is hers as his eyes flicker from one to the next. He seems relaxed, though. Relaxed but curious, like the building is familiar but he's forgotten what it looked like.

"Who the fuck are you?" I spit.

I don't recognize him at first or second glance, and that annoys me.

"Who are you?"

I wrap my arm around Sierra and slide her behind me, not appreciating the way he looks at her. We're already in front of her apartment, seeing as hers is the one directly beside the staircase. It helps settle me knowing that he's not already too close to her space yet.

Cocking my brow when he takes another two steps toward me, I meet him half-way and place my hands on his narrow shoulders. I squeeze hard before shoving him back.

"Tell me who you are before I drag your sorry ass outside."

"What are you doing here, Logan?" Sierra asks, sounding

exasperated with this *Logan* guy. I find comfort in that. She's behind me again, running her hand up my spine.

The little prick takes the short distraction as an invitation to sneak past us, ducking under my arm when I try to catch the back of his dress shirt, and slides into Sierra's apartment. Sierra must have unlocked the door while I was busy trying to get his name.

Grunting under my breath, I follow Sierra into the apartment, slamming the door shut behind us. Logan is standing by the kitchen island, shaking like a leaf with what I would assume to be an ungraspable amount of adrenaline.

It's probably burning his blood, making it thump in his ears. His chest is probably tight, the thought of seeing Sierra give another guy even a spare glance making his vision tint with red, darkening around the edges until all he can focus on is him.

I know that's how he feels, because it's how I feel. The only difference between us is that I'm not the one watching her touch another man, attempting to comfort him.

Sierra leans up on her toes, both hands gripping onto my right bicep like it's the only thing keeping her grounded, and presses her lips to the top of my shoulder in a short, sweet kiss, and that's his final straw. His control snaps, and he's suddenly in my face.

With a loose jaw and wild eyes, Logan swings his fist in the air, the hit sloppily aimed at my face. I catch his fist mid-swing, wrapping my hand fully around it and squeezing. I don't stop squeezing when he tries to pull his arm back toward him, or when he hisses through his teeth at the pain. I stop when she asks me to, sounding only half like the Sierra that I've come to know.

"Let him go. He's not worth it," she says under her breath, staring up at me with a silent plea in her steel-grey eyes. "I just want him to leave."

I drop his hand, and he pulls it to his chest immediately,

staring down at it like he can't believe it's not broken. It would have been easy to shatter his hand in mine, and I hope he knows that I didn't do just that because I chose not to.

I peer down at Sierra, and the vision rattles me. She clings to my side like an adorable, Sierra sized koala bear, and I feel a piece of me crack wide open at the sight, baring that small, yet significant part of myself to her whether she realizes it or not.

There's no mistaking the feelings that have begun flapping away in my chest. Yet I can't find it in myself to run and hide from them. I realize now that I actually want them. I want *her*. Not just for one night, but for every night. I don't want to drive her home after having her in my bed, making it smell like her. I want to fall asleep beside her warm, naked body and make her breakfast in the morning. I'm not a cook, but I can try.

I want to learn her every quirk and flaw. I want to hear about every important moment in her life, good or bad, I don't care. I just want to *know* her. She deserves someone who will put the effort in. And I'll be damned if I let another guy seize the opportunity before I can.

It's Logan's voice that pulls me out of my head.

"You sneaky little bitch. It was you that told Maeve where I was tonight, wasn't it? Were you messing around with this guy when we were together, Sierra? Is that why you won't give me another chance?" He's rambling, eyes flinging around the room, pupils blown and cheeks flushed.

Sierra tenses around my arm and moves impossibly closer to me.

The pieces of the unfinished puzzle slowly start to come together as I recognize the fancy buffed dress shoes and ironed suit jacket from the hotel restaurant earlier. Logan is the guy that was grabbing on Sierra like she was his to touch. The thought of that alone is enough to have every muscle in my body coiled tight, ready to throw him to the ground and teach him the proper way to throw a punch.

"You're nothing but a stupid whore," he spits at her, focusing on the way she clutches to me. "You're not worth the trouble."

"I'm going to give you one chance to calm down and leave before I break your skull." My tone is dark, the threat obvious. "Nobody talks to Sierra like that. Do you understand me, or should I show you what I'll do to the next person who raises their voice or calls her a whore?"

Logan slides his venomous stare to me, his brows bunched together in thought. This guy really has no idea who I am or what I do for a living, because if he did, he would know that I don't like repeating myself when it comes to scum like him. It's much easier to hit someone instead. They don't second guess you then.

"I don't take kindly to people who find it so easy to talk to women like that. And I especially don't like it when that woman's mine."

Sierra tenses briefly before relaxing again. I almost steal a look at her, but chicken out when I realize I might not be prepared for how I'll feel if my slip of tongue impacted our relationship negatively. It's better not to know.

"Oh yeah? And what are you going to do about it if I don't, pretty boy? Stay out of it. This is between her,"—He moves a hand between him and Sierra— "and me."

I wrap an arm around Sierra's waist on instinct and pull her tight to my side, palming her hip in an attempt to calm myself down before I do something I don't want her to see.

"Go home, Logan. I didn't tell Maeve anything. But regardless, she's your problem now, not mine. You made sure of that."

Logan's Adam's apple bobs. "I know that you talked to her, Sierra. You never could keep your mouth shut when it came to other people's business."

She flinches against me as he continues to scare her. I bite my tongue when alarm bells start blasting in my ears. Holy mother of *fuck*. This guy is fucking dead.

I'm already in front of him, punching him square in the nose before he can blink. The solid crack in the air has my ego swelling as he stumbles backward, shooting his hand up to cradle his shattered nose as blood begins dripping onto the floor.

I unclench my fist and wince at the pain shooting through my knuckles but shrug it off as I move in on him again. He flinches when I grab him by the collar of his shirt and start dragging him behind me all the way to the front door.

I pull it open and shove him through the doorway, fighting off a satisfied grin when he trips over his own feet and falls to the floor, unable to catch his balance.

"If I see you here again, you'll be taken out on a goddamn stretcher. Now fuck off." I slam the door in his face and turn around just in time to catch Sierra as she jumps into my arms.

Sierra

Braden catches me without difficulty, capturing me in strong arms as I wrap my legs around his waist and thank him by placing my lips firmly on his.

I thank him in a way that feels so much deeper than with common, expected words. He carries me toward my bedroom, shifting us so my butt is perched on his left arm.

With his now free hand, he grips my nape, tilting my head and deepening the kiss. A sudden wave of appreciation has my skin buzzing and belly flooded with a few sets of flapping wings.

I've never been a girl who cheered for violence, but

watching Braden slam his fist into my cheating ex-boyfriend's face—*shit*. From the bulging of the veins living in his forearm, to the flex of his bicep when he swung, I was a goner. I've wanted to pounce on him from the second he called me his woman.

Usually, I would have bristled at the dominant claim, but it had my legs feeling like jelly instead. He might not have meant it, and may never say it again, but I've placed that shit in my memory. I won't forget it.

With a sly swivel of my hips, I feel his arousal press against me and whimper, all past thoughts suddenly overpowered by the liquid heat pooling between my thighs. My palms lay flat on his shoulders before curling into them, pulling at his shirt to bring us even closer together. Our chests brush, a jolt between my legs making me gasp at the sensation that comes from my nipples rubbing against his solid pecs.

"Cold?" He pulls back and grins broadly, his dimples making a beautiful appearance. Brown eyes slide from my face to my chest then back again.

I feel his happiness in the very center of my chest as I shake my head. "No. I'm perfect."

The silence wrapping around us would usually make my skin itchy, but the only thing I feel right now is a sense of peace. A sense of *belonging*. I want to grip the feeling in my fists and shove it deep inside, storing it for a time where I know I'll inevitably need it.

I'm placed gently on my back in the middle of my bed, and can't help but gawk at the man in front of me. I wonder how I got here, with this power house of pure masculine energy and power towering over me, looking at me like I'm something more than a workaholic with a crooked relationship history and family drama.

I frown as skepticism creeps into my head, and the peace slips away.

It's Braden's whispered words that blanket those pesky

thoughts. They're just four simple words. Words that shouldn't have my breath catching in my throat, but do so easily.

"You're so fucking beautiful."

Cautious eyes trace my face. It's like he's scared that his confession will make me run from him and he's looking for something to prove him wrong. But I don't run. I don't think I could regardless of how hard I tried.

The tension leaks from my muscles and I relax. Then comes a moment in time where his expression is completely open, his walls temporarily pulled back. There's a trust there that says more than words ever could.

With a deep groan, he's hovering above me, knees between mine and hands gripping the headboard. I arch up into him and take his mouth, distracting myself from the feeling of heaviness that's fallen over us.

My bottom lip is pulled between his teeth as he nips on it before soothing the sting with a stroke of his tongue. The heat flaring in his brown eyes makes my thighs clench and tighten around his hips, the want to have him touch me is becoming a torturous need.

Again, he does what I want without me having to ask. It's a sort of recognition that has a lump forming at the base of my throat. He's begun to know my body just like I have his.

I swallow back a whimper when he begins undressing me, taking his time to trail his fingertips over every inch of my body. An involuntary shudder works its way up my spine.

"Stay with me, my little fighter. We're nowhere near done yet."

The raw need burning in his eyes sets my insides on fire. An incessant throb builds in my center and I lift my hips, desperately seeking friction. With a steadying breath, I grab the back of his neck and pull him toward me. I barely catch the battle being fought behind his heated stare before he's burying his face in the crook of my neck with a sigh that shoots straight to my clit.

Wet lips part against my hot skin as Braden begins marking it with strong sucks and peppered kisses until he nips at the area beside my collarbone.

"Braden," I whisper.

I could spend hours with his mouth on my body, worshipping me in the way only Braden can.

With a shaky exhale I drop my forehead to his shoulder and hold him against my bare chest. The threat of losing his touch is too consuming right now. I hate that I feel this way. That if he were to push himself away and leave me, right now, it would hurt—*badly*. It wouldn't be like last time. I wouldn't be able to pretend that it doesn't bother me. He would leave his name etched in my skin. I'm just not sure how deep it would be yet.

My eyes nearly roll back into my head when his fingers finally slide over my upper thighs before slipping between them. He pants against my neck while parting my lower lips and dragging one finger through my wetness, right up to swirl it around my throbbing clit. My breathing becomes heavy as I close my eyes.

My bottom lip slips between my teeth when he groans, "Always so wet for me, baby."

I spread my thighs wide to give him the encouragement to slide a finger inside of me. He does, before quickly adding another, alternating between a slow and fast pace while curling them inward, pressing down on the spot that has me snapping my eyes open with a sob.

"That's right. Let me hear you. Tell me how good I make you feel."

My neck is suddenly cold and it takes me a second to realize that Braden's staring down at me now, no longer pressed tightly against me. His lips are swollen and red as they sit slightly parted. When his tongue swipes out to wet them, I know that I clench around his fingers, my thoughts overrun by memories of having that tongue slide along my pussy until my thighs are shaking.

"Answer me, baby. Tell me how good I make you feel and I'll feast on that sweet, wet pussy until you beg me to stop," he demands with a sharp twist of his fingers.

"Good. *So good.* Please, Braden. I need it."

I'm long past feeling embarrassed by how badly my body needs him or how quickly I fall apart around him. There's no point. I can't stop it, nor do I want to by denying myself the feelings he invokes with a single touch or drop of his voice.

Being with Braden like this is the only time where I'm not worrying about a deadline or working myself up over simple everyday tasks. I'm just Sierra. A very horny Sierra who would do just about anything for a mind-numbing orgasm at the hands of a giant, Hulk-like man who knows what my body needs before I do.

Braden's moving down the bed with a groan of approval. I squeak in surprise when two large hands grab under my ass and pull me down the bed so that I'm sprawled out like a starfish. Gripping the skin beneath my knees, he throws my legs over his shoulders and buries his face between them, swiping his tongue from my entrance to my clit, swirling it in a clockwise motion while keeping his eyes locked on mine.

His stare is soft—unbelievably so as he repeats the motion over and over, watching me writhe beneath him, a string of profanities falling from my lips.

I reach for him, finding it hard to suck air into my lungs. My head is swimming, my thoughts clouding. I say his name like a plea, voice thick with need. Words fail me as I gasp and whimper, but he knows what I want. What I *need*.

I'm close, *so* close. I can feel it trying to consume and blind me. My fingers thread themselves in his hair and pull hard as my back arches, hips threatening to shoot off of the mattress. But he reaches up and uses a flat, firm hand to keep me down while also taking hold of my hand and lacing our fingers together with a squeeze.

"That's it, baby," he coaxes, drawing out my orgasm like magic with a jab of his tongue inside of me. "Let me taste you."

I sob unintelligible words as white-hot pleasure shoots through my veins. My muscles tense, thighs shaking and squeezing around Braden's head as he keeps fucking me with his tongue, letting me ride out my high on his mouth.

The intensity of my orgasm has drained my energy, leaving me exhausted. I crack a smile and watch Braden use the back of his hand to dry his mouth before crawling over my body and collapsing on top of me.

"Get off me," I wheeze. "You're too heavy."

He presses a kiss to my cheek, chuckling when I start hitting his back. A roll of my body has me feeling the hardness beneath his jeans and I'm slapped with a pang of guilt. As I'm about to reach down and touch him, he nips my jaw, pulling my attention to his boyish grin.

He pins me with a look. "Don't. I'm good."

I want to argue, but nod instead, a feeling of warmth flooding my stomach. "Well then, I'm serious, you behemoth. Roll over."

With a hard pinch to the side, he finally rolls over and lays on his back, head tilted to the side so he can still look at me. Heat climbs up my neck and stains my cheeks when he continues to stare, completely straight faced.

"What?" I ask.

"You're gorgeous when you come."

I burst out laughing. "Shut up and go to bed. I'm tired."

The humour dancing in his eyes has me smiling long after I'm under the covers and he's flicked off the lights and crawled in beside me. His body rubs against mine as he wraps his big arms around me and pulls me close.

"Thank you," I whisper after a while, running my fingers

up and down his abdomen. The hard, warm muscles flex under my touch.

"For what?" I can hear the smile in his voice.

What am I thanking him for? The orgasm? The company? The sense of calm? I let out a long, tired breath before whispering, "Everything."

He presses a kiss in my hair and hums. "Anytime, baby."

I don't even bother telling him not to call me that before I let him hold me as I fall asleep.

19

Sierra

"Auntie!"

My niece rips open the front door and rushes toward me, hugging my thighs with a tight squeeze. Her bursting energy has me smiling softly when I reach down and plant an exaggerated kiss on her head.

"Hey, kiddo. Have you been behaving?"

"Of course!" She flashes me a toothy grin, her left hand planted on a jutted hip.

Wearing a pair of dark blue jeans with iron-on patches across the knees and a shirt with a beagle eating a donut triple its size, she couldn't possibly be any cuter.

"That's what I like to hear. Now where's your momma?"

I reach up to smooth the hairs that have blown out of place by the wind outside. When my fingers get caught in a giant knot, I know it's already too late to salvage it. Leaving my hair down after my shower seemed like a good idea at the time, however that may just have been because Braden didn't exactly leave me much time to get ready after sneaking in the shower and eating me for breakfast.

Liz turns toward the back of the house and points to the patio door. "The backyard. We're raking leaves!"

"Let's go then. We're wasting daylight," I tease.

The young, spitting image of my sister bolts toward the door. I pull it open for her and watch, amused, as she sprints off to one of the three piles of orange, brown, and yellow leaves. Clare stands with a rake in her hand, adding to the already giant third pile.

I whistle to grab my sister's attention, and wave when she lifts her head, smiling so wide her white teeth shine in the sun. She throws the rake in the pile of leaves without hesitation, pats her hands on her coverall-clad thighs, and sidesteps the battery operated, hot-pink children's car resting on the grass before walking over to me.

"What are you doing here? Not like I mind the surprise visit." She pulls me into a tight hug.

"I was in the neighbourhood. Figured I might as well visit my beautiful sister while I'm here."

"That's what I like to hear. Come inside. I have iced tea in the fridge. Liz, come inside when you're done playing in the leaves!"

A hand clamps around my wrist as Clare pulls me inside, a slight bounce in her step. Her beaming attitude isn't exactly a rare sight, but it still has me curious. She's usually happy, but not *this* happy. I mean, happily raking the leaves? With today's wind?

No, not a chance.

I sit down on one of the bar stools lining the small kitchen island as she grabs the pitcher from the fridge and pours me a large glass. Placing the dew-covered glass in front of me, she flops down beside me.

"You're starting to freak me out," I say, raising my brow. "What's up with you? You look like you just got lai—" *Oh.* "You got laid, didn't you?"

"That obvious?" Her blue eyes sparkle.

"Oh yeah. Who's the lucky guy?"

"His name is Joel. He works at a mechanics shop only a

few blocks away. Isn't that amazing? We've been on a few dates."

"A few? And I'm just hearing about him now? You break my heart, Clare."

"Oh, shut up." She swats my arm. "I didn't want to say anything unless I felt like it could really be something. He wants to meet Liz."

I try to keep my feelings from showing on my face, but my surprise is evident when I ask, "He does? So, it's actually serious then."

She nods once, suddenly stiffer than a board. "I think so. I don't want to rush into it, though. Not when Liz is involved. Plus, I have no idea how Max will react to another man in his daughter's life. It's always been just him."

Hearing the name of her ex-husband is like nails on a chalkboard.

"He doesn't really have a say in your love life, Clare. Not completely, anyway. It's kind of inevitable that you would both find other people. I'm sure he's had his fair share of women over the past three years."

Ever since my sister separated from Liz's dad a few years ago, I don't think Clare has even thought about dating anybody else. I guess in her own way, she was holding out hope that they would end up working out their issues and find their way back to each other. That's just not how life works, though. Not in my experience, at least.

Max and Clare were always the couple that I looked at and fawned over, hoping that that would be my future one day. They met in high school and dated all the way through college before getting married the year after graduation.

When they got married, everyone thought they would be together until they died. But the reality of life got in the way. It twisted and pulled apart their ideal future until it cost them their memorable love story.

"I know," she breathes, swallowing thickly.

"I say go for it. If you're ready, that is. Don't rush into anything."

"I don't really have time to take things slow, Sierra. I don't really have men lining up on my doorstep. Nobody seems to want to date a thirty-year-old divorced single mom."

"Apparently Joel does." I throw her a wink and place a reassuring hand on her shoulder. "Have faith. What's meant to happen will happen. I promise."

"I guess." She smiles slightly.

"Where did you two meet? Actually, when did you meet? How long have you been keeping this a secret from me?"

It doesn't matter to me where or when she met this guy. I just want her to be happy. She deserves happiness more than anybody that I know. I owe her everything.

"Relax, Nancy Drew." Resting her chin on her palm, she smiles at me. "Remember when I popped that tire back in June? On the way back from the beach? We didn't have the spare so we had to call a tow truck."

I nod. "That was what, three months ago?"

She smiles sheepishly. "Yeah."

"You kept him a secret from me for three months? Oh, man. You *so* owe me, Clare Bear."

She lifts one shoulder in a shrug but I can see the humour flicker in her blue-green eyes.

"Yes. But we didn't start dating right away. He is the lead mechanic at the shop where the tow truck dropped my SUV off, but he wasn't the one that fixed my tire. I didn't meet him until the next time I brought it in. Liz had stuck a barbie doll somewhere under my hood when I was refilling the windshield fluid and I didn't notice until it had melted all over the inside and I couldn't get it off."

My attempts at stifling my laugh fail and I lose it, laughing hard enough that tears swell in my eyes. "I can just imagine you right now. 'Hi, sorry, but my daughter melted a barbie all over my engine. Please help me.'"

A tightness grows in my stomach as I brace myself on the counter, my shoulders shaking. I peek through closed eyes and see Clare staring at me with a look that says "shut up or else" but don't stop laughing until she punches me in the shoulder.

"Stop it." She's blushing.

"I'm guessing he was sweet to you then? Didn't laugh in your face?" I swipe away the tears that have fallen.

"No, he didn't. He was very professional."

I smirk. "Professional? Is that how he wound up between your sheets?"

She glares at me. "No. He wrote his number down on the invoice and glared at the other mechanic when he started teasing me about not using the inside of a car as a barbie dream house or something stupid like that. I don't remember."

There's a sense of pride and happiness that grows in my chest while watching how dreamy she looks talking about Joel. It's enough to have me accepting him already, regardless of not meeting him yet. Any guy that makes my sister smile like that is good in my books.

"Anyway," she says. "Don't think that I haven't noticed the glow to your skin either. You look different. *Happier*."

Do I? I brush off the comment. "I feel the same."

Her stare burns into my face and I take large gulps of my drink to try and pretend that I don't feel it.

"Don't even, Sierra. Have you forgotten that I'm your big sister? That title comes with younger sister reading skills."

"Is that so?" I scoff. Her intense stare doesn't waver as it wears me down way too fast. "Fine! Put that damn look away. I've only been sleeping with someone. It's not serious like you and Joel."

I risk looking at her again just to see her roll her eyes. "Yeah, okay. Try again."

"I'm serious! We're just having fun. Trust me, he isn't a

relationship kind of guy." My fingers dance on my leg as I bounce it.

"He's gotta be hot then, right? What's his name?"

I'm flushed when I answer, struggling to keep my voice from wobbling when just the thought of his name has me wanting to rub my thighs together.

"Braden. And yeah. He's really fucking hot," I burst, raising a hand to my cheek to feel the burning skin.

She taps a contemplating finger on her chin and hums. I feel my brows lift with curiosity. "What? You don't like that name or something?"

"Braden," she says slowly, pronouncing each letter like she's never spoken them before. "Braden." This time she rolls the r.

"Jesus Christ, Clare. You're weirding me out."

She swipes a hand in the air. "I was just trying to see how well it rolled off the tongue."

I shake my head at her ridiculousness. "Well? Don't leave me hanging. Does it fit the bill?"

She tosses me a wink. "It's not bad. I'm sure he makes up for having such a usual name in other ways. Tell me, is he tall? You're far too tall to be with a short guy."

"Clare!" I chastise regardless of the smile that stretches across my face. "Don't hate on short guys. Majority of them know their way around a woman's body better than most of the tall guys I've ever met. But yes, Braden is pretty much a giant. Even compared to me. I reach his chin."

She looks surprised. "Really? Well then. I certainly can not wait to meet this guy."

"Keep dreaming, Clare Bear. I don't see that happening any time soon—if ever." I can see that she wants to push me on it, but knows better than to try.

I'm grateful when she easily changes the subject to ask if I'm free to come with her to Liz's fall talent show. After agreeing, we make our way back outside to join my niece in her leafy paradise.

Clare and I exchange smiles, both of us starting to laugh before we grab Liz and toss her into the only pile that she hasn't yet destroyed. Her squeal of excitement is like a shot of serotonin. And just like that, I'm home.

20

Braden

"No."

My tone leaves no room for judgement, it's too cold and void of emotion. Betrayal like I've never known rears its ugly head.

Dad's brows move to his hairline as he stares at me, mouth gaping as if he's surprised for some ungodly reason. He was either completely naïve to my feelings, or just doesn't know me as well as he used to.

Whichever it is, I don't care. It's the same either way.

He wants to leave.

"What do you mean, no?" he echoes, and I catch the movement of his fingers curling around his bottle of non-alcoholic beer.

I clear my throat. "Sorry. *Fuck* no."

"Watch it, son," he growls.

Dark eyes burn into the side of my face with a look of rage I've seen only a few times over the course of my life. I continue to look straight ahead, refusing to meet his stare. "I meant, why not? What's keeping you here? The gym? Forget about it. We'll buy a new one in Toronto. Hell, if you come with us, I'll buy you three."

There's no holding in my humourless chuckle. "Really? In case you've forgotten, you drained every last fucking penny you had for the rock on your fiancée's finger. And what about Tyler? You know, your other son? Don't you think maybe he's something that I don't want to leave behind? I'm actually surprised you're so okay with it."

"Tyler spends half the year on the road, Braden. Location doesn't matter to him. Gracie does. And it wouldn't be fair to take her from her family, especially while they're building a family together. Anyway, I already spoke to him today. He turned me down."

I feel the judgement in his words like a sucker punch to the gut. The disappointment that my father's feels with how I live my life makes me want to throw my fist through a cement block. The way I refuse to commit to one woman pisses him off—disappoints him. I know it stems from his own past mistakes and regrets, so it's not surprising he projects on me, wanting me to be better than he was.

For a second, I debate throwing Sierra in his face to spite him, but stop myself when I remember that while I may want her to be mine to some degree, it's not like that between us. Our relationship, or whatever you would call it, is messy, filled with a never-ending list of questions I don't have the answers to yet.

Every time that I feel myself give in to her pull, I yank back before I give it a chance. The thought of her with another guy makes me want to go postal. I get possessive and lose myself in her presence and the way she makes me feel like I could rule the whole fucking world. But all it takes is one reminder of how broken I am in the world of relationships and commitment to shut down again.

Seeing Sierra makes me happy. I care about her, and don't want her with anyone else, I won't deny that or how selfish it makes me. But I won't let myself give more than that. I don't know how. I'm happy with how things are now. Anything else would be far too complicated.

I would only be digging myself into an even deeper grave in Dad's eyes if I admitted that to him right now.

"So, because I'm not married and expecting a kid, I have nothing to lose by uprooting my life to fit into *your* plans? *Your* future? You can't just expect me to come with you because you're too scared to do this on your own."

I meet his eyes when he slams a fist down on the top of his new kitchen table. His bottle shakes, and the small porcelain jars of cream and sugar clatter. I hold his stare intensity as I press my tongue to my cheek.

His mouth is held in a firm line that's only broken when he opens it to speak, his refusal to my claims at the ready. But I cut him off with a raised hand in front of me that has a rumbled, angry curse falling between us.

"If you're not scared, then sign over the gym to me and go. It's going to be mine someday anyway. You know I'll take care of it. If there's nothing here for you to come back to, then you really can start over with Lana."

He visibly flinches. Adam's apple bobbing with silent emotion, Dad's eyes fall to his hands as they rest open on the table, drawing my attention to the calloused, wrinkled skin.

Years of fighting show in the countless white scars etched on his knuckles. Each one represents a memory—a win or a loss. The thick calluses are from the years of hard manual labour he endured with my grandfather, building houses for countless years while he worked for the money to buy his gym. Rampage.

"The gym isn't everything, Braden." He uses his thumb and pointer finger to smooth out his scrunched brows. "I hope that someday you'll be able to see that."

I'm saved from this conversation by the ringing of my phone. Sliding it from the pocket of my jeans, I see a name on the screen that doesn't surprise me in the slightest. I'm surprised Tyler waited this long to call me. Dad must have told him that he would be talking to me this afternoon. The asshole's probably been waiting all day to call me and gossip.

"Need to answer that?" Dad asks. He stands up and moves to get rid of his still half-full bottle of warm piss. I know my dad well enough to tell when I'm being dismissed, so I swallow down the rest of my questions, and take a steadying breath to keep myself in check.

Following his lead, I silence my phone and stand up. "No. I do have to leave though. I'm sure we'll talk about this again later."

I stay in the kitchen long enough to catch his barely-there nod before heading for the front door. After slipping my sneakers on, I throw a pained goodbye in his direction and rush out of my childhood home feeling more fucking weighed down and pissed off than I have in a long time.

MY MUSCLES ACHE. They're on fire, throbbing deep to the bone. A clear warning that I've spent far too long in front of a punching bag. Still, I haven't even *begun* to touch on the feeling of rage that's been swirling my insides around with a hot poker since I left my father's house.

I still can't believe it. Moving across the country for some ditsy Barbie Doll that he hasn't even known for a year?

I've been replaying our conversation in my head for hours. *The gym isn't everything, Braden.*

That's bullshit. Maybe he's happy to give it up, but I'm not. This gym—boxing at this gym—is all that I have. I gave up the only other thing in my life that has ever made me happy to help run this damn place. I threw away what could have been a professional career in hockey for this place. For him. And he's just going to leave it all behind. Like it's nothing but a speck on a map of his past. A *blip*. Vancouver is our *home*. I'll be damned if I let him leave it all behind just to chase some young tail.

"You don't think he's actually serious, do you?" Tyler mutters gruffly, his swift punches not faltering as they make the swinging leather bag cry out in pain. I know he's hurt by our dad just as much, if not more, than I am. And he has every right to be.

Whereas I grew up with our dad, he wasn't so lucky. He grew up only knowing his abusive piece of shit stepdad and drugged-up mother. The same mother who kept both Tyler and our dad in the dark for twenty-years.

It's almost a sick joke, really. I've known him as a friend for five years, and only as my blood brother for two of them. His mother dropped the bomb on all of us the night she disappeared from his life. She wasted no time in hightailing it out of Vancouver after finally spilling the beans about my father's secret love child. It was the definition of a mic drop moment.

But more than anything, it was a punch to the balls. For Dad especially. He knows it wasn't his fault that he missed out on so many years of Tyler's life, but that doesn't make it any easier of a pill to swallow.

Ever since that night, Dad has been trying to make up for his absence whenever possible. Until now, I guess. Now the girl clawing on his arm is more important than his damn family—his *kids*.

"I think he's dead serious," I spit. "He wouldn't have brought it up if he wasn't."

"I don't see how he could expect us to follow him out there. I would rather chew off my own tongue than play for Toronto's hockey team," Tyler grunts while wiping a towel aggressively down his face, leaving the skin red.

"I'm sure Lana would be your number one fan." I nearly choke on her name.

"I don't understand. Vancouver is our home. Gracie

would feed me my own cock if I even considered uprooting us."

That has my scowl cracking. Talk about a sight I would pay a hefty penny to see. Gracie Hutton may be small, but damn she's vicious.

"I don't care how hot the girl is. Nobody could make me leave Vancouver," I say.

Tyler remains silent for a long moment, and I have a feeling he's going to tell me that that could change someday, but he doesn't. I don't doubt for a second he would follow Gracie to fucking Mars if she asked him to. But Tyler and Gracie are different. They're the closest thing to soulmates I've ever seen. There's nothing odd or abrupt about their love and adoration for one another. It's pure and raw.

"I don't think he'll do it. What about the gym?"

Tyler takes a drink from his water bottle, looking around the gym. It's closed to the public right now, so it's just us. Technically, we should be open, but I couldn't risk anybody hearing about Dad ditching out on us. It would have opened a can of worms that I don't have the strength to pry back shut right now.

This gym is home to the majority of my childhood memories. The good, the bad, and the fucking ugly.

I spent more time here than I did anywhere else. Hell, during my rebellious teenage years I practically slept here. These chipped brick walls and cushioned floor mats kept me sane during a time where I feared I would never be able to get a grip on my angry at the world attitude.

I was pissed off at my parents for splitting and not being able to keep it civil between them, even at the best of times, not even for me. It took years for me to get my head out of my ass. And even then, I was still an asshole most of the time.

I knew that Dad was aware of the fights held behind his back, but he still let me get my ass beat time and time again without so much as a shrug in my direction. He never mentioned them when I came home from the gym to shower and sneak food from the fridge with bloodied knuckles and bruised eyes, or when he would drop me off on the curb outside of my grandma's house.

He didn't say anything when I wandered into his office requesting the first aid kit after getting absolutely rocked by a guy three times my size. And he definitely didn't offer me any sympathy when I broke my nose for the third time in a year because I refused to wear headgear out of pure stubbornness.

At the time, his lack of attention to my dangerous hobby served as a catalyst, encouraging me to keep going and going until he finally acknowledged the fight I had inside of me. With every win came a sense of hope that I wouldn't be as invisible to him as I thought that I was. I wanted him to be proud of me. I craved it with every fiber of my being.

With his time spent between a divorce lawyer, financial meetings regarding the gym, and training a full list of aspiring boxers, the only time I saw him was right before I left for school.

He would be leaning against the countertop with a steaming cup of black coffee in his hands when I came to grab my lunch. I would get a brisk wave and a tired grunt. Then we would go our separate ways until I saw him at the gym after school.

Now that I think back on it, I realize he was just trying to teach me a lesson. I was never invisible to him. He was going through a hard time too. I could never excuse the shit that happened between my parents during their divorce and the years that followed, but I can give them some leeway.

Every loss I took taught me the benefits of not giving up when shit got hard. My body hated me for it, but I'm not sure that I would change much from back then if it came down to it.

My stomach pitches as I turn back to my bag and swing at it. My arm locks due to my lack of concentration and I hiss from the burning pain that explodes through my shoulder when I make contact with the punching bag.

"Fuck!" I shake out my arm and rip my glove off, tossing it a few feet away.

"Told you to stretch," Tyler sings, earning himself an eyeful of both my middle fingers.

"And I told you to stop being such a loser, but here we are," I shoot back, trying not to cringe from my lame insult. I massage my shoulder and grit my teeth when it begins to throb.

"Wow, good one. What are you, ten?" Throwing off his own gloves, he grabs his water bottle and squirts a stream of water over his torso.

"Are you leaving now? I'm nowhere close to done and you're just pissing me off."

He rolls his eyes. "You need to go home before you hurt more than just your shoulder." He's right. I have a match in three days. Getting injured is not in the plans.

"I can't handle Clayton right now."

"Okay, so go somewhere else. Just not here. I can't stay here all night and babysit your raging ass."

Sierra's bright smile dances through my head, grabbing at both my chest and my groin. She would tell me to grow the hell up if she saw me right now. Her smile would be there, though, teasing and distracting me. I wouldn't be able to keep my hands off of her, seeing her in my domain, having her watch me do what I love.

"Ah, there it is," Ty chuckles, tossing his gloves in his bag before zipping it up. "Anything I should know since we last talked?"

"Huh?" I clear my throat, focusing on him again.

"Are you really going to keep pretending with me? I've seen that look before. *In the mirror.*"

"She's just a friend." The words feel wrong in my mouth.

"Right. Have fun with that then." He laughs to himself

and tosses his bag over his shoulder. "Just be careful, Braden. I thought it meant nothing when I was just sleeping Gracie too. Next thing I knew, I was telling her I loved her while standing butt-ass naked in her living room. It sneaks up on you and knocks you on your back."

"Well, I'm not you." I paint on a fake smile. This is not a conversation I want to have with him right now. Everything is still so new to me, I'm not ready to admit my feelings to anybody else yet.

"Alright." He throws his hands up in surrender. "If you're so sure she means nothing to you, then I believe you. Just figure yourself out and calm down. Have sex or get drunk, I don't care. Just don't hurt yourself." He moves toward me and punches my good arm, saying, "Call if you need anything."

I punch him back. "Will do."

21

Braden

I DON'T KNOW WHY I TEXTED SIERRA, BEGGING HER TO LET ME come over, or why I'm knocking on the front door knowing how close I am to the edge of losing my sanity, but here I am. And I'm dying to be inside of her.

Sierra pulls open the door wearing nothing but a loose-fitting pajama shirt that falls mid-thigh. Her hair is thrown up in a messy bun and there isn't a speck of makeup on her face. She looks stunning.

Magnificent, really.

"Is everything okay? Your text worried me," she mumbles, inviting me in and shutting the door softly behind me. I walk inside without muttering a word, kick off my shoes, and turn to face her.

Her concern for me is written all over her face. I rasp, "Come here."

She doesn't hesitate before walking straight into my chest, wrapping her arms around my middle as I pull her flush against me, sighing out in near instant relief. My hold on her is tight, like I'm terrified she'll run and leave me here. But she doesn't. Instead, she relaxes in my arms, strong puffs of air fanning across my chest as we stand in the middle of her apartment, neither of us wanting to let go.

My eyes close when she starts running a hand up and down my spine, warm fingers soothing the ache in my chest. A moan of appreciation falls from my mouth, and I kiss the top of her head, keeping my lips there for a few seconds, not wanting to lose the contact so soon.

With a reluctant sigh, her grip loosens the slightest bit and she leans back, looking up at me with worried eyes. My immediate reaction is to pull her back into my chest, but I loosen my hold on her with a soft sound of annoyance.

"Are you okay?" she asks gently. "Talk to me. I'm here for you."

The hand that was rubbing my back slides around to my front before climbing up my chest and gripping my nape. She gives it a slight squeeze, and smiles a small, toothless smile that fiddles with my chest, unlocking something she wasn't planning on letting me keep away from her for much longer. I try to be upset with myself for letting her get so close, but can't find it in myself to do so. Not right now, at least.

"Let's sit down, yeah?" I wince at the emotion in my voice.

She drops her arm from my neck and grabs my hand instead, leading me into her lamp-lit bedroom. "The couch is super uncomfortable. I picked it up at a thrift store downtown after . . ." She hesitates for a moment, chewing on the inside of her cheek before straightening her back. "I got it after I moved out of the apartment Logan and I shared. All of the furniture was his when we were living together, so I had to stare over. I didn't mind because the last thing I wanted was a reminder of him and my ex-best friend having sex on the couch. You know?"

I don't bother hiding my surprise. "He cheated on you with your best friend? If I would have known that, I would have hurt him worse for you, fighter."

She lifts a shoulder in a shrug before sitting down on the edge of the bed and tapping her fingers on the white duvet.

"I was upset for a long time. It was more betrayal than anything else."

"How long were you together?" I would rather swallow gravel than think of her with anyone else, but I'm too curious to stop asking questions. I want to know her. I almost feel like I *need* to.

"Four years. I only had one boyfriend before him, and none after. I guess the idea of trusting someone again has never appealed to me."

"Or maybe you just haven't found anyone worth trusting."

She seems to gnaw on that for a while. "Or maybe I have, but I'm exactly sure what to do with him yet."

Surprise collars my throat and threatens to toss me off a tall cliff.

My mouth is dry as I try to pull together a reply. She doesn't let my silence bother her, though, as she says, "Your turn. What made you come here tonight? And don't tell me it's because you missed me."

She meant it as a joke. But I did miss her. It wasn't the reason for the aching pain of betrayal or the sharp burst of pain in my shoulder from behaving carelessly in the boxing gym, but it is the reason that out of anywhere that I could have gone to try and get myself back under control, I'm here. With her.

The fear of being open and honest with her about how I'm feeling is numbing. I've always prided myself on being confident, fearless. And I almost feel like I've let myself down in some way by not taking a risk that could end up paying off in the end out of fear of the unknown.

Maybe if I knew exactly what I wanted from her, I would be able to articulate that to her, and maybe it would put us both at ease. But I'm like a fish out of water here. I don't know my head from my ass. The only thing I know is I can't get enough of this woman, nor do I want to anytime soon.

I'm in front of Sierra before she has a chance to be surprised, gripping under her ass and hoisting her up. Her legs wrap around me without hesitation before she presses against me with a heavy sigh and a roll of her hips. Needing to taste her, I take her mouth in a heated kiss that I hope allows her to feel the ache that's settled beneath my rib cage, only calmed by her.

My tongue slips between the seam of her lips before working deep inside her mouth, possessing her in a way I've never craved before. I taste the mint-chocolate chip ice cream she must have been eating before I arrived, mixed with the pure, addictive taste that belongs to Sierra and don't hold back my groan. She swallows it, sucking the air from my lungs as she does so.

We both need to breathe, but neither of us are willing to break apart. I'm a man possessed, too utterly captivated by the feel of her plush mouth moving against mine with a familiar possessiveness to think of my own needs.

With another roll of her hips against me, I jerk my hips and brush my cock against her underwear clad pussy, relishing in the feeling of warmth radiating from her. I drag my open mouth across her flushed cheek and under her jaw, nipping on the skin before tugging on her ear.

"I need to be inside of you, baby."

"Then take me. Please, Braden."

"That's a good girl," I growl, sucking hard on her neck before pulling back and crawling on the bed, keeping her tucked beneath me and holding her to my chest as I do.

Only once I've moved us to the top of the bed do I release her, watching as she falls to the bed, a toothy grin looking up at me. There's a shatter in my chest as she breaks me open again and slithers farther inside the crack, owning me in a way that should have me terrified.

Slim fingers begin pushing my shirt up my torso, and I yank it over my head before removing the rest of my clothes.

"Take it all off, my little fighter. This is going to be hard and fast. I don't have the patience for slow and steady right now. Have to fuck you."

Need to own you like you do me.

She does as I say with lust-blown pupils and swollen lips. As soon as her shirt hits the floor and her bare flesh is right there in front of me, I curse.

"You have the most gorgeous tits." I suck a rose-tipped nipple into my mouth with a moan, flicking it with my tongue before letting it slip from my lips and blowing on it, watching as it grows needy for me. I pay the same attention to the other one, but bite down on it gently before pulling back and sucking on the skin beneath her breast, marking it.

She cries out when I reach down to cup her and feel the smooth, wet skin beneath my palm. "*Shit*. Jesus Christ. How long have you been this wet, baby? You're soaking my hand."

Her head falls back against the pillow, and she arches her back, pushing against my hand with a twist of her hips. I slide a finger through her slit and curse as it sinks inside her tight hole with no resistance.

With my thumb pressed to her clit, she cries out. I slide in a second finger, jack knifing them when I feel her begin to pulse around them. Desperate noises spill from her pretty mouth as she grinds against my fingers, needing release.

I only plan on having her come around my cock tonight. Not my fingers, and not my tongue. She can soak my face in her cum when I take her again later. I need to feel all of her right now.

She sobs with frustration when I slide my hand from her pussy and grip myself with it instead, using her wetness to cover the throbbing length. I give my shaft a couple hard pulls as I watch her catch her breath—thighs spread wide to reveal glistening pink flesh.

The tightness in my spine lets me know that I won't be lasting long tonight, so I don't wait any more time before rearing back and burying myself deep inside of her, feeling fingernails rip into my back as Sierra cries out with the sudden fullness.

I reach up and grab the headboard, squeezing my eyes shut when I thrust into her again, cursing under my breath as she tightens around me like a fucking fist. I'm barely holding on as I thrust ruthlessly, slapping my hand on the headboard over and over again.

"Braden!" she cries as she comes quivering around me, scratching at me like an animal.

Grabbing the back of my neck, she tilts my head down, forcing me to watch her fall apart. The unguarded affection in her silver eyes has a piece of me shattering, crumbling into a pile of dust laid at her feet as I fall right there with her. I grab both of her hands from around my neck, sliding them down my skin and dropping to my elbows before intertwining our fingers together beside her head. My thrusts become sloppy, and I shoot deep inside of her with a mangled grunt.

Our chests rise together rapidly, both of us falling into a dark, dangerous pit that I don't ever want to crawl out of.

I collapse on top of her with her name on my lips.

Where it belongs.

Sierra

A clang sounds from the kitchen, jolting me awake.

The bed is cold, hauntingly so as I notice the other half of my blankets are pulled up and tucked under the barren pillow. The unmistakable scent of Braden still lingers on the sheets, providing a thick sense of comfort that I didn't know I needed.

Standing up with the comforter wrapped around my naked body, I suck in a sharp breath at the sharp pain between my legs and carefully walk—or waddle, more like it —to my closed bedroom door. With my heart thumping nervously, I slowly twist the knob and pull the door open an inch.

A shirtless Braden stands fumbling with the frying pan I see resting on the stove. I can hear the quiet grumbles of a few incoherent words as he slides a flipper under a frying egg and attempts to flip it.

A girly giggle I hardly recognize slips through my grin, catching his attention as he jumps back from the oven. He spins around on his sock-covered feet wearing a nervous expression on his handsome face that I find utterly adorable. My grin doesn't dare falter as I open the door fully and walk toward him.

"Did I wake you up? Shit. I tried to be quiet," he rambles, a tinge of red moving up his neck.

Woah, is the great and mighty Braden Lowry blushing? At something I said? I don't know what universe I woke up in, but I don't think that I ever want to leave.

"Nah, I was already up," I lie.

He brushes off my fib. "Are you hungry?"

The fire alarm begins blaring through my apartment, no doubt waking up my neighbours, but I could care less. I catch sight of the large puffs of grey smoke floating behind Braden's broad shoulders and rush past him. A small flame singes the corner of a hand towel, one that he has left resting directly on the burner. I burst out laughing before I can stop myself.

"Were you planning on serving me this for breakfast?" I ask, quickly grabbing hold of the burning cloth before dumping it in the kitchen sink and turning the tap on. After the flames are extinguished, leaving nothing more than burnt fabric behind, I spin around to see Braden's rigid figure, waves of annoyance radiating from his shoulders, and a scowl on his mouth.

"And now I'm never cooking again."

"If that's how you cook, then I must agree with that brilliant idea." I giggle again, a sense of happiness falling over us and filling my belly with warmth.

"You didn't have any toaster waffles or I would have just made those."

"It's okay, Braden. Everybody has flaws," I tease, loving the way his eyes narrow at my subtle insult. I kiss away his pout.

"Careful, Sierra. Don't test me when I'm tired," he replies slyly, pulling me back to his chest and holding me when I go to step back.

I don't mind being held so tightly to this strong man, especially after the sweet gesture he just made, so I cuddle into him, pressing my cheek to his chest. "When did you get up, anyway? It's still really early."

"I couldn't really sleep. Too much on my mind."

"Oh, okay. I know that we didn't really get a chance to talk about what upset you yesterday, but I'm here if you want to talk abou—"

"No. I'm okay. Thanks, though." His voice is hard, the complete opposite of earlier, but I try not to let it weigh on me.

I'm not surprised by the change, but I can't help but let his quick rejection tear at my chest—even just a little bit. Especially after I shared a piece of my past with him last night.

I pull away again, and this time he lets me. The simple brush off has my throat tightening as I turn back to the sink and nod before my face can betray me.

I want to give myself a shake at the way this makes me feel. He's nothing more than a mindless screw. I can't afford to let myself feel anything for him. It won't end well. He's not somebody that can give me what I need. Whatever that may be.

Awkward silence envelopes the kitchen, only intensifying my annoyance with myself. Just say something. *Get out of this situation.* "Well, thanks for breakfast any—"

"Do you want to go get some food?" He cuts off my rambling with his own, taking me by surprise. I think I even gasp. "I mean, since I almost burnt your house down. It's the least that I can do."

Is he asking me on a date? Or is he just starving and doesn't want to go alone? Shit, why does it matter?

"Sure," I reply, spinning back around and shrugging as if his offer doesn't affect me.

He scratches at his forearm and forces a smile.

"Okay. Uh, did you want to shower?" His eyes widen immediately and I nearly swoon from how nervous he is. "Not like . . . together, right? I mean, unless you want to? It's not like we haven't done everything else under the sun." His shaky, booming laughter is enough to crack through the awkward tension.

"If we shower together, we won't ever make it to breakfast. Let me go first. I don't trust that you won't use all the hot water." I rush past him.

He stops me when I get within an inch of him by grabbing my wrist and tugging me to his chest. "You're not going anywhere without kissing me."

My stomach swirls as I hide my burning cheeks by reaching up and gently pressing my lips to his, smiling to myself when he does the same. His thumb brushes my warm skin before he pulls away, clearing his throat.

"I'll be back!" I squeak and beeline it for the bathroom. I'm about to close the door behind me when I hear him scolding himself.

"What is wrong with you? Focus, dude."

What's wrong with *you*, Braden? More like what's wrong with *me*?

———

I'M RUNNING a brush through my wet hair for the final time when Braden strolls inside my room with nothing but a Sierra sized towel wrapped around his hips. A strong sense of need sweeps through me, making my legs shake as I take in the strongly carved muscles that cover his entire torso.

Small droplets of water linger on his tan skin, slowly slipping beneath the towel. My mouth dries as I beg for the towel to drop.

Seemingly reading my thoughts, Braden doesn't give me as much as a sliver of a warning before the towel falls to the floor, exposing every inch of him to my greedy stare.

"What are you doing?" I breathe, raising my hand to shield my eyes when he starts walking to the pile of his clothes from yesterday.

A ridiculous throb beats between my thighs at the pure masculine energy radiating from his shoulders. It's addictive, drawing me in until I drown beneath it. A morning beard covers his jaw, and I ache to run my palm across it, to feel the prickling against my skin.

"Crap, I guess I have to go commando," he sighs, ignoring my question altogether when I hear the zipper of his jeans rattling around.

"You're ridiculous."

"You've never minded looking at my cock before, Sierra."

I can hear the smugness in his voice as he pulls a tight, grey short sleeve shirt over his stomach.

"I guess things change."

"Oh?" He cocks his brow and lets his darkening eyes slither up my body. "Is that so?"

"Mhm," I hum.

"What was that?"

"Oh, screw off." I shake my head at his cockiness and anxiously smooth down my hair. His bottom lip juts out in a sudden pout that has me fighting back a grin.

"I don't think so, buddy. I'm hungry for this breakfast that I was promised."

"I'm hungry too, but not for breakfast." His handsome face has become serious and hard, amber eyes blaze with want.

My lungs fail to bring it enough of the thick air around us when he starts moving toward me, his stance suddenly becoming predatory. With wide-eyes, I gulp and mutter, "The only way you're getting anything is if you feed me. With *food*."

His deep chuckle meets my ears as I pull my eyes to his and take in the easy expression he's now wearing, blessing me with a dimpled smile that has my cheeks beating with heat.

It's rare and even more unbelievably beautiful.

22

Braden

MORNING-AFTER BREAKFASTS HAVE NEVER BEEN MY THING—clearly. But seeing the shine in Sierra's eyes when the waiter brought her stack of strawberry pancakes to our table seemed to be enough to drag me over to the dark side.

I'm sure her hands would have been clapping in front of her when the plate was pushed across the table if it weren't for the several eyes roaming carelessly around the restaurant. She would hate to draw attention to herself, although I'm not sure why.

Most of the gorgeous women I've met have loved attention. Maybe that's one of the reasons that I find myself so drawn to Sierra. She's the most beautiful woman I've ever met, but she doesn't let it define her. It's sexy as hell.

Her megawatt smile punches me directly in the chest as she looks up at me from her stack of pancakes. My lips lift in a lazy smile, and I lean back against the booth, tilting my head slightly.

Her long hair is pulled up into a lump on the top of her head again, allowing me to soak in the full extent of her natural beauty. I've always been a total sucker for freckles, and of course, she has plenty spackled across her porcelain skin.

She raises a curious brow when she notices my intense staring. "You know, food is way better when you eat it while it's still warm."

I look down at my plate full of assorted meat. "Might have a point there, baby. You do know your meat." It's a ridiculous, child-like tease, but when she rolls her eyes and her shoulders shake with a silent laugh, a strong sense of pride swells in my chest.

After a few moments, she's back to eating her pancakes, and I'm watching her again, content with just sitting here, soaking in her presence.

"I didn't know that you loved pancakes so much," I say, and shove a piece of crispy bacon in my mouth.

She swallows her mouthful and slides her tongue along her bottom lip to clean off the blob of red syrup that I can't seem to take my eyes off of. I watch her tongue disappear again before she speaks.

"My sister used to make me a stack every Sunday morning. It was our thing."

"You have a sister?" And why haven't I asked about your family before now?

"Yeah. Clare is a few years older than me. Her daughter, Lizzy, is the cutest thing ever." Sierra smiles wide, stabbing another piece of pancake. "My parents weren't really around when I was young, so Clare went out of her way to be a mother figure for me in a way. We're really close. Best friends, I guess you could say."

"She sounds great. You'll have to introduce us sometime."

She seems as shocked by my offer as I am, but recovers quickly, nodding once. "She'd like that. But what about you? Do you have any siblings? Or is Clayton your loaner brother?"

Laughing lightly at that, I grab my glass of orange juice in my palm and gulp down half of it while staring across the table. "Clayton could only be so lucky as to call himself my blood brother. My actual brother, Tyler, is the opposite of Clay in almost every single way."

"Isn't that a good thing?"

"Depends on what type of guy you like, I guess. Clayton is loud, obnoxious, and judges people before getting to know them like the little shit he is. Tyler is the silent broody type who doesn't care enough to judge you. The only people my brother has let get close enough to judge would be his wife, myself, and a select few friends."

Sierra nods, her brows scrunched as if she's thinking hard about something. It makes me nervous, and I begin to feel desperate, not wanting her to shut down and run out of here.

"What else should I know about you, my little fighter?"

"Like what? I doubt you want to hear about my hobbies." Her forced, mocking laugh stings worse than I care to admit. I try to push off her backhanded insult with a tight smile.

There's no way I'm going to let her stop me from finding out everything that I can about her. She's got me too interested now. I can't keep being held at arm's length.

"And if I do? Don't be shy, Sierra. Tell me something interesting."

"Alright then," she hums and taps her chin. "I started a new job at a decent sized marketing firm pretty recently. I think that I might actually have a chance at getting somewhere in my career for the first time in what feels like forever."

I find myself enthralled with the way she speaks about it with such confidence and pride. It makes me grin, as if I'm proud of her for doing something that she's so happy with.

"That's great," I praise, reaching across the table and covering her hand with mine.

The shock that flashes across her face has me coughing awkwardly and pulling my hand back, shoving it in my lap as the unfamiliar burn of rejection scalds the palm of my hand. I want to have the right to hold her hand whenever I want to, and I don't do well with rejection.

I'm not sure what I was hoping for when I asked her to go for breakfast with me, but I know that I didn't want to leave her so quickly. I needed more time with her. It didn't matter what we did or where we went. I just needed to be with her.

I've been going around and around with my feelings for weeks, tearing myself up inside over what I wanted to do with them. But I don't think I want to keep fighting them anymore. Not if fighting them means dealing with the constant pain in my chest that only Sierra's presence can soothe.

I don't know what this all means, or if she feels even slightly the same in her feelings toward me—if there even are any beyond our shared lust for one another—but I can't stay away from her anymore. That much I do know. I would rather take my chances than keep torturing myself.

"Have you always wanted to do that?" I ask.

"Yeah. I've worked really hard to get where I am."

Her words make me think of her boss and my jaw tightens. I think he would love for her to work just a little harder—

As if sensing my discomfort, she swaps the attention to me. "What do you do? You've never talked about your work."

"I train and fight at my dad's boxing gym. I don't do anything as glamorous as you."

I crave to feel the same amount of pride in what I do as she does. I'm not ashamed of my job, but I can't help but feel like it pales in comparison to hers. When it comes to being even merely successful, I left that up to everybody else I know.

"That explains Logan's broken nose. You have one hell of a punch," she giggles, eyes sparkling. My chest puffs at her compliment before deflating just as quickly. "Maybe I could come watch you sometime?"

Her question takes me off guard. She wants to come watch me beat someone up? She doesn't seem like the violence type, although she did enjoy watching me hit Logan. But isn't that different? He at least deserved that. The guys that I fight do it solely because they love the feeling of it.

There are no chances to back away once the beating starts. They're stuck there until the pain brings them to the brink of surrender.

"I never took you for the violence type," I tease. "But if you really want to go, I have a fight tomorrow night. I can get Clayton to pick you up."

"Oh, you wouldn't be picking me up?" Sierra doesn't meet my eyes when she asks, and the pink colouring her cheeks has me grinning so wide that I'm sure she thinks I'm a lunatic.

"I'll be at the gym too early getting everything ready. But I promise Clayton will take care of you. He won't spend another day on this earth if he doesn't."

Sierra seems happy enough with my answer, her eyes burning brighter than a few minutes ago. The way she's looking at me has my breath catching in my throat as I struggle to swallow back the urge to jump over the table and sit down beside her. I want to pull her tight enough that we could be super glued together.

The waiter returns and slides his eyes over Sierra's empty plate of pancakes before asking, "Everything going good over here? I would say so."

He's teasing her, but I know immediately that I don't like it. I want him gone ASAP. Especially when Sierra flushes with embarrassment and drops her eyes to her lap.

No, I don't think so. Nobody embarrasses Sierra but *me*.

Grinding my teeth together, I push my plate toward him, letting it scrape across the table to grab his attention. I speak when his eyes finally fall on me. "I want the bill."

His chin dips in acknowledgment while he reaches in his apron and pulls out a piece of paper. After he places it down on the table, I swipe it with a forced smile.

"Thanks, Wilson." I scowl, eyeing the shiny nametag on his chest.

"I'll be back in a few minutes with the machine." I don't acknowledge him, and he leaves without another word.

"You don't have to pay for my food." Sierra reaches across the table and attempts to grab the bill from my hand. I pull it to my chest before she has the chance.

"If you want it so bad, you can always come and grab it." I cock a taunting brow, daring her to try.

She huffs. "You're a child."

"Not the first time that I've heard that, sunshine."

"Sunshine? Really? Is little fighter not good enough anymore?"

"Are you saying that you like it when I call you my little fighter?" I smirk, obsessed with the way she can't help but fight me on everything. I sit further into the booth and cross my arms for a few seconds, waiting for her to push me on it but she doesn't. "That's what I thought, baby."

"Where is that damn waiter? It's been longer than a few minutes," she rambles, physically flustered.

Her fingers brush at her hair, toying with the fallen ends. She slips her lip between her teeth, chewing on it anxiously.

Oh yeah, I got her right where I want her.

23

Sierra

"JUST OPEN THE DAMN DOOR, SOPH. I'LL BE OUT IN A minute!" I shout from my bedroom, annoyed with the incessant knocking that's been going on for the past minute.

The knocking finally stops as I'm shrugging my jean jacket over my shoulders. My reflection in the stand-up mirror on the wall makes me cringe. I spent three hours getting ready, and this is what I managed to come up with? Black skinny jeans and a light washed jean jacket? Jean on jean?

There's no way that Sophie will ever let me out of the house in this.

"We needed to leave five minutes ago, Sierra!" Sophie's voice carries through the closed door.

I rip the jean jacket off and throw it across the room, watching it smack against my desk. Why does it even matter what I wear? It's not like Braden will even see me in the crowd full of people shouting and cheering, pushing their way around the fighting ring like a possessed mob. Okay, that might be a bit of a stretch.

Boxing has never been anything that I've really cared about nor watched before. I have no idea what to expect once we get there.

The almost inaudible dinging of my phone grabs my attention. Picking it up from its spot on my mattress, I feel my lips lift in a small smile.

Braden: Wear something gold.

Gold? I don't think I have anything gold. Wait, how did he know I was struggling with what to wear?

"Sophie!" I shout seconds before footsteps pound against the floor outside of my room. The door flies open, and Sophie's grin aggravates me instantly.

"I see you've been talking with the half-wit out there," I growl, folding my arms.

"Heard that!" Clayton shouts from somewhere in the living room.

"Don't care!" I shout back and look back at Sophie, sighing, "I need something gold. Help me." I mumble the words.

"Got it." She marches toward my closet and starts tearing through the rows of clothes. Hums and haws make their way from the closet and clothes start flying around the room. The telltale sign of a migraine blurs my vision and I groan, long and heavy. Massaging my temples, I flop down on my bed.

"Please tell me that I have something to wear," I sigh. "I hate that I care this much about this. Who am I, Sophie? You?"

She slings me a glare over her shoulder before returning to the clothes. "You like him."

"I do," I mumble before I chicken out. "Is that stupid?"

"Absolutely not, S. Didn't I tell you that friends with benefits never works?"

I don't answer. I refuse to give her the satisfaction.

"It's okay. I know the truth. That's enough for me," she adds before I hear a few clangs from across the room. I keep my eyes on the ceiling. "Yes! Now we're talking."

Keeping my hands pressed flat on the bed, I push myself

into a sitting position and watch Sophie pull a metallic gold, off the shoulder top from a hanger before tossing it to me. The tag pricks my finger before I rip it off and quickly tuck it under my pillow, feeling only slightly embarrassed that I didn't even remember I bought it ages ago. It's stunning, so it was probably one of my impulse buys.

I run my fingers along the silk like material and begin to feel nauseous, nerves burning a hole in my stomach. Most of the time, I avoid unfamiliar places and situations. Fear of the unknown is real, and it sucks. But there's no way I'm going to let fear ruin this for me. Not this time.

I want to put myself out there and experience something new and thrilling. And I guess I have Braden to thank for that. He makes me want to slip out of my comfort zone and breathe in new experiences. It's one of the reasons why I think I'm so addicted to being in his presence.

So, I'm going to let go, at least for tonight. The world can go back to normal in the morning.

"Thanks, Soph."

"Yeah, yeah. Just get changed so we can go," Sophie replies. She sits down on the bed, eyeing me curiously.

"You're not going to leave so I can change?"

She looks at me with pleading eyes. "Please don't make me go out there again without you. Clayton is driving me crazy."

"Fine." I nod with understanding and take the shirt to the bathroom to change.

A few minutes later, we're all situated inside Clayton's Jeep. To say I was surprised to find how absolutely pristine he keeps the interior is an understatement.

The smell of leather and cologne is thick in the air, but I can't say that I mind it much. There's not a single wrapper or fleck of dust anywhere that I can see, and I've snooped through the backseat after letting Sophie take shotgun, much to her frustration and Clayton's pleasure. I can tell that it doesn't bother him much having my best friend sitting so close to him, unable to run and hide from his ridiculous puns and that damn attentive stare that makes a girl feel like she's been placed under a microscope. Sophie, on the other hand, looks like she might jump out of the moving vehicle at any given moment.

"Please tell me we're almost there," she begs.

The street lights move over the front seats every few seconds, shining enough light for me to catch the daggers she's shooting in the side of Clayton's head.

"Oh, please. I can list at least five girls who would love to be sitting where you are." Clay clicks his tongue while strumming his hands against the steering wheel.

"Yeah, right," she scoffs.

"You don't have to be jealous, gorgeous."

"Fuck you."

"You always could."

"In your dreams, asshat."

With a quiet sigh, I lean my cheek against the cold window and tune out their pointless bickering. My eyes slide shut, letting the darkness calm down my jittery nerves.

I'm not sure what to expect tonight. The only thing I expect is to see a completely different side of the laid-back, quick-tongued playboy that I've come to know.

When he first told me that he boxes for a living, all I could think about was seeing him break Logan's nose, and suddenly I couldn't stop myself from asking to go watch him. I'm way more excited than I originally thought I would be to watch Braden in his element. Maybe if I had been spending more time getting to know what makes him *him*, instead of just how he works his dick, I would have been able to realize he was a fighter to begin with.

The scar through his eyebrow and the fresh ones over his knuckles seem more important to me now, like pieces of the puzzle I swept under the couch and forgot about. Even the way he walks—completely confident in himself and his ability to drop anyone who so much as thinks of making a wrong move without breaking a sweat—screams fighter.

I always assumed it was just his ginormous ego that called to me, making my clit swell with need with the briefest flash of his smile. But maybe it was his strength and power instead. They both radiate from his broad shoulders like sound waves, calling to me at a frequency that has my head doing a doubt take, not grasping as to how this man has such easy control over me.

"We're here," Clayton grumbles. We come to a jolting stop as he slides the Jeep into park and whips open his door, walking into the dark. I look at Sophie, my eyes wide with surprise when he slams the door behind him.

"What did I miss?"

"Nothing. Let's just go before he abandons us."

I nod quickly and open my door. The noise hits me like a freight train as soon as I step outside. There's no music playing, the noise comes solely from shouted voices, the clear aggression behind them taking me by surprise. I grab hold of Sophie's hand and squeeze when she steps out and gasps.

"We're going to die," she groans, eying the bulky guys standing in front of the front door, chatting with Clayton. There's a glowing red sign above the door that spells Rampage. "I pissed him off so badly he wants to have us killed."

"We're not going to die." I hope. "Come on." I gather up my confidence and pull her toward the men.

"About time!" Clayton yells when he notices us slowly creep up to him. "This is Roy." He points to the taller but leaner of the two men and I get a grin of welcome from him before we're moving onto the bulkier man. "And this is Brooks."

Gulping, I force my lips to spread in a welcoming smile. "Nice to meet you. I'm Sierra."

They both return my smile with more genuine ones. The

shockingly handsome, much stronger looking one—Brooks, I think, offers me his hand. I'm taken aback by the strength of his grip when I place my hand in his, shaking it before dropping it back to my side. I eye him curiously, focusing on the familiar, thick bushy brows, prominent cupid's bow and amber-coloured eyes that I could have sworn I've looked into quite a number of times.

I nearly sputter an embarrassed laugh when he winks at me, informing me subtly that he caught on to my gawking.

"I've heard all about you, Sierra. The pleasure is all mine," Brook's says in a low rumble.

My cheeks burn as I grow confused. Heard all about me? From who? Clayton? I go to offer him a forced smile, but he's already moved on, slinging a massive arm around Clayton's shoulders. *Okay then.*

"And I'm Sophie." I hear from beside me, the voice suddenly entirely at ease. When I catch the slight flutter of her eyelashes as she stares up at Brooks, I know that it's time to go.

"Hello, Sophie," he chuckles, shaking her hand like he did mine.

"Should we go? I think we're already late, Clayton." I expel a heavy breath of relief when he turns to me, nodding. He says his quick goodbyes to the two men before pushing open the door and holding it for us.

"Come on, Soph." I grab her hand again and yank her past Roy and Brooks, forcing her to follow Clayton inside. When we finally make the front doors, she turns to me, visibly annoyed.

"You're such a pussy block, S."

"I spotted a few grey hairs in that man bun. He's way too old for you," I mutter.

"Whatever."

Our shoulders knock together when we're brushed off to the side by a couple of dominant looking women shoving their way through the growing crowd around us. Panic slices up my spine as we become surrounded with large, sweaty bodies.

Steeling my spine, I refuse to let fear rule me tonight. So, with a shake of my head that I hope is enough to clear out my worries, I turn my attention to the view in front of us and steady myself.

Oh, shit. I definitely wasn't prepared for this.

24

Sierra

THE CROWD IS TERRIFYING.

Countless loud voices scratch at my eardrums as we slowly venture further into the gym, Sophie's hand still clasped in mine.

The cement floor looks cold, but the air is hot and sickly humid. I feel too exposed in my current clothes. My skin crawls as several pairs of eyes drag their way up my body when we begin pushing our way deeper into the mob.

We follow Clay as best we can, but it's hard to keep him in focus while being shoved around. At this point, the only thing keeping me from turning around and running away is that Braden wouldn't have been okay with me being somewhere I could get hurt. Or I hope not, at least. He has faith in me and the people here, and I hold onto that like a lifeline.

Sophie gives my hand a hard squeeze, and after a quick look around, I realize we've lost Clay in the mess of people around us.

Slipping my lip between my teeth, I attempt to stand on my toes and search the gym. It's not so easy, though. Not in an entire building full of mostly tall, brown-haired men.

Searching for Clay in here is like searching for a needle in a haystack.

"Just keep going straight!" Sophie shouts.

Her eyes are wide as they move over the people pressed up against us with seemingly no sense of personal space. With a huff, I stick out my elbow and push, leading us even further into the crowd. I duck my head down and yank Sophie's hand, forcing her to follow me. It works like a charm until a tree-truck sized arm pushes out in front of me, nearly hitting my cheek. I freeze. The arm presses against my collarbone, forcing me to stay still.

My heartbeat picks up, and nerves start to twist my stomach into a boulder sized knot. I follow the length of the arm until I find a sharp jaw. The thick scar trailing the length of the bone only fills me with even more unwanted fear.

"Are you lost?" the stranger asks, his voice so hoarse it causes a shiver to run up my spine.

"No," I respond quickly. The stranger's dark eyes light up with humour as I lie to him.

"You sure?" He looks past me to ask the question to Sophie this time. Her grip on my hand tightens.

"We're fine. Thanks."

He cocks his brow, serving me with a look that makes me feel like gum beneath his shoe. "Let me take you—"

"Fuck off, Tavares. They said they're fine," a different voice says. The rumble comes from a stern-faced, tatted-up man.

The arm drops from in front of me as the asshole takes a step back, jaw clenching fiercely. Clearly, he doesn't like to be told no. Fancy that.

"Always walking around like you own the place, Tyler," he spits.

The two brawny men stand firm and broad in front of each other, but I don't miss the way our tattooed saviour shifts himself in front of me.

"Always walking around harassing women, Tavares," Tyler replies, not taking his narrowed gaze off of the guy.

Thankfully, Tavares doesn't seem to want to make a scene and spins on his heel with a mumbled curse before walking off.

"Where the fuck is Clayton?" Tyler moves to face Sophie and me, growling a curse under his breath while running a large hand through his head of short black hair.

I shrug both shoulders. Tyler's towering height, slim waist, and wide back instantly remind me of Braden, and I nearly smack myself upside the head when I remember where I've heard his name before.

"You're Braden's brother, right?" I ask him. The knots in my stomach begin to unravel.

Tyler dips his chin and smiles, looking as if the past few minutes have already been forgotten. He's happy to be introduced as Braden's brother. I think I like him already.

"You're Sierra and Sophie, right? I know that my brother may be a fucking idiot most of the time, but he wouldn't be stupid enough not to have somebody here with you. So, tell me where Clayton is, and I'll knock him around a bit for the lot of us."

"That's us. And I wouldn't fight you on that one. We're lucky that we ran into you. It's insane here. Is it always so crowded?"

He tilts his head side to side in an "eh" gesture. "Mostly just when Braden fights. The guy's got quite the fan club."

For some reason, I expect to hear jealousy in Tyler's tone, and am relieved when the only thing I pick up on is pride. Knowing that Braden is surrounded by people who care for him so deeply spears me with a warm and fuzzy feeling.

"As great as it is to meet you, Tyler, I would really love to get out of this crowd," Sophie cuts in, a note of frustration in her voice. I'm reminded of where we are and wince, taking a step closer to Sophie and clutching her elbow.

"Follow me," Tyler says with a firm dip of his chin.

I watch in awe as the crowd parts for him, leaving more than enough room for us to catch our breath.

He leads us through a vast archway that separates the front half of the gym from the back half. There are two men standing in front of the entrance but they let us through with a quick nod in Tyler's direction.

A gasp gets stuck in my throat as I take in the new space. It's much bigger than where we just were, and painted with dark lighting that barely manages to highlight the giant, elevated boxing ring that's been placed in the middle of the room. There's an empty hallway to the right of us that I assume leads toward a locker room, and two others, each one on an opposite side of the ring. There are large square lights around the platform that are turned off, leaving it dark.

Anger sizzles in my blood when I spot Clayton leaning against the thick velvet ropes lining the edges, his cellphone pressed to his ear. His body is completely relaxed, not a care in the world as to where Sophie and I may or may not have ended up as he continues chatting with whoever's on the other end of the call.

"Forget something, Clay?" Tyler asks, stalking toward him with a thick sense of power.

I snicker when Tyler brings his hand up and smacks it against the back of Clayton's head. The angry man seems to pull Clayton's head from the clouds as he spins to look back at us, eyes wide with worry.

"Yeah, or maybe a couple somebody's?" Sophie hisses. I can tell she wants to walk over there and beat some sense into him, so I tighten my grip on her elbow and ignore the glare beating into my temple when she whirls to face me.

Clay stays silent for a few seconds, as if he's running through every possible reply for the one that will piss us off the least. But unfortunately for him, there won't be a good enough answer when it comes to a pissed off Sophie. Or me, for that matter.

"See, what happened was I had to take a piss and the bathrooms up front are always so dirty, so I had to use the ones back here, and then by the time I was on my way back out, I saw that Tyler had you—"

"You didn't even give it to her either, you dumbass," Tyler grunts, snapping his attention to my bare neck before pinning Clayton with a deadly glare.

My brows pull inward as my eyes dart between them. "Give me what?"

It's Clayton who answers me, wearing a sheepish smile that looks completely out of place on his clean, sharp features. "Braden's lucky chain. He gave it to me this morning, and told me to have you wear it tonight. I meant to hand it off to you in the car, but Sophie distracted me."

My lips part. There's a warm, buttery feeling wrapping me up in a tight embrace while doves take flight in my belly, their wings flapping so hard I nearly reach down and place a hand on my stomach to see if I can feel them from the outside.

"Oh," I breathe, flushed all the way to my toes. "Can I still wear it? I mean, if it's not a big deal?"

Holy shit it's hot in here. Am I sweating?

I thought I had a greater understanding of the extent of Braden's feelings, but I apparently highly misjudged the depth of how much he cares for me. I expected to find him swimming near the top of the ocean, not deep enough that his stomach could brush the sand. The realization has my heart thumping to an off-tempo beat.

"He would string me up a pole by my balls if I didn't let you wear it," Clayton snorts, reaching into the front pocket of his jeans and pulling out a thick silver chain.

The silver is dull, worn, and well loved. Something that feels a hell of a lot like love swells inside of me before I shove the feeling out of sight.

With tentative fingers, I pluck the chain from Clayton's outstretched hand and hold it gently, like I would a piece of my great-grandmother's fine china. I let it fall from one hand to the other, shivering as the cold metal tickles my palms.

The return of voices has me closing my fist around the chain and spinning around. I watch the crowds begin filing in around the ring, the excited whoops and hollers making me tense up.

"Let me put it on you before you drop the damn thing and lose it," Sophie murmurs, the pitch of her voice slightly higher than normal.

Eying her with a scrutinizing look, I see the swoon in her eyes and breathe a laugh.

After I've dropped the chain in her open palm, I feel the cold bite of it over the burning skin of my throat before she quickly clasps it and moves to my side again. "There. Now let's find somewhere to stand before we're stuck sandwiched between a bunch of sweaty old men."

Tyler nudges my arm and points to the empty space a few feet down the ring, directly underneath one of the giant lamps that have turned on sometime during our exchange of Braden's chain. The reminder has me reaching to the hollow of my throat and toying with the silver chain between two fingers.

Sophie and I follow after Tyler and Clayton as they lead the way before stopping and moving so we're sandwiched between them. The protective stance has me smiling.

In all honesty, it's a relief having these two as our bodyguards for the night. Even if Clayton isn't exactly the ideal candidate.

It only takes a few minutes for the building to fill. Hands and arms push against my back, pushing and pulling me as best they can before they're shoved back by either Clayton or Tyler. I can tell that the two men are becoming frustrated, but they try not to show it, keeping their mouths shut and their bodies tight.

It's not until the ceiling lights transform from a bright white to a mesmerizing, shimmering gold that they break out in beaming smiles. A brick drops in my stomach as excitement begins to buzz under my skin.

Smoke crawls over our feet, slowly rising in the air until it toys with the bottoms of my leather pants. It swirls higher and higher before spilling over the edges of the boxing ring. I spot Brooks waiting beside the entrance to the hallway closest to us, and nearly choke on an inhale when a massive, shirtless figure begins moving toward him, meeting up with him in what feels like no time at all with a set of giraffe-sized legs. The voices around me become louder as each dawning second passes by until my ears beg to be covered, beginning to ache.

Suddenly, two rows of beaming white teeth come into focus, and I smile too, completely enamoured by the stunning confidence behind the star-studded smile. It's a smile that breeds a sense of victory and worship that even I can't ignore.

There's a deep, husky voice shooting through what sounds like a microphone, but I ignore it, too busy watching the way Braden's massive biceps stretch above his head and toes tap on the floor with a sort of grace that I never expected from such a big man. It probably sounds ridiculous, considering boxers have incredible balance and control, but seeing the fluid way he moves his body has my mouth gaping in surprise.

Fingering the chain around my neck again, I watch Braden as he finally makes his way into the shimmering light. A shiny black robe hangs loosely from his shoulders, leaving his defined chest bare for all to see. My mouth waters as the individual muscles flex on their own accord, almost as if to torture me.

An unmistakable itch of jealousy worms up my body at

knowing that his miraculous body is on full display. It's a ridiculous feeling, considering he isn't even mine to begin with, but that doesn't help settle me as much as I wish that it would.

Forcing my eyes to move from the solid abdomen in front of me, I drop them to the gold, mid-thigh length shorts that fit snugly to his muscular legs. The material stretches tight as he expertly hands his robe over to Brooks, who I'm beginning to piece together might be his father, and pulls open the velvet ropes to climb inside the ring.

My eyes become saucers when I steal a glance at my gold attire, finally feeling the pieces fall together.

Well played, Braden. Well played.

He raises a fist in the air as the excited hollers continue to praise him, no doubt adding to his already enormous ego. I can't find it in me to care, though. I'm too busy letting a heavy sense of pride shine in my eyes as I stare at him, not daring to move my gaze from his handsome face.

A cheek splitting smile spreads across my face as soon as his wandering eyes clash against mine with enough emotion to pull a whimper from my throat.

A beyond obvious, cheesy wink from my playboy boxer is all it takes to forget about everything and lift my own arms in the air to join in the excited cheers, happier than I have been in years.

25

Braden

D<small>AD</small> <small>LEANS BACK AGAINST THE WALL WITH A DEEP SCOWL,</small> <small>HIS</small> arms crossed hard enough for the skin to bulge. "You ready?"

I slip the smooth black and gold robe over my shoulders and give a cocky grin to my reflection in one of the wall-length mirrors hung along the locker room wall.

"Always."

Boxing matches are a more common event in Rampage now that we spent the money updating and expanding the building to accommodate a separate fighting ring and more people. The renovations wouldn't have even been a possibility without my brother loaning us the money, but we've more than paid it back over the past year by hosting these matches. They bring in more cash-flow than we expected. Especially once the high-rollers get interested.

Everything went as planned today while I was getting the usual last-minute jobs done, but I felt the pressure harder than most days. It was easy to recognize why.

Tonight is special. Not because I get to show up countless fighters with my well-worked-for skills, but because for the first time ever, I have someone out in the crowd that I'm actually trying to impress. I don't want Sierra's first experience watching me fight to be a disappointment. My pride couldn't take it.

Usually, I'm too concentrated on the guy in front of me to care about the pussy I'm going to be getting once I step out of the ring a winner. But this isn't just any ordinary pussy out there tonight. This is Sierra we're talking about. Just the thought of demeaning her to the word pussy has my throat burning with the threat of throwing up.

"I ran into Clayton earlier. He introduced me to a couple of his friends," Dad says, accusation flickering in his voice. My brow raises, pushing him to elaborate. "I'm assuming that they're also your friends?"

"Happy you picked up on that, old man." I snort. "Yeah, Sierra's mine."

His eyes widen slightly and he chokes on a laugh. I don't know why, but the reaction has my face hardening to stone. "She's *yours?*"

My eyes narrow into slits. "Yeah. What about it?"

His hands come up in front of his chest, held out in surrender. There's a curiosity behind his calm composure that has me sliding an invisible guard up.

"I didn't know you were dating anyone. That's all."

"Dating?" I choke on the word. "I wouldn't go that far. We both know that I wouldn't even know what to do with that sort of label."

Dropping his arms, he moves toward my locker and grabs my gloves before offering them to me. I take them with a bit more force than necessary and stretch out my wrapped hands, feeling the black material stretch around the knuckles.

"Relax, buddy. Honest mistake." He laughs. "So, you're just friends, then?"

Just friends? Somehow that label is even worse. "Ah, slow down there. I never said that."

Shaking his head, he sits down on the bench in front of me and clasps his hands in his lap. He looks like he feels out of place with his twiddling thumbs and clouded eyes floating around the room. Dad hasn't fought in a long time, not after he tore his rotator cuff one too many times. He misses it. I hate that he has to sit back and watch me, unable to feel the liberation and freedom the way that I do.

"Just don't get distracted out there. You don't get days off for any of the injuries you're going to get trying to impress one of the girls you're banging."

"The only girl I'm banging," I correct him, feeling the need to clarify it for him. For a guy deciding to get hitched to someone half his age, he's immensely judgmental of everyone else's relationships. Although, does what he thinks really even matter?

"Do you really think so low of me?"

"Yes," he replies without hesitation. I inhale sharply, my mouth dropping into a frown. "Sorry. Of course not, Braden. My perfect child. The poster child for monogamous relationships. I must be thinking of my other son who was sneaking girls into my house in the middle of the night since he was fifteen. Oh wait, my other son is happily married."

Ignoring the hurt spearing my stomach from his low opinion of me, I slip my gloves on and strap them like always.

"Okay, okay. I get it. Point taken."

"Just stay focused on the fight. If Sierra really is the only girl you're seeing, maybe she should come around the house sometime. I'm sure Lana would love to cook for her," he offers.

"Sure. If that'll get you to lay off, then consider it set in stone," I reply, although I have a feeling that Sierra would rather eat rocks than what Lana calls cooking.

The surprise in Dad's eyes is evident as he watches me, intent on making me squirm and admit that I would rather spoon out my own eyes than go for another awkward dinner with Lana. But when I keep my mouth shut like a good little boy, he gives my shoulder a squeeze.

"Jesse lacks stamina. Strike first and the win is yours. Good luck."

"Thanks, Dad." I grin and his hand falls from my shoulder. As he makes his way to the entrance, I start to bounce in place, shaking off the nerves. The cheers reach my ears and I know that it's time.

Any prior thoughts that I have disappear as I shake out my arms and walk down the hallway. The usual fog begins to crawl up my legs as golden light pours over my shoulders. Screaming voices pierce my eardrums as I confidently shrug out of my robe and hand it over to Dad.

I pull at the velvet ropes and step inside the ring, basking in the adrenaline and screams of encouragement from the crowd. My feet repeatedly tap the pad as I let my eyes start sifting through the crowd, desperate to find my golden girl. And when I do, my arm shoots to the ceiling in a victory-like celebration.

She wore what I asked. Pride surges through me when our eyes meet, my lungs constricting in a way that has me wanting to clutch my chest. I fight off the feeling and let a smile light up my face, aching to scream a hurray at the ceiling when she smiles back, shining from head to toe with pure, unfiltered bliss. The gold top clinging to her skin is a near-perfect match to the colour of my shorts and gloves. She looks exactly how I pictured.

I swear my heart slides to my throat when the light catches on the silver chain wrapped loosely around her dainty neck, the shine capturing my attention and holding it hostage as the room blurs behind her.

There was a part of me that didn't expect her to wear it. To snuff it up to her pride and refuse to wear something of mine when I haven't even told her how I feel. But she *is* wearing it. And I don't think that I ever want it back. The rush of contentment that falls on my shoulders fills me with more than enough confidence to make this a quick, easy fight.

I've never wanted to bail on a fight so bad in my life. I need to touch her, tell her that she's mine and there's no longer any room for discussion.

When I hear my opponent's name being called out, I force myself to pull out of the trance and collect myself. After shooting her a cheesy wink that has her throwing her arms up to cheer me on, I finally turn my attention to Jesse.

He makes his way through the ropes, meeting me in the center of the ring with an icy scowl that I can't wait to sink my knuckles into. He's about an inch or two shorter than me, but wider. Much wider. If it weren't for the constant drug tests we run before matches, I would assume that he's become good friends with a performance enhancement drug named Steroid. His size doesn't shake me, though. I've trained and fought bigger guys than Jesse. He might be stronger, but I *know* that I'm faster on my feet.

Keeping my eyes from drifting to where I know Sierra stands watching is a new form of torture. *No distractions, Braden. Forget she's there.* The reminder has me shaking my head as if the simple movement would somehow do what I've been unable to do for weeks now.

My dad has moved to the crowd now, and I spot him holding my mouthguard from between the ropes. I slip off one of my gloves and pop in the guard, gnawing on the silicone out of habit. It's always driven my dad crazy, but fear of pissing off the old bastard has never stopped me from doing anything.

I slip my glove back on before tapping my hands to Jesse's extended ones. Taking a step back, I raise my arms to protect my chest seconds before the round begins and Jesse throws the first punch.

———

As the hot, thick air starts to fill my burning lungs once again, I let my arm hang from the hand of the referee in celebration of my hard-earned win. It only took six rounds for Jesse to give up a win that he was never going to get, but it was a hard, exhausting six rounds. I'll be sore tomorrow for sure.

I know Dad's waiting outside the ring—having seen him take off in that direction as soon as I claimed victory—ready to collect my exhausted body in case I drop dead any minute. Which, if it happens, I wouldn't be surprised.

Jesse deserved way more credit than we gave him. He was faster than I expected for being so massive, more domineering, too. But sloppy with his tells, like a rookie. Like Clayton. That's what cost him the round, not my speed or experienced throws.

As soon as my arm flops back against my side, I carry myself to the edge of the ring and let Dad help me through the ropes and back to the locker room.

"I hate you," I hiss when he doesn't make enough room for both of us to fit side by side through the entrance. My side bumps the door handle and I wince, gnashing my teeth.

The locker room has never looked more inviting as I fall onto the wooden bench and squeeze my eyes shut, trying to ignore the throbbing coming from the left side of my face.

"You didn't strike first," Dad points out. He sits down beside me with a large medical kit. I have no clue when he went and got that, but I don't give a rat's ass as long as it helps with this fucking pain.

"Oh fuck off, you old shit."

"That was insane!" A shrill voice bouncing off the walls only deepens the throb in my forehead as I throw my hands over my ears.

"Your eyebrow!" Sierra gasps, pushing her way past an exhilarated Sophie to crouch in front of me, concern swimming in her silver eyes.

Suddenly the only touch I feel is hers as she drags her

thumb above what I can only assume is a decently split brow. My eyes close at the gentle touch as the throb becomes a thing of the past.

"How bad do I look?" I grit out, flinching at the sting in my bottom lip as I speak.

"You've definitely looked better," she says. Her beautiful face is all scrunched up with concern. I want to reach out and grab onto her, but her fingertips leave my face before I can, and I'm left with a raw feeling of disappointment.

"Here, let me," I hear her tell my dad before he's getting up and leaving the locker room.

"You want me all alone, huh?" I ask, watching her with an intensity that I'm sure she feels in her gut. She scrunches her lips to the side as she focuses on what she'll need to use to clean me up.

"Obviously," she teases.

After a few silent seconds, a wet towel is pressed to my brow, bringing a burning sensation with it. There's an unguarded sense of worry on her face, and I would be lying if I said it didn't fill me with pleasure to have her want to fix me up. I want to bottle up the look in her eyes and keep it for a bad day.

"Your concern is adorable, baby. But I always thought our first time roleplaying nurse and patient would involve a bed, not a wooden bench."

She replies by pressing down *way* harder than necessary on the cut, laughing lightly when my features twist in pain.

"Hey, hey. Take it easy. I'm wounded." I grin, ignoring my sore lip and reach up to wrap my fingers around her small, dainty wrist. Her skin is warm and soft and I want nothing more than to go home and feel every inch of it pressed against mine. "I'm just teasing, my little fighter. I really do appreciate your help."

She seems pleased with my more *sincere* words as she pulls

the cloth away from my face and nods. "You shouldn't need stitches, but I'm guessing you already knew that."

I did, but it's adorable that she still felt the need to tell me. "You know what I do need, though?"

She cocks a brow, entertaining the question.

"A celebratory kiss. I did win for you, after all."

Sierra rolls her eyes, only making me inch closer to her, not buying the uninterested facade. I slowly grab the wet fabric from between her fingers and set it down beside me. Her cheeks darken, eyes wandering off behind me.

"Shy doesn't suit you, gorgeous," I mumble, gently pulling her attention back to me. My fingers itch to touch her warm cheeks, to run them down the soft skin that her long lashes flutter against like the wings of a butterfly.

I watch as she rolls her lips, almost as if the voice in her head is telling her the same thing as mine. *Calm the fuck down.* It's an impossible task on most days, but as I fall from a boxing induced adrenaline high with Sierra knelt in front of me, her concentration so focused on fixing me up and making sure that I'm okay, impossible has taken on a whole new meaning.

"You neither," she counters. "If you want something, why don't you take it? The Braden I know would rather be castrated than let his nerves sho—"

"Is that a challenge?" I cut her off, sliding my fingers from her wrists to her elbows before gently pulling her from her kneeling position and onto my lap.

"Does it sound like one?" she breathes, wiggling her ass on my thighs. My eyes darken, heat flaring in my groin as she rubs against my hardening cock with a knowing smirk.

"You're playing a very dangerous game, fighter." My gaze is hungry, straight primitive as I become transfixed on the way her chest rises and falls so quickly, her attraction to me so obvious. It's like looking in a goddamn mirror.

Two small, warm hands fall to my shoulders, fingers slightly kneading at the sore muscles. "Sorry," she whispers.

I let out a content sigh and press my forehead to hers, basking in the charged energy that's begun to circle us. With a large open palm, I hold the side of her face, my eyes anchored to hers as I trace the shape of her lower lip with my thumb. Sierra tugs it up in a smile that I easily return before sliding my hand to her nape and pulling her toward me. My eyes slide shut and our lips brush, the touch so gentle that I struggle to catch my breath. My pulse is fast and thumping like a kick drum. *Fuck.* It feels like I've just run a marathon.

Suddenly my hand on her neck isn't enough, and I'm gripping her hip with a splayed palm, kneading it and using it to pull her closer. A groan slips between us when her leather-clad center slides against my cock, our clothes the only thing keeping me from taking her right here.

"Braden," she whimpers, the sound so soft, like a desperate plea.

Her fingers move from my shoulders, finding purchase at the back of my neck a moment later. I wish that I didn't love the sound of my name on her lips as much as I do. It only fuels my need to hear it fall from those pretty lips that much more.

"I knew we should have just waited in the car," my best friend grunts, joining us again. The locker room door slams shut a few seconds later. Sierra jumps away from me at the sound of his voice, struggling to stand on her own feet, and leaving my lap unbearably cold.

Annoyance slithers under my skin but I try to ignore it, not wanting to piss Sierra off.

But one look at Clayton's arrogant smirk and my attempt at calmness crashes and burns. "Clay. Can you please get the *fuck* out of here?"

The prick turns to point at the blonde beside him. She's already glaring at him, arms crossed firmly. "Wrong person, brother. Take it up with this one. I wanted to go, but she refused to leave without Sierra."

"Which clearly was the wrong decision," Sophie speaks up, embarrassment flushing her cheeks. Her eyes flick between Sierra and me with a fierce sense of curiosity.

"I'll take good care of your friend," I promise her before straightening up beside my girl and properly introducing myself. "It's nice to officially meet you, by the way. I was afraid that Sierra was going to keep me hidden in her closet of dirty secrets forever."

With a pinch to Sierra's waist, I kiss the top of her head and pull her back flush to my front, wrapping my arms around her as my light laughter brushes her hair.

Sophie's nose crunches in evident disgust as she watches us. "I bet. Anyway, I'm out of here. Call if you need me, Sierra.

Without sparing either of us a second look, she clutches Clayton's hand in hers, taking him by surprise, and heads for the door, letting it close behind her.

I'm not sure what the two of them have planned tonight, but I'm glad I won't be finding out. Clayton hasn't gotten laid in a very, very long time, and if Sophie is anything like Sierra, she'll eat him alive.

I stare at the woman leaning back against my chest and smile, feeling completely at ease. With a sigh, I slide my thumb under Sierra's shirt and rub the smooth skin above her pants. "You jumped away from me pretty quickly back there. You don't happen to be embarrassed by me, do you, baby?"

As if commanded by my words, she spins around in my arms, placing her hands on my chest to steady herself. "Why? Would that manage to chip away at your giant ego?"

"No." I shrug. "But it would make what I have planned for you later a bit more interesting."

Her eyes double in size, and I don't miss the way her throat bobs with a massive swallow. The thought of taking her home and hearing her scream my name while I fuck her against every surface in my apartment has my cook hardening, pressing into her back. Mental pictures become a distraction. I'm more than happy to take her to my place and keep her in my bed for hours—days even.

"Who said I was coming home with you?" she croaks, pushing back against me just enough to let me know that she can feel exactly what she does to me.

"Me."

"Always the gentleman," she scoffs but nods toward the heavy gym bag resting a few feet behind me. "Let's go then. I work tomorrow morning."

With a helpless grin that has me feeling like a little boy, I push myself off the bench and collect my shit. Pulling open the locker room door, I wait for Sierra to walk past me before letting my right palm connect with her ass. Her shriek is immediate, bringing a chuckle up my dry throat as she spins around with her eyes narrowed.

"My God, you're an actual teenager."

"You say it like it's a bad thing. We both know you love it."

"Just shut up and take me home."

"Yes, ma'am."

26

Sierra

"KNOCK KNOCK."

Peeling my eyes off my computer screen, I blink past the burn from staring at the bright screen for hours and see Cole leaning in the doorway to my office. He's wearing a light grey suit today with the sleeves uncuffed and rolled twice, paired with shiny black dress shoes. His aura is confident and arrogant, like he knows some big secret that nobody else does.

I haven't had to spend too much time alone with Cole over the past two weeks, but this is the first time that he's come across this way. Most of the time, he's too concerned with trying to butter me up to let his true colours show. But I've always known this arrogance would make an appearance sooner than later.

Most men like him have a strong arrogant side, one that doesn't usually appear until they have you wrapped around your finger, unable to let their true personality turn you away, already too enraptured by them to care.

"Hi, Cole. What can I do for you?" I clear my throat and plaster on a smile.

Cole was the last person I was hoping to deal with today. It's just past lunch, and having been plagued with a killer migraine this morning, I skipped it, not trusting my stomach to handle anything other than a glass of flat Ginger Ale.

"Let me start by saying you look beautiful today." Cole says the compliment with a grin that I see right through. I'm anything but beautiful today.

With my finger combed hair and wrinkled clothes, I look ridiculously unprofessional. But after being woken up in the early morning with Braden's tongue between my thighs, I fell back asleep way too late and slept past my alarm. It's a miracle that I even made it today in the first place. I can't say that it wasn't worth the risk, though. Because it definitely was.

In the past two weeks since my first ever boxing match, Braden's only managed to slither farther under my skin. When I'm not at the office, I'm with him. And in the moments that we're not together, the thoughts of him consume me. I *let* them consume me. I should be more frustrated with how far inside my chest he's managed to bury himself, and I hate that I ache for him to stay there forever.

My house, his house, dinner, the movies, we've been doing it all. I feel like a teenager again with all of this so-called "dating." At least, I would consider it dating. I know that Braden does too.

We haven't exactly put a label on what we're doing, but he's been adamant that he hasn't been seeing anybody else, and I haven't even thought about anybody else since we first met. I'm sure that if I asked him for a label, he would give me one. But what pisses me off the most is that I can't get myself to ask.

Labels bring something heavy and expecting to a relationship. The word girlfriend comes with the expectation of putting your partner above and beyond everything else. And I can't do that. I can't promise that I'll put my life, my *career*, on the back burner for him if he asked me to. The ugly sinking feeling taking up shop in my stomach is exactly why I refuse to label our relationship. It would ruin what we've built. I know it would.

I turn back to Cole with an ache in my chest. My boss seems to think his compliment permits him to drag his eyes down my torso in a way that leaves me itching to wrap myself in a blanket. I swallow the wad beginning to form in my throat and stiffly say, "Thank you."

"I also wanted to stop by to personally escort you to the meeting happening in the boardroom in just a few minutes. It's going to be a jaw-dropper."

His words bring back the confusion that I felt when I opened up my emails this morning to see a meeting with the entire firm scheduled for today. It wasn't posted on the calendar Friday, so it had to have been added over the weekend, although it's highly unusual for such a big meeting to be planned on such short notice. A Monday no doubt.

"The meeting, right. Did I miss an email about it? It wasn't on the schedule before I left on Friday and I wasn't told about it until a couple hours ago in your email."

"Oh, no. The meeting was pushed up a few weeks. I understand your confusion, but I promise it'll make sense soon. Are you ready?"

Weird, but plausible. The tension drains from my muscles at the realization that it wasn't my fault. After working at my previous job and missing the due date of our marketing pitch for one of my boss's highest paying clients, I now make sure to check my calendar twice a day, terrified of making the same mistake. That mishap cost me a shit load of respect and nearly my job altogether.

With a reluctant nod, I stand and brush my sweaty hands down my skirt. Cole's excitement is borderline revolting as he watches me closely, not moving from his spot in the doorway until I'm mere inches in front of him.

"Let's go then." He holds out his arm for me to take and with hesitation, I do.

Luckily, the board room is only a few doors down from my office, leaving only a couple of minutes of awkward silence between us. I can tell that he wants to talk to me, but I avoid him as best I can while being so close to his side. His good looks don't have the same appeal as they did just a few weeks ago. It's like someone has reached inside my brain and flipped off the *Cole is attractive* switch. And if I were to guess who that somebody was, I'm sure that I would be right.

When we reach the glass door, I peer in and wince. A room full of people packed in like sardines waits a few feet away. Some sit, some stand, but the one thing everyone has in common is the confusion etched on their faces as they look toward the front of the room. Clark Brenton stands stiffly at the head of a long, dark table, assessing each and every person with a scrutiny that has my skin itching.

It's so quiet that you could hear a pin drop when Cole opens the door and leads us inside. Heads turn and curious, maybe even envious eyes observe me. When Cole turns to face me, I let my arm fall limp to my side. I flinch when he pats my lower back, his pinky brushing the top of my ass.

He mumbles quickly, "Have a seat and enjoy. I look forward to talking to you afterward."

I manage to nod before moving to the lone empty chair that rests against the back wall. Clark's voice echoes with authority as he begins to speak. A shared sense of nervousness floats along the room, sitting heavy and thick. Looking from one set of rigid shoulders to the next, I realize that I'm not the only one who has no idea what this meeting is about. None of us do.

A gorgeous blonde sits with perfect posture on the left side of the table, two chairs down from where Clark stands, his thin lips moving as he addresses the room. A sleek, well-ironed navy pantsuit covers the woman's athletic build. It matches the colour of her eyes perfectly. I notice that after they've narrowed in on me, lit with barely controlled anger.

The intensity has me swallowing an invisible lump. It's then that I begin to feel watched. Turning my head slowly, I see several sets of eyes on me. They all look at me like they've found me tossing kittens onto a busy highway.

The intensity behind their sudden hatred has me touching the base of my neck, feeling my raging pulse beneath my fingertips. Suddenly freezing, a shiver racks down my spine.

"The expansion in Toronto will only push our clientele to the next level. And with the team management selected, I have no doubt we'll be up and running in no time," Clark announces.

A list of several names appears on the screen at the same time that my hand flies to my mouth. Mine rests five spots from the top.

Sierra Caster - Marketing Manager

What. The. Fuck?

I meet Cole's eager stare from across the room, fully aware that my jaw hangs unhinged, but not giving enough of a shit to reattach it. This is some sort of ploy to get into my pants. It has to be. I haven't earned this job. Hell, I haven't even been here long enough to earn my choice of fancy coffee creamers in the staff lounge.

It feels wrong—*dirty* even. Like I slept my way to a promotion when I haven't done anything of the sort. Everyone has to be thinking the same thing. I can feel it in the way they look at me, like they're disgusted by me.

Women shouldn't need to sleep their way to the top of anything, let alone a job. Every feminist bone in my body is snapping right now while trying to convince me to throw two middle fingers into the air and scream *fuck you!* It's what I should do, right?

The boardroom is silent, everyone either staring at me or pretending they're not while they are. It's brief, subtle flicks of their eyes or full-blown stares. Nothing in between. And as soon as Clark dismisses the meeting, promising to set something up for the members of the Toronto team this week to discuss the job, there isn't a moving limb in the room.

I feel like the walls are closing in on me. The longer I stay here, facing more judgment than ever before, the harder it is to breathe. The panic in my chest has my breath catching with every inhale. I start to cough as I fumble out of my seat on wobbly knees, I ignore it.

Need to get out of here. Need to breathe.

Grasping at my chest, I sprint to the door and shove it open, the cold air on my face sticking to tears that I didn't know were there. My fingers fumble in my pocket until they grip my phone, pulling it out as I dial the number of the only person I need right now.

With a shaky hand, I lift the phone to my cheek and listen to the dial tone. I brace myself along a dark, quiet hallway and choke back a sob.

"Well, if it isn't my favourite girl. What do I owe the honour?"

Braden's voice is like a wrecking ball, smashing apart the last remaining columns holding me up as I crumble. I can feel the tears streaming down my face, scorching the skin where they fall.

"Baby," he whispers, and I hear something like protectiveness in his voice. It settles down on me like a weighted blanket, comforting me in a small way that I didn't think was possible. "Where are you? I'm coming to get you."

My head falls to the wall behind me as I place a hand over my mouth and try to silence my cries, suddenly overwhelmed with shame. My next words come out watery and weak. "Work. Brenton Marketing. It's downtown. I'm in a dark hallway on the third floor."

I hear him shout something to someone and then the slamming of a door before he speaks again. "I'm on my way, sweetheart, and I'm going to stay on the phone with you until I get there. You don't have to say anything if you don't want to, but there's no way that I'm hanging up this phone knowing how upset you are. Got it?"

I nod, regardless of the fact that he can't see me. "Got it."

The burn in my eyes doesn't let up, even when the ridiculousness of the situation starts to settle in. I should be embarrassed to have called him, but I'm not. He won't judge me for this, and the need to have him here, holding me against that strong chest of his is enough to ward off any more of those thoughts.

Inhaling a shaky breath, I slide down the wall, sitting my ass on the cold floor. I put my phone down on the floor beside me and pull my knees into my chest, tucking my head between them and wrapping my arms around myself until I form a ball. Quiet, subtle sounds come from the phone as Braden drives. I'm not sure how long I stay there, crying silently into my legs, but by the time my cries have turned into small sniffles, I hear footsteps thumping down the hall.

I lift my head slowly, feeling the tense muscles pull, aching from being stuck in the same position for so long. A watery smile forms on my lips when I see Braden running toward me, hair disheveled, eyes wild as they roam my face and body, like he's searching for even the slightest injury. I think he becomes even more worried when he sees that I'm not physically injured.

A squeak escapes my dry mouth when he bends down and swiftly lifts me off of the ground, holding me tightly against his chest like he's trying to protect me by shoving me inside of him, someplace nobody can hurt me. My back touches the wall, and I wrap my legs around his waist as he holds me, one arm looped beneath my butt and the other in my hair, his face in my neck.

I press my wet face to the soft cotton of his t-shirt and breathe him in, letting the scent of laundry detergent slither under my skin and calm me. We don't speak for a long time, too busy soaking in each other's comfort.

"What happened, sweetheart?" Braden's finger's tighten in my hair and his nails scratch at my scalp, the sensation making me whimper.

"It's not as bad as it seems. I just . . ." My vocal cords are scratchy and hoarse as I trail off, unsure of how to describe what really upset me. He probably won't understand why being given such an amazing position pulled this sort of reaction from me, and if the roles were reversed, I'm sure that I wouldn't understand it either. But my pride is too big for me to appreciate it when I know that I haven't earned it.

"I don't like hand-outs," I mutter. "And I especially don't like them when what's expected of me in return is something I'm not comfortable with."

I whisper a curse under my breath when Braden turns to stone against me, the arm beneath me bulging and beginning to shake. If I didn't know better, I would have mistaken his rage for the inability to hold up my weight much longer. Lifting my head, I look at him through damp lashes. The way that he glares at the wall behind me has a ball of emotion clogging my throat.

"What do you mean by that, Sierra?" His words ache in the worst way, settling deep in my gut.

I swallow thickly while touching his scruffy jaw. Suddenly, his cold brown eyes move from the wall to me, pinning me with a look tainted with the desire to punish. "Did somebody say something to you? *Fuck.* Did somebody *touch* you? I'll kill them." He spits the words like he's disgusted by them. I flinch, and his eyes soften slightly, his grip on my hair loosening.

"Nobody touched me," I promise him. "I was handed a promotion. One that I'm certain I got because of my boss's attraction to me. I don't want him to expect me to want to owe him for it, but I think that he will."

"He can't have you. Tell me what you need me to do and I'll do it. That pompous prick won't know what hit him."

"I don't know what to do," I whisper.

215

"We'll figure it out. I promise. That bastard won't be getting anything from you."

Braden pushes me further against the wall while moving impossibly closer to me, like he needs to reassure himself that I'm really here. The possessiveness that he's showing sags in my stomach before settling between my legs. I tense around him, my thighs beginning to shake.

Embarrassment and shame are two feelings that I should be feeling while I attempt to dry hump Braden in a dark hallway at work, tear stains on my cheeks and snot stuck to my nose. But lust and an aching appreciation have taken over, blinding me.

Braden's face falls in my neck again and he shutters a breath against my skin, thrusting up slowly between my legs. "We need to go home, baby."

I nod quickly, anxiously, unable to pretend like that's not exactly what I want. "Then take me home."

27

Braden

"ALMOST THERE," SIERRA SOBS, CLENCHING HER THIGHS tighter around my head.

The reflex encourages me to suck harder on her clit, knowing that's all it takes to send her flying into oblivion. Her squeak of approval echoes in my ears and makes me grin against her wet flesh, pushing my fingers deeper and faster inside of her before curving them inward and pressing against the place that sends her to space.

"Braden!"

Her back arches away from the shower wall, water cascading down the valley of her chest from the shower-head above her. When her fingers release their grip on my hair, and she gifts me a lazy smile, I slowly lower her legs from my shoulders and stand up. Her pupils are blown as I push against her, moulding her body to mine.

"That never gets old." I smirk and push my hair back and out of my face as the water falls directly on top of me.

Gripping her waist, I take a step back, pulling her under the water, savoring the moment her eyes flutter shut when the warmth runs over her goosebump covered skin. The way her features relax makes me smile, and I find myself counting the freckles that splatter across her pale skin like the softest brown paint flicked from a brush.

Two, ten, fifteen. Moving from her hairline, down her small, button nose, to the tiny triangle above her top lip. I lose count of them the second her eyes open, transfixed on me in a way that has my breath catching.

"Stop staring at me," she murmurs.

"I like looking at you." Her gaze falls to the water beneath our feet and I raise my brow. "That surprises you?" It shouldn't, and if it does, I've clearly been doing a shit job of making her feel as good about herself as I thought I was.

"No," she rushes, but her stiffening posture says the opposite. With a shake of my head, I have my finger under her chin, tilting her head up.

"Look at me," I plead. She swallows quickly but does as I say. "You're stunning. I don't know how you don't already know that. I'm sure you hear it all the time. And I have no idea how you ended up with me."

When she doesn't reply, I feel my stomach start to churn. Maybe that isn't what she wanted to hear? Fucking shit. My lips roll and I pull back into myself, wanting to hit my head against the shower wall.

"Braden," she calls quietly, attempting to reel me back in when I let my hands fall to my sides. With what little confidence I have left, I nod and open my mouth to take back my words, but her lips are on mine before I have the chance.

With wide eyes, I watch as her hand moves to cup my face. Her touch is gentle, almost impossible to feel as her palm presses against my stubble covered jaw.

"I have heard it before. Just not from you."

———

I CONTINUE to drag my nails up and down Sierra's back as she rests her head on my chest and a flat palm near my collarbone. Her body curves into mine like it belongs there. She's much calmer than she was a few hours prior, and I find myself finally able to relax.

I'm not sure what exactly happened in that shower, but I have to admit that I feel pretty good about it. What I don't feel good about is what happened earlier—when I picked up my phone only to hear her heart-wrenching cries and how broken she looked when I finally got to her.

I expected the worst. The entire drive to that fucking building, I was preparing myself to find her in a state that would test me in ways that I've never been tested before. The imprints of my fingernails in my scalp are probably still there, forever scarred from the aggressiveness of each hand I ran through it, of every clump yanked out of worry.

I knew that I would have done anything she asked me to right then. There wasn't a single unforgivable crime that I wouldn't have committed for her.

But then I saw her there, not a scratch on her body, and felt my heart stop. Somehow, knowing the damage was invisible was worse than anything I had prepared myself for. With no injury, there was no easy way that I could have patched her up. The damage was inside, damaging her beautiful soul.

I had never felt as helpless as I did right then, with her in my arms, clutching onto me just as tightly as I was clutching onto her.

Cole Travis painted a bullseye on his own back. And I plan on being the one that takes the shot at it.

"You awake?" I whisper.

"Mm," she moans, rubbing her cheek against my peck.

I hate that I'm about to poke and prod at something that I should leave alone so that she can rest, but if I don't get more information soon, I think I'm going to damn near explode. "You wouldn't happen to want to tell me more about what happened earlier, would you? I'm going out of my head here."

"No. I'm sleepy."

"Sierra," I sigh, wrapping my arm securely around her waist and tugging her so her stomach is pressed flat to my side, eliminating all distance between us. "At least give me something."

"Fine," she mumbles. "Work sucks. Are you happy now? Can I go to bed?"

I pinch her side. "No. Not good enough. What was the promotion you got? Why do you feel like you didn't earn it? Is it that much of a career boost?"

My muscles tense as the idea of her being anywhere near her boss after this. I don't notice that my grip on her side has tightened until she gently peels away my fingers.

"Relax, Scrappy." She pushes out a laugh and drops my now relaxed hand back on her waist. "It's pretty much what I've been working for since I graduated. It's not my end goal, but it's a giant step in the right direction. They offered me a marketing manager position, which is what I was close to earning at my old job. But I was there for *three* years. Yeah, it was a harder company to work for and I didn't have half of the opportunities that I've been given here, but maybe that was the first red flag that I missed.

"Cole took an immediate interest in me, and I was so excited about the fancy office and client opportunities that I became naive. I didn't realize that being so appreciative toward him would be taken as something that it wasn't."

"Don't blame yourself for the actions of a man who has tried to use his power to take advantage of you. No woman, especially one as intelligent as yourself, should need to bow to the feet of a man just to feel like a person. It's incredibly revolting to me that you have had to worry about a smile being taken as something more than you intended it to, and that showing appreciation for being treated like a decent human being at work could lead to you owing somebody something. It's not fair, baby, and I'm so fucking sorry that you've been dealing with that."

She's silent for a few seconds, but the arm laying across my chest tightens. "They want me to move across the country."

"Across the country?" I mutter. Fear spears my insides before collaring my throat, squeezing and squeezing and squeezing.

"The promotion is for a job in Toronto. The company is expanding. I would be going with a small team."

The hand I have on her waist slacks. I want to jump up and run, but my limbs are too heavy. The thought of leaving right now and not knowing if she'll be here when I get back makes me gnash my teeth together.

The weight of her admission falls heavier than it would have had my father not been leaving too. Toronto, Toronto, Toronto. Everything is about fucking *Toronto*. What a coincidence.

I feel betrayed, even though I have no right to feel this way. There's something much deeper, more unforgiving that flares under my skin and sizzles in my veins, boiling my blood. *Abandonment.* A feeling that I buried a long time ago, back when my parents decided that I wasn't enough to heal the broken bridge between them. A feeling that severed my relationship with my mother for years, and still crackles in the air when a disagreement gets a bit too loud and out of hand.

A young boy can't even begin to understand how fractured and broken a marriage has to be for vows to be broken and a single piece of paper to be signed. All of the shouting and the screaming doesn't make sense. The countless nights spent at a house that's not his, just so that he can escape the angry voices don't, make, sense.

All it takes is for those memories to come swinging back for me to roll out from under Sierra and sit on the edge of the bed, my back to her.

"Toronto is shit," is my only reply. The words are rough and emotionless.

"Wow, thank you for your helpful input." I can hear her

moving around on the bed. "I don't know why you bothered asking if you were just going to be a dick about it."

"Give me a break." I laugh humourlessly. "What do you want me to say? Break a leg? Enjoy the weather?"

She inhales sharply before I hear her feet hit the ground and begin stomping around the floor. "I don't know what your deal is, Braden. You asked and I answered. You're being ridiculous."

"When are you going?" I grind out, staring at my bedroom door as I debate storming out like a child.

"A few weeks maybe. I never really stayed around to listen to the fine details, in case you forgot."

The only words that register in my mind are the first three.

A few weeks. *A few fucking weeks.*

That's all I have left.

28

Braden

I WASN'T SURPRISED TO FIND SIERRA GONE WHEN I WOKE UP this morning. Shit, I was surprised that she stayed the night at all after the way we ended our conversation. I was spiteful and she didn't deserve my harsh comments. So when I said I was going to sleep on the couch, she didn't fight me on it. I was too grateful that she was even bothering to stay to try to push my luck of sleeping in the same bed as me.

But just because I wasn't surprised that she had snuck out in the middle of the night—no note or anything—doesn't mean that I'm not disappointed. Running away from our problems isn't going to work for me. Not anymore.

I slide my phone back into the pocket of my jeans and wait anxiously for the elevator doors to open. It's uncomfortable being stuck in such a tight space with a bunch of pricks wearing expensive suits, everyone pretending to listen to the lame elevator music to avoid awkward conversation. But that doesn't matter. I'm here for Sierra, not to make small talk with a bunch of businessmen.

A sigh of relief pushes past my lips when the metal doors slide open with a brief *ding*. The space is somewhat familiar, but not enough that I know where I need to be going. I was too busy searching for Sierra yesterday to really take much else in.

I do remember how the white tile flooring sparkled from the sun's reflection through the tall windows, the potent smell of coffee that reminded me of being stuck inside of a Starbucks, and how out of place I felt wearing sweaty gym clothes in such a professional building. But come to think of it, it probably wasn't my choice of attire that had me feeling so out of place.

It was quieter yesterday, not a lot of chatter or shoes clapping on the tile like there is now. But I tune it out, knowing that if I let myself start thinking about anything other than seeing Sierra, my first stop would be Cole Travis' office.

The woman working the desk gets more familiar the closer I get before I realize that she was here yesterday. Her hair is almost so platinum blonde that it looks white, greyish even, and her otherwise pretty blue eyes are incredibly dull as they stay strained on the thin computer screen.

Clearing my throat, she looks over at me, blinking slowly while assessing me. "How can I help you?" she asks slowly.

"I'm looking for Sierra."

The woman blinks slowly again and raises her hand to point to the hallway to the left of her. "Third door on the left."

"Thanks." I head down the hallway at a quick pace before stopping in front of Sierra's closed office door, my fingers twitching restlessly at my side. I swallow the ball in my throat before rapping three times.

It takes a few seconds before I hear her soft voice. "Come in!"

Turning the doorknob, I push open the door and grin. Even hunched over and frustrated, she looks gorgeous. Her tired eyes fall on me when she lifts her head and quickly brushes a few stray curls out of her face. With her lips slightly parted in surprise, she blows out a harsh breath.

"What are you doing here?"

Okay, not the welcome I was hoping for. "Hello to you too, fighter."

"I'm serious. Why are you here? I don't have time for your games today," she snaps at me, and I know that I deserve it. The purple bags under her eyes make me wince. Did she sleep as badly as I did last night?

"Look, I'm sorry for being a total ass last night. You just took me by surprise."

"What am I supposed to do without my favourite lady?"

Her eyebrows scrunch before she stares at the pile of papers on her desk. "I haven't even made my decision yet."

"I know. Which is why I owe you an apology." I clear my throat. "I also came by to ask you something. It's the worst possible time to ask you this, but just know that there's no pressure or anything." It's now or never.

"Okay." She says it without sparing me a glance.

"My dad's getting married this weekend, and he won't stop bugging me about asking you to come. Something about him not wanting his son to show up alone and all that. I don't know. It doesn't have to be a date or anything. You could come as a friend or somethin—"

"What day is the wedding?"

"Saturday. You wouldn't need to be there until after the ceremony. Dad and his fiancée are keeping the ceremony really small. Just them, her parents, Tyler and me. I could pick you up as soon as it's over if you want." I scratch the back of my head nervously and fight off the urge to kick myself in the ass. I feel like I'm back in middle school asking a girl to sneak away at recess and share a yogurt with me.

"You can pick me up after the ceremony is done. Just let me know what time I should be ready by." She's finally looking at me again, her beautiful face beaming with mischief. "But you have to promise me something."

"Anything."

"You have to dance with me."

I throw my head back and laugh. "It's funny you think I'll be doing anything but."

Sierra

"So, it's a date," Sophie states as casually as ever while continuing her aggressive search through the endless racks of clothes in the third boutique we've stumbled into. We have yet to find a store that has the "perfect" dress, and my feet are beginning to throb.

"It's not a date. Braden just needed someone to go with him." At this point, I don't know who I'm trying to convince more—her or myself.

Braden never said it was a date, he actually was pretty adamant on it *not* having to be one. But I want it to be. I don't particularly like being introduced to a casual fling's family and friends. Why bring other people into a relationship that isn't going anywhere? I don't see the point.

The entire situation with Cole and Toronto has created a crack in our relationship, one that I don't think can be fixed simply with apologies and hot make-up sex. Braden is hard to understand at most times, but now more than ever. I'm terrified to tell him that I've made the decision to go to Toronto. He won't give me a chance to explain myself before he runs without giving me a chance to explain myself.

"You're ridiculous," Sophie scoffs. Wrapping her fingers around the metal rack she was just sorting through, she turns to me with a heavy scowl. "Clearly, you're into him. And boy, does he do an awful job of hiding his feelings for you. He never takes his damn eyes off of you, always watching like if he looks away for a second somebody else might snatch you up and steal you away."

I stare at my bare toes as they stick out of my strappy sandals and shake my head, flushing. "It doesn't matter, Soph. I'm leaving, in case you forgot. I told Clark this morning after I got off the phone with you. I shouldn't even be going to this wedding. It's going to make telling him that much harder."

Her eyes nearly pop from their sockets. "He doesn't know yet? Dammit, Sierra."

I divert my gaze, shame falling heavy in my stomach. "I would have told him today, but you should have seen how nervous he was when he showed up at my office. It would have ruined everything." I drag my fingertips down a mauve-coloured velvet dress before clenching it in my hand, fighting off the sting in the back of my eyes.

"Oh, you silly girl. I told you that this would happen. Friends with benefits doesn't work. Haven't you learned that from the thousands of movies about it? The couple always ends up in love."

"I don't need an 'I told you so' lecture right now, Sophie. I don't know what to do." I tip my head back and blink at the ceiling, pushing back the guilt-laced tears that have begun to collect in the corner of my eyes.

"Are you finally going to admit to yourself that you have real, big girl feelings for him? That's probably a good place to start."

My voice is small and chalked full of regret. "I already have."

It was impossible not to. I did an awful job of keeping the lines drawn between love and lust, and now I'm going to break my *own* heart. And Braden's. He doesn't have to tell me how he feels, I already know. He's done just as awful of a job hiding how much he cares about me as I have.

Friends don't act the way we do unless they feel something

227

beyond an ache between their legs. They have to feel one in their chest too. One far stronger, impossible to ignore.

I wanted to say no to this promotion, to moving to Toronto. But regardless of how I got it, I couldn't turn it down. I promised myself that I wouldn't let anything get in the way of my personal successes. Of my career. Cole is just one boss of many, he won't be around forever. He'll get bored of me once he realizes he won't get anywhere with me. He'll move on and back off. But an opportunity like this may not come around again. I would be stupid not to take it.

The thought of leaving Clare and Liz makes my stomach hurt to the point that I want to kneel over and scream. They're the only family I really have, and I don't want to leave them. But when I drove to Clare's last night with a bottle of cheap wine and tears in my eyes, she was persistent that I go. That I stop worrying about them so much.

She pulled me into her arms and hugged me like she used to when we were kids. We cried together, and then we laughed to the point of crying again. It was the first time that I felt like this might be the right decision. And I've been clutching onto that feeling ever since, too terrified that it will disappear if I let it go.

I have all of my ducks in a row. All but one.

Sophie touches my arm, pulling me out of my head. "You need to tell him, S. And not just about Toronto, but also how you feel. It isn't fair to him if you don't."

"I know that I do. Shit, I hate that he doesn't know that I'm crazy about him. Even when he makes me want to yank my hair out piece by piece." I smile for a second before it slips away again. "The thought of leaving him here hurts more than I was expecting."

With all of the sleepless nights spent with my legs tangled in his, our belly-aching laughter that kept Clay up night after night, and the helpless fluttering of my heart with every whisper of my name on his lips, I never stood a chance. I have no idea how I'm supposed to go back to how my life was before eating Italian takeout on the floor between Braden's legs, watching reruns of Law & Order became what I looked forward to at the end of the day.

"Have you thought about asking him to go with you?" Sophie asks after a minute of silence, her lip tucked between her teeth. She watches me nervously, like she's afraid of what my reaction will be.

"Yeah, right." I snort, the sound angry. "Braden isn't the type of guy to chase after a girl he isn't even officially involved with. And his entire life is here. I could never ask him that."

Sophie doesn't reply with words, only a simple nod of her head as she turns back to a rack of cocktail dresses. I didn't mean to come off harsh, but that idea isn't something I want taking root in my mind. There's no need to make this any worse than it's already going to be. I won't be able to handle it.

29

Sierra

HOLY. SHIT.

I don't know whether to get down on my knees for this man right here in my apartment hallway or throw myself at him, knowing that he'll catch me without hesitation. The way my heart thumps so rapidly against my chest bone is terrifying, but I revel in it. Heated amber eyes burn into my skin as he looks me up and down, striking a match to the arousal in my blood and setting my insides on fire.

My stare carries the same intensity as his, if the groan that rumbles in his chest is anything to go by. I ache to reach out and touch him, but force my hands to stay by my sides as I soak in the model-worthy image in front of me.

A navy-blue suit jacket stretches across his shoulders, and the top three buttons of his white dress shirt are unbuttoned in that sexy *I don't care* way. His thick thighs push the boundaries of his slacks, and I begin to wonder if they would rip if he bent down. Giant biceps swell within the tight restraints of his suit jacket when he places two hands on the doorframe above me, swallowing the space between us.

Moving my gaze, I stare at the hands gripping the doorframe and swallow, feeling my underwear grow damp. The veins in his hands seem more prominent to me tonight, thicker, sexier even. An array of simple black rings are placed neatly on three of his five knuckles. It's a different look for Braden than I'm used to, but I would be lying if I said that it wasn't curious as to how the cold metal would feel pressed up against my center while he's finger deep inside of me.

His hips push against me and for the first time tonight, I meet his stare. My lips part at how softly he's looking at me, like he wasn't just eye-fucking me a second ago. It brings a chill to my skin, and I shiver against his chest. If there wasn't a familiar hardness pressing against my stomach, I would have assumed that I imagined the past few minutes.

"Maybe we don't have to go to this wedding after all." His words are gruff, raspy and thick with need.

"Would you prefer that I change?"

I hear a low chuckle and warm breath fans my face as he moves closer until short beard hairs scratch the underside of my jaw. One hand moves from the door frame to settle on my hip, the heat from his palm soaking through my dress, warming my skin.

I suck in a breath, my eyelashes fluttering when he rubs his nose against the beating skin of my neck, nipping at it gently before darting his tongue to the sore skin, lapping at it with a groan that falls between my legs. He backs away too soon, and a finger is placed under my chin, tilting it upward until our eyes meet again.

Braden softly mumbles his next words as if he isn't sure of them. As if he doesn't understand them himself. "The dress is perfect. *You* look perfect."

I find myself lost in the way he looks at me—like I'm *his*. Like he'd tear apart anyone who tried to come between us. My heart swells to ten times its size and calls out to him, desperate for more of his attention.

And just like that, both of his hands touch me, one palming my hip, burning a hole through my dress while the other plays with the thin strap on my shoulder, his thumb slipping beneath it and rubbing slow circles into my skin. He licks his bottom lip and tilts his head to the side. "I just don't know if I want anybody else to see you like this. I want this to be for me and *only* me."

"It is all for you." My breath catches in my throat when his hand moves up my side, cupping the side of my breast and squeezing. "Thank you. For the compliment. I wish I would have known that you had a blue suit because I would have gotten a blue dress. But I guess a dress is a dress, right?" My cheeks flame with embarrassment, nerves sizzling under my skin.

"Relax," Braden whispers. He's right there, so close that I can taste the bubblegum he must have chewed on the way here. My nipples harden and push through the tight material of my dress. I arch my back so they brush his chest, whimpering from the contact when they do, but needing more.

Braden shifts the hand massaging the side of my breast before gripping the full weight of it. "Tell me, baby. Did you skip the bra on purpose? Were you hoping that I wouldn't be able to keep my hands off of your perfect tits?" He squeezes the heavy breast in his hand before dragging his thumb across the nipple. "That I would have to have a taste before I paraded you around, letting other men see how fucking amazing you look in this dress?"

My knees threaten to buckle, his words like a zap to my swollen clit. I open my mouth but no words come out. I try again, but cry out immediately when the top of my dress is yanked down and my nipple is sucked between Braden's lips. His tongue moves in slow, teasing strokes before flicking at it. He feasts on the sobs that follow every strong suck, and groans in approval when I wind my fingers in his hair, pulling every time his teeth brush the sensitive tip.

His mouth leaves my skin with a *pop* and I gasp at the sudden coldness that envelopes my wet breast. "We can go inside," I mutter, almost adding a please before I think better of it.

The grin that spreads across his face is evil, maniacal even. "No, my little fighter. From now until the end of the night, I'm going to be a *perfect* gentleman, and you're going to keep those soaked panties on so that you remember exactly who you're coming home with tonight. I can't have you forgetting who it was that made that pussy so wet, now can I?" He clicks his tongue to the roof of his mouth and winks.

I blink twice, wishing that I was angrier with this show of possession that I really am. But no. Instead, my panties only become damper, causing them to stick to the slick flesh beneath them.

Pushing up on my toes, I grab his jacket by the lapels and gently press my lips to his. He responds quickly, like I knew he would, but only with a light caress of his mouth, nothing more. A sigh escapes me at the sudden change in tempo.

I pull him closer, just needing to feel his body against mine, and grin into the kiss when he does the same, palming my cheeks in those big hands, making me feel dainty and small.

If only he knew just how much of me he really did hold in his hands, all of it so easily breakable.

We break apart after a few more seconds, my breath escaping in one big puff while he simply laughs, eyes bright and sparkling with mischief. "My, my, Sierra. Are you trying to trick me into breaking my own rules and having my way with you in this hallway? Who knew you were so naughty."

"You say it as if it's a bad thing," I tease, dropping my hands with a step backward.

"It couldn't be farther from a bad thing, sweetheart," he says while I grab my clutch from inside and lock the door. When I return, Braden extends his elbow toward me and I take it, letting him guide us outside and into his car.

It's not exactly a horse drawn carriage, and I'm not

wearing glass slippers or a dress made just for me by my fairy Godmother, but the man on my arm could very well be my Prince Charming.

———

BRADEN and I have just walked hand-in-hand through a wide, pink daisy covered archway when I hear a cheerful, vibrant voice yell, "Well if it isn't my handsome brother-in-law!"

The welcome comes from a petite blonde with a gorgeous sparkling silver, knee-length strapless dress fitted tightly to her slim figure. As she hurries toward us from inside the ballroom, I notice Braden's brother, Tyler, following closely behind her, his head shaking as he watches her.

"And he brought a date!" the woman shrieks. The striking blue in her eyes contrasts against her silver dress effortlessly. It isn't until she turns to the side, briefly stealing a glance at her husband as he settles beside her that I see the protruding baby bump. I want to congratulate her, but decide to do it later.

"You act like I didn't tell you that I was, Gray," Braden replies with a chuckle while snaking an arm around my waist and pulling me close. "Sierra, this is Gracie. Gracie, this is Sierra." He introduces us just seconds before I'm tugged away from him and enveloped in her small arms.

My body tenses for a small moment before I laugh and return the hug. "It's nice to meet you."

Gracie pulls back but keeps her hands on my shoulders, holding me in place as if to inspect me. "Are your eyes naturally grey? Or are they silver? Either way, they are gorgeous!"

Her outgoing, sweet as honey personality takes me by surprise in the best way. Tyler seems like such a hard person to get to know, so I think I just assumed that maybe his wife would be the same. "They are both grey and natural. I used to hate them when I was a kid." I laugh nervously.

"I hope you don't anymore! They're *so* unique," she gushes.

"Thank you."

"Okay, princess. Don't scare away the only girl that can stand Braden's presence," Tyler half-heartedly scolds, placing a kiss in her hair and rubbing her swollen stomach. "Let's go find our table before the reception starts."

Gracie rolls her eyes but agrees anyway. Her reaction has Braden laughing, his palm now comfortably resting against my lower back.

"Fine. But I'm so not done with you, Sierra. We'll see you in there?" she asks, her tone hopeful.

"Where else would we go?" Braden teases, earning himself a smack on the arm that has him wincing.

"Alright, smart ass." She gives him the finger before turning back to me. "I'll see you soon."

As we watch Gracie wrap her fingers around Tyler's forearm and nearly drag him back into the ballroom, I let out a small giggle.

"Something funny?" Braden asks, flashing me a beaming white smile.

"I like her."

"Yeah? She's definitely something."

"I found it refreshing. She seems genuine." Like the type of person who knows exactly when to be warm and compassionate, but also cold and merciless when she needs to be. She reminds me of Clare. Maybe that's why I like her so much already.

Braden nods in response and turns us so we face each other. Lines form across his forehead as mouth turns down, a heavy feeling twitching in the air. "She's the reason for my brother's happiness. It's hard to think about where he would be right now without her." I grab his hand and squeeze as he clears his throat along with all of the worry that was present just seconds ago. "Anyway, we should probably head in. You ready?"

"I think so. I used to love weddings as a kid." There was something magical about watching two people announce their love for one another so publicly. It gave me butterflies and only grew my obsession with fairytales as a little girl.

"It's been a long time since I've been to one. I'm glad you're here with me." Braden presses his lips softly to my forehead and I lean toward him, closing my eyes.

"Me too," I whisper before he pulls back and interlocks out fingers. "Lead the way, handsome."

30

Braden

I'VE NEVER BEEN A FAN OF WEDDINGS. BUT THAT'S PROBABLY because I don't ever want one.

Weddings are pointless, futile. They're an excuse to spend thousands of dollars on the idea and hope of forever. You invite hundreds of people, some of whom you probably haven't seen in ten, fifteen years, and stand in front of a priest just to proclaim a love that you already know you feel. The day is over before you know it, and life carries on like it did before you were handed that flimsy piece of paper. The one that tells you that you're tethered to someone for the rest of your life. For better or worse, right?

But what happens afterward? After the honeymoon phase washes away and you realize there's no going back. The years go by and you begin to hate the way your partner handles stress, or maybe they work too much and are home too little. You realize that you're not happy, but that damn piece of paper says you have to stick it through. You have to grow to hate each other before the topic of divorce is brought up.

That nasty seven letter word still makes my skin itch. Divorce. Even years later I remember exactly how it felt when my mother sat me down at the kitchen table and told me that her and Dad were getting a divorce.

"We're just not happy anymore," Mom had said, as if I hadn't already known that. As if I hadn't spent most of my life watching them grow to hate each other.

There was a reason I immediately understood why she had chosen a night that he was out of town fighting to deliver the news to me, her things already packed. They hadn't been alone together in the same room for months, too busy ripping each other apart, so why would I have expected that night to be any different?

She dropped me off at my grandmother's that night and I didn't see her again for two years. It was two years that I spent confused, hurt, and worried. I didn't know where she was, or who she was with. Dad would let me know that she was alive and well every few weeks, saying he had talked to her and that she was fine.

I was seventeen when my mother came back from a two-year trip trekking across Europe with Antonio, her new fiancé. It turned out that they met in Italy, at some hole in the wall bistro or something like that. He was visiting his family for a few months, and as my mother would say, *the rest is history*. It took me years to forgive her for leaving, too betrayed to hear her out.

And it wasn't until I saw how easy it was for my mom to move on and be happy once the chains of marriage were broken that I promised myself that I wouldn't make my parents' mistakes. That I wouldn't marry someone just to lose them a few years down the road.

I don't need a piece of fucking paper to tell me that I'm going to spend the rest of my life with someone. That's not how it works.

I have no idea why my dad wants to get married again, let alone throw another huge party. But I've tried not to spend much time thinking about it. If he wants to keep making the same mistakes, then who am I to stop him?

It's Sierra that brings me out of my head, her voice putting me at ease. "This really is beautiful. Did they plan it themselves?"

I turn in my seat until our knees brush. Her eyes are already waiting for mine. I reach over and place my hand on her thigh, squeezing the bare skin over her knee where the dress has ridden up. Toying with the hem, I smile, happy to have her with me.

Fuck, she's a sight for sore eyes. All warm, pink cheeks and bright eyes that hold the power to consume me with a single look.

"I can only assume that Lana hired someone to do the work. She seems like the type," I mumble and pull my attention to the tacky vase placed on the center of our table. The number of frilly, pale-pink flowers peeking out of the top makes me cringe. Talk about overkill.

"Braden," Sierra scolds, placing her palm on top of the hand I have wrapped around her leg in what seems like an attempt to pull me back. "I'm sure if she did hire someone that it was for a reason. Some people need help planning something as big as a wedding. If this is just the reception, I can't imagine how beautiful the ceremony must have been."

It was definitely something. "You're lucky that you weren't there. I almost fell asleep at the altar."

Huffing, Sierra removes her hand from mine and wraps it around her wine glass instead. "You're helpless."

"Weddings aren't my thing, babe. I'm not going to apologize for it."

"You don't have to apologize. But you don't need to be a dick either," she scoffs before taking a sip—or more like a gulp—from the crimson liquid in her glass. "I actually happen to love weddings. A wedding is supposed to be one of the best days of your life," she sighs, the faint ghost of a smile on her lips.

I sling my arm around the back of her chair and lean in so my mouth brushes her ear. "Let me guess, you've been planning yours since you were a little girl? Did you used to dress up in one of your mom's dresses and pretend you were a bride?"

I meant for it to be a joke, but I sound more mocking than I intended to, and when hurt flashes across her face, I know that she caught it too.

Her smile falls and she begins looking around the room to avoid looking at me. Guilt falls like a rock in my gut. "If you don't like weddings that's fine, but don't be a prick to everybody who does. This day isn't about you and your arrogance, it's about your dad and his new wife," she replies after a few seconds, her words muttered low enough to only be heard by the two of us and not the entire table.

Thank God for that. Gracie is already pinning with me a glare that has my blood cooling.

Suddenly, a hand is placed on my left shoulder, causing me to flinch in surprise. With an uncomfortable cough, I turn to see my mom, her attention glued onto the annoyed woman beside me.

"We didn't know that you were here yet, Braden. And with a guest at that," she half-scolds. If it weren't for the slight smirk on her lips, I would have assumed that I was about to receive a lecture.

Sierra jerks beside me as she takes in the woman beside me before introducing herself. "You must be Braden's mother. I could recognize those timeless cheekbones anywhere. I'm Sierra." She extends her hand confidently as she slips into business mode.

I register her compliment and smirk. So, she thinks I have timeless cheek bones, eh? Can't wait to tease her about that later.

Mom's eyes widen for a split second, a clear response to Sierra's outgoing, genuine gesture as her grip on my shoulder tightens ever so slightly and her other hand grabs Sierra's.

She's happy with the compliment, although I'm not sure why she's surprised by it. My mom's features really haven't aged over the years. She isn't old by any means, but she definitely doesn't look fifty. I don't think that she's ever even found a gray hair among all of the chestnut brown.

"Please, call me Tia." She grins. "I can't say that I have ever had one of Braden's girlfriends make me blush so easily. Thank you, Sierra. You are just lovely."

When Sierra's cheeks darken to match Mom's, I step in with a chuckle. "Okay, I get it. Sierra's special. How about we not scare her away."

There has to be a thousand questions running through my mom's head right now, considering that there's only ever been two past girlfriends in my life, and I would never have taken either of them to such a family-filled event. Not willingly, at least.

"I'm sorry, Sierra. I have loose lips." Mom laughs with a slight roll of her eyes. "I'll leave you two for now. But I'll be back. Don't disappear before I have a chance to chat with you some more."

"Wouldn't dream of it, Tia," Sierra replies, flashing her a genuine smile that has my heart thumping a bit too heavily.

"Well, alright." My shoulder is squeezed once more as breath tickles my ear. "I like her," Mom whispers and walks away, leaving my chest filled with pride.

Me too, Mom. I really fucking like her.

Sierra

"Did I tell you how beautiful you look yet?" Braden asks, the words kissing the skin of my shoulder seconds before his lips do. I tighten my arms around his neck and hide my growing smile in his dress shirt, welcoming the familiar smell of his cologne.

The music playing around us has been slow for the past few minutes now, seeing as we're one of the only pairs left on the dance-floor. Most guests left when Braden's dad and new bride did, but some hung around, reveling in the classy music and free bar.

I didn't mind staying and surprisingly, neither did Braden. We've just been hidden in our own little world, swaying slowly to the music, clutching each other like we fear the other might vanish in thin air if we let go.

"You did. A few times." Heat warms my cheeks as I pull away just enough to stare up at him.

There's an unmissable playfulness in his eyes, one that always sparks when he's happy. *Really* happy. The thought alone of him feeling so lighthearted and giddy while in my presence makes me feel prouder than I probably should.

"Well, I'm going to tell you again," he murmurs, kissing my hair. "You look stunning."

"You're feeling generous tonight."

"You have no idea."

"Is that so?"

Much to my surprise, Braden has kept to his word all night, never touching me in anything but a gentlemanly way. But as nice as it's been, there have been a few times that I've wanted nothing more than for him to reach under the table and slide a hand up my dress. I'm pretty sure that that's just my hormones talking, though.

"Give me one more dance. Then I can show you what I mean."

"I already know what you mean," I poke, loving the way

his lips tug to the ceiling when I tease him. "But I'll give you the pleasure of one more dance."

He doesn't reply right away. He pulls me closer instead, close enough that my chest moves with his with every sharp inhale. "Did you have a good time? I know that Gracie can get a bit nosey."

"It was great." I press my palm to his chest, directly over where his heart beats. "And you really love to rile her up. Poor girl."

"Poor girl? Did you forget what she did to me tonight?" Braden looks traumatized as he gags. The repulsion in his eyes makes me laugh, choking on air mid-laugh.

The pissed look on Gracie's face when Braden gave her a noogie will be forever in my memory. I was genuinely surprised when she didn't try and attack his balls as payback. That's usually my go to revenge move.

However, Gracie preferred a much subtler form of revenge. She had the chef swap their plates before they were brought out, making Braden choke down whatever vegan meat she ordered while she pretended to dig into his steak. How he didn't notice the difference in texture or smell is beyond me. But the way he struggled with the silent retching while gulping down mouthfuls of water straight from the pitcher was hilarious.

"I don't think I could ever forget." My forehead falls to his chest as my body shakes with silent laughter. There's no point in holding it in, Braden can pretend that he's still annoyed but I know that he loved the whole thing. His playful nature is too strong to be wounded by some fake veggie steak.

Braden's hands move from my hips to my sides before his fingers are digging into them. I shove away from him, squealing and swatting at him. "You think it's funny that I nearly threw up all over the table? Wait until I get you home, little fighter. You won't be laughing then."

"Stop! Stop!"

His head falls back with a loud laugh, his eyes twinkling beneath the party lights. Tears blur my vision as my abdomen begins to ache. Our eyes meet and my belly fills with warmth.

A portrait of pure joy is staring right at me in the form of a truly beautiful man. One with bushy, scarred eyebrows, eyes the same shade as expensive whiskey, and a smile that could turn even the most ruthless of people into a puddle of goo at his feet. Braden is protective in the best ways and also playful enough that in those few moments where you find yourself stuck in the realities of being a grown-up, he can make you feel like a kid again.

He's everything that I've been needing and begging for.

"You're really beautiful," I choke out before my eyes bulge and then shut. Our laughter slowly dies, and the air begins to tighten.

His mouth falls, and he lets out a wavering exhale. "I will never hold a flame to your beauty, baby. I promise you that."

———

I STIFLE MY YAWN. "How far are we?"

We left the reception a few minutes ago, once the music cut and the few stragglers left. The blisters on my feet made it impossible to walk to the car without limping, so of course, like the gentleman he promised to be, Braden swept me off of my feet and carried me the rest of the way. I think it made me fall for him that much more—that much deeper.

It also makes my telling him about Toronto that much harder.

The car comes to a jolting stop, my body lurching forward and the fabric of the seat belt digging into my skin. With wide eyes, I turn to see Braden already undoing his seatbelt, turning the headlights off, and sliding his seat back.

"Are you okay?" I shriek, looking through each window in

an attempt to find a reason as to why we're currently stopped on the side of an empty street instead of at home.

"I'm way too horny to be driving right now," he groans and I watch him palm the thick bulge in his slacks.

"You're kidding," I scoff and push out a relieved sigh. "I thought you were having a heart attack or something, jackass."

"A heart attack? Do I look like someone that would be having a heart attack? I'm healthy as a horse, sweetheart. Don't worry about me," he boasts and pats his thighs. "Now come over here."

I stay in my seat. "You want to have sex here? On the side of a road? What if somebody sees?"

"Who cares." Lifting a shoulder, he starts to unbutton his dress shirt, revealing a sliver of his taut chest. "Don't tell me you're too chicken, Sierra."

I narrow my eyes. "I'm not chicken."

"Then come over here and ride my cock."

My clit swells at his dominant tone, my panties becoming damp. Swallowing, I watch his fingers skim expertly down his shirt before pulling it open. I itch to reach out and feel the familiar ridges covering the tanned-skin, craving the heat of him beneath my fingertips. But I keep my hands to myself, wanting to watch him first.

He reaches for his pants now, fiddling with his belt buckle until it flaps open and pulling down the zipper of his slacks. My thighs clench together as I try to soothe the throb between them, keeping my eyes trained on Braden so he can see just how desperately I need him.

It feels impossible to keep from touching myself. My nipples swell behind my dress, and I can't help but palm my breast, whimpering when my inner walls pulse in response.

His eyes meet mine as he lifts his hips and pushes his pants and boxers down his legs. My lips part when he grabs his hard cock with a tight fist. He gives his shaft a few slow, hard strokes before swiping the bead of pre-cum away.

"Well? Do you want an invitation, Sierra?" His voice is gravelly, raw.

The arrogant question slides off my back as I unbuckle my seatbelt and climb over the center console. With my thighs pressed to the outside of his, I sit down on his lap and nearly cry out when my core brushes the hard ridge of his cock.

My teeth sink into my bottom lip as my hands find purchase on his shoulders for balance. A firm hand grips my face, squeezing my chin and tilting my head down. Braden takes my mouth in a desperate, dirty kiss, sucking the air from my lungs. My tongue licks the seam of his lips and he parts them for me with a throaty groan that I feel vibrating deep in his chest.

I've never been so attracted to somebody in my life. Braden invokes something carnal in me, something that's been hidden for as long as I can remember. It makes me desperate and unhinged, like I have no control over my body. It's scary, even a little terrifying. But I've begun to harness those feelings, using them to take control over this man in a way that I never thought was possible.

Our kiss is frantic, *hungry*. It's as if this is the last time his lips will taste mine and we both know it—a thought that I don't let poison my mind as I grind against his bare shaft, searching for the release I need so desperately.

I feel him reach between us and pull my panties to the side, exposing my drenched pussy. My head falls back with a curse when he cups me, pressing his palm against my clit.

"You're always ready for me."

I suck in a sharp breath and buck against his hand, my hips swirling. One long finger teases my entrance before sliding inside, agonizingly slow.

"More," I breathe, twisting my hips again as blinding lust heats my blood. My nails dig into his shoulders, and I press my face into his neck, pressing my lips to his pulse point and sucking on the racing beat beneath it.

Two more fingers thrust inside of me, swirling and bending to hit my sweet spot before retreating fully with a wet, sloppy sound. "If I don't get inside of you right now, I might fucking die, baby," Braden grunts before I feel the swollen, wet tip of his cock press against my entrance. He coats himself in my wetness before slapping my clit with the head, my thighs shuddering as I struggle to hold myself up.

The heat in his amber eyes has me unable to look away and watch him as I lower myself onto his shaft, sinking inch by inch until I've taken all of him.

I feel so desired, so beautiful that I can't catch my breath. My throat constricts, tightening to the point I have to gasp, like an invisible hand is collaring it, choking me until black rims my vision and the world stops. But there's nothing there. Nothing but bright, world-burning, unadulterated love for the man in front of me. A stinging sensation builds behind my eyes, my vision blurring.

I love him.

But I have to leave him.

"Braden," I whimper, sliding the dress shirt down his shoulders and gripping onto the muscles resting there in an attempt to ground myself before I fly away. Something warm and wet slides down my cheek, and I swipe it away quickly, hoping he didn't notice. I refuse to cry right now. This might be the last time . . . *no. Don't think about it.*

With a throaty groan, he grips me tighter and thrusts his hips, burying himself so deep I cry out. My head falls back and I close my eyes, blinking back the blinding pain that ricochets through my chest.

Braden's hands slide through my hair, gripping it tightly like he always does when he uses it to move me how he wants me. Closer, farther, it's his choice. Just how he likes it. I don't put up a fight, too utterly weightless.

"Tell me that I'm the only one who gets to fuck this pussy," he orders, thrusting into me relentlessly while shoving my dress down my shoulders and rolling my left nipple between his calloused fingertips.

A sob tears up my throat when I feel the familiar pull in my stomach. "You're the only one."

Lifting my hips, I take back some control and begin to ride him. I try to memorize how it feels to be filled with him, the smooth, thick size of him pulsing as he gets closer and closer to his release. My nipples drag against his bare chest as I arch my back and place my palms on his thighs, using him to increase our pace.

His large hands cup my face and I'm right there, shaking in his lap like a leaf in the wind as tears scorn my cheeks, falling to his chest. Those amber eyes fill with something broken, something too heavy to carry as his thumbs begin to catch my tears, wiping them away frantically as he says my name like a curse.

He drives inside of me hard one last time before stilling, my walls continuing to pulse around him, the last of my orgasm draining what little energy I had left. "You're mine, Sierra. *All mine.*"

I nod over and over again and collapse against him, seconds before his arms wrap around me, holding me to him like he's scared I'll open the car door and run. But I can't. Not right now.

31

Sierra

"YOU'RE ABSOLUTELY RIDICULOUS," I SQUEAL, ATTEMPTING TO hide my smile in Braden's shoulder as he carries me bridal style down the hallway to his apartment.

There was no way that he was about to let me out of his sight after what happened in the car—which thankfully, he hasn't mentioned since—so I wasn't surprised when he insisted that I stay the night with him. There wasn't any way that I was going to say no either.

This is exactly where I want to be.

"I think you mean absolutely jaw droppingly handsome, sweetheart," he mumbles, kissing my head.

Keeping me held firmly in his arms, he manages to use his key to unlock the door before pushing it open with his foot.

Loud voices erupt through the doorway, and I lift my head in search of the culprit, hoping that we didn't walk in on something that's going to be burned in my memory for the rest of my life. But when I find Clay lying outstretched on the couch, feet hanging off the edge, a box of half-eaten pizza on the coffee table, and a horror movie playing on the T.V screen, I laugh.

"Why aren't you gone?" Braden asks gruffly.

Clayton shoots up and reaches for the remote, turning the sound down a few notches before resting eyes on the two of us.

"Well, if it isn't the two lovebirds. Finally home, are we?" He drags his attention to the clock above the T.V. "It's two in the morning, in case you forgot how to read a clock."

"And?" Braden shoots. His eyes drop to mine, sending me a warning before my feet are placed on the floor. "I didn't know that I had a curfew, Dad."

After pulling my dress further down my legs to avoid giving Clay a view of my goodies, I cross my arms and pin him with a look. "At least we were out doing something. What's your excuse?"

"Plans changed. Figured I would save my liver for the night and watch a movie."

"Smart." Braden snorts. When he laces his fingers with mine, I look up and see him already staring down at me with soft, muted eyes. "You tired yet?"

My mind screams yes but I shut it up, shaking my head instead. "I can stay awake for a while longer."

With as little as a nod in my direction, he pulls me behind him to the living room. And when Clayton makes no move to share the couch, Braden sits down in front of it, his back leaning against it. Grinning, I watch him pat his lap and hold his arms out in front of him. I settle on his thighs without hesitation.

He bends forward and presses his mouth to my ear. "Keep your hands to yourself, yeah? We have company."

A shiver racks through me at the thought of trying anything while Clayton sits only a few feet away. Braden's hands wrap around my waist and pull me as far against his chest as possible.

"I will if you will."

"Best behaviour, baby. Scouts honour." He pats my sides.

Clayton turns the volume back up, cutting our conversation short as we turn our attention to the young woman screaming for help on the screen. I attempt to ignore the consistent flutter in my chest with every soft stroke of Braden's thumb against my side, but fail miserably. His body heat wraps around me tighter than his arms do, and I find my eyes starting to droop as his heart beats quickly against my back.

There's only one thing that runs through my mind before it all goes dark.

In just a few days, this is all going to disappear.

Braden

The bed is cold when I wake up, my least favourite feeling as of late. I don't have time to get frustrated by Sierra leaving because I hear her voice in the apartment, muffled by my closed bedroom door. The sound makes my lips lift in a smile as I sit up and stretch my arms behind my head. I look down at the pink pillow resting beside my black one and gnaw on my lip.

I've never been the guy to let a girl so much as keep a sock at his house, let alone half of the kind of shit that I find littered around here now. There's no room that's safe from the Sierra invasion, but I can't find it in myself to give a shit. It's so natural to me now seeing an extra toothbrush on the bathroom counter or a pair of booty shorts in my laundry basket.

Maybe that makes me a pussy-whipped loser. Who the hell knows.

Reaching down beside the bed, I stretch my arm out to grab a t-shirt from the floor but freeze when my nightstand starts buzzing. As I move to pick up the vibrating phone, I hesitate when I notice it's Sierra's.

Do I, or don't I? Is there a rule that says I can't pick up her phone when it rings?

With a shrug of my shoulders, I grab it and flip it over, raising my brows at the caller ID on the screen. My pride gets the better of me and I answer the call with a clenched jaw.

"What do you want?"

"Who is this? Is Sierra there?" Cole asks, his tone cautious. *Good, he should be nervous.*

"It's her boyfriend," I all but growl at him, surprising myself when I use the title. We've never really discussed placing a label on our relationship, but this fucker doesn't need to know that.

"Right." He clears his throat. "Well, is Sierra available to talk? We need to discuss her flight times."

My eyes narrow as my stomach clenches, worry building in my spine. "What do you mean, flight times?"

"Yes. Flight times. For her move to Toronto next week," he says, as if I'm a complete idiot for not knowing what he's talking about.

"She hasn't decided if she's taking your creepy ass offer yet, dickbag," I grind out, gripping my jaw tightly. "You're messing with the wrong fucking girl, Cole Travis. Don't think that I won't break you in half just because you're my girl's boss. I promise you that she would not sympathize with you in the slightest."

"Is that so?" He sounds bored. And fuck does that piss me off. "I'm sorry to be the one to inform you, but she has actually taken my offer. Maybe you should have a talk with your girlfriend before throwing such careless threats around. It seems that you're not on the same page. Please make sure you tell her to call me after you have your much needed *talk*."

The dial tone rings in my ear after he hangs up on me. I squeeze my eyes shut and dig deep for any ounce of calmness left in my ice-cold body.

I know that I haven't exactly been the most open about what exactly I wanted from this relationship, but I assumed she knew me well enough to know that I didn't think of this as a fling. I might not be ready to offer her a future of forever, but I would *try* and give her something close, if that's what she wanted.

The thought of not having her anymore is like being stabbed from back to front with a serrated knife only to have it ripped back out again. The mere idea of it makes bile sting my throat and my heart crack down the middle.

After spending the past couple of months getting to know each other, I would have hoped that she would have told me about something as big as her taking a job across the country. If not for her own conscience, then for me. Because if she is planning on leaving, then I don't know why the fuck we've been wasting our time together, building something that would only burn to the ground.

With a fire raging in my chest, I toss her phone on the bed and stand, nearly ripping my door off its hinges as I open it. I spot her leaning against the kitchen counter wearing a baggy shirt and pajama pants as she laughs at something Clayton must have said.

Unable to hold myself back, I yank off the Band-Aid without warning. "When were you going to tell me that you took that fucking job?"

When she spins to stare at me, wide-eyed and tense, I know that Cole was telling the truth. That fucking weasel was telling the truth and she's been lying to me for *days*. What a slap to the face.

"Brade——" she squeaks, but I cut her off with a dark chuckle.

"I never took you for a liar, Sierra. It definitely doesn't suit you."

"I never lied to you. I hadn't decided yet," she mumbles, staring at her toes, her neck a dark shade of red.

Guilt flows off of her in waves, but I don't let it affect me. I refuse to back down from this.

"That's not an excuse. You had plenty of time over the

past few days to tell me. I've been with you constantly. But you were going to wait, right? Until when? The day you left? Well sorry to ruin all of your fun, but I know now and I'm done wasting my time."

"Wasting your time? Nice," she scoffs, looking at me again with narrowed eyes.

"If I would have known that you would be leaving, I wouldn't have bothered letting you meet my parents or leave your shit all over my house! You made everything so much more complicated," I hiss, running a hand through my hair and pulling at the ends.

"Well, it's great to know that it's so easy for you to throw me away and move on with your life. It's not like I'm moving to another country! We could always try to make it work."

"I'm just going to go," Clayton mumbles, earning himself a glare from both of us as he scurries off to his bedroom.

When his door shuts behind him, I spin back to Sierra, a dangerous mix of betrayal and hurt building deep in my chest.

"Try to make *what* work? As much as I love fucking you, I'm not going to fly across the country to have an endless tap of your pussy." I laugh humourlessly, ignoring the ache in my chest when I see the new shine in her silver eyes. My protective walls slide back up, where they should have been the entire fucking time. I was a helpless idiot to think it was okay to let them down.

"Good to know," she whispers, shoulders dropping before she's walking to the front door, not sparing me a second look.

I'm hot on her heels, aching to push her against the wall and fuck this decision right out of her. I don't want her to leave, but the words don't stop flowing from my fat mouth, deepening the rift that's now formed between us.

"I wish you the best of luck. I'm sure Cole will be there for all of those lonely nights," I say.

She slips her shoes on quickly and opens the door, hesitating in the doorway. "I knew that you wouldn't come with me. That's why I didn't say anything. I knew that telling you I took the job would have meant the end of us. I should have told you; I know that. I just wanted more time."

And then she's gone, stepping into the hallway and disappearing from my life.

I can't find it in myself to chase her, or close the door once she's gone, no matter how badly I try. Instead, I send my fist through the wall and watch the drywall dust float in the air, too numb to care that my blood now drips on the floor.

32

Sierra

My feet ache and my arms feel like warm string cheese. The box I'm holding wobbles as I attempt to move it from my bedroom to the living room. To some, it might seem pointless to move a singular box from one room to another just a few feet away, but with the number of boxes cluttering up my bedroom, I'll take whatever free space I can manage.

Waking up in the middle of the night to go to the washroom, only to end up stubbing your big toe on a heavy box and falling on your ass isn't how I would like to spend my last two nights here.

My sigh of relief replaces the sound of my laboured breathing when I finally place the collection of picture frames on the floor. The glass clatters as the poorly packed frames bang around inside the box.

Too drained to care, I just stretch out my cramped arms and kick the mess of broken glass away.

That's a problem for another day. And it's not like I have many family pictures inside that box, anyway. Most of the frames are filled with lame quotes that at one point in my life, made me think that I could take on the world. At this point, I don't think that I could take on the world even if I woke up gifted with every superpower known to man.

I head for the fridge in desperate need of some water. The cold fridge air makes me sigh with a weird mix of relief and pleasure. My eyes burn from exhaustion as I fight to keep them open, knowing full well how nasty my under-eye circles must be by now.

I haven't slept more than three hours a night in the past three days. Since leaving Braden's house, I've been lost in a sea of regret and confusion, unsure of where to go now. My future is flashing in front of me in the shape of a giant question mark.

I don't know if I've made a huge mistake, or taken a risk that will end up paying off in the end. I'm sure if my mother knew what I did she would praise me up and down, so proud of me for putting my career before anything else.

Is that what I want? To have made a decision that would have pleased my mother of all people?

The bottle of water meets my sweaty palm as I unscrew the lid like a maniac and finish the contents in a few gulps. The plastic crunches when I twist it and throw it toward the recycle bin, not bothering to look if it ended up on the floor or not.

Three light knocks on my front door have me smiling, knowing exactly who's on the other side.

"Coming!" When I pull open the door, my smile pulls into an even wider grin.

Clare stands with Liz on her back, legs wrapped around her waist in a bear grip. Both girls radiate happiness and love. It's an addicting, nearly overwhelming aura that I still haven't been able to fully comprehend. How could I? The only time I've experienced a bond even remotely the same is with my sister. And even then, it's not the same as what she has with her daughter.

"Auntie!" Liz shouts and jumps down from Clare's back.

She rushes toward me and hugs my leg tightly before pushing her way inside and heading for the colouring book and crayons I left out for her on the couch.

"She'll be busy all night now. Smart move." Clare steps inside, shutting the door behind her. "It looks awful in here. Are you sure you're leaving in two days?"

"Don't remind me," I sigh and walk to the kitchen. "Want something to drink? I have water or wine."

"Go easy with all the options, sis." She laughs. "Did you leave any glasses unpacked or are we drinking it from the bottle?"

Pulling open my cupboard door, my lip slips between my teeth when I realize I haven't been drinking from a glass for a few days now. "Bottle?"

"From the look of your overflowing recycle bin, it looks like tonight isn't the only time this week you've been drinking straight from the bottle," she says, attempting to hide her curiosity with an otherwise harmless poke.

"You caught me." I shut the cupboard again before pulling a mostly full bottle of red wine from the fridge and suck back a few sips.

"On second thought, you can enjoy that on your own."

I try to find the judgment in her voice but come up short. Not that I'm surprised. My sister is the least judgmental person I know. If anybody is going to understand my sudden obsession with booze, it's her.

"Thanks." I wipe my mouth with the back of my hand and hold the bottle by my side.

"Wanna talk about it?" Clare pulls a barstool away from the small kitchen island and sits down, her brows pulled in tight, round eyes locked on mine.

"There isn't anything more to talk about." I sit in the seat beside her. The bottle rests on the countertop as I lean forward on my elbows and close my eyes.

"That's a lie," she scoffs. "Have you talked to him since? If you leave without at least trying to talk to him you know that you'll regret it, S."

Right. I forgot that she was the one who brought me home Sunday morning. There was no way that I could have avoided explaining the situation to her after I started sobbing in her SUV.

"He doesn't want to talk to me. He's probably banging someone else as we speak."

The thought alone of another girl in his bed makes my skin burn and my top teeth scrape the bottom ones in an almost animalistic action. I know that I lost the right to care about who he spends his nights with, but I can't help that I still care. I care way too much, and I have no idea when or *if* I'll be able to stop.

His words still echo in my ears, burning fresh in my mind when I try to fall asleep at night. *"As much as I love fucking you, I'm not going to fly across the country to have an endless tap of your pussy."*

The crack in my chest deepens, my love for him burning a hole inside of me. I hoped that he had felt even relatively similar feelings for me, but I know that it was a far-fetched idea. We were never meant to be forever. I was just a step in the right direction for him. A reminder that he doesn't always have to hide that big heart of his behind that playboy facade.

"I doubt that." Clare's soothing voice breaks me out of my jumbled thoughts. "If he felt even remotely close to what you felt for him, I guarantee he's wondering how to reach out to you."

A laugh breaks through my frown. "You don't know him. He's not the type."

"No?" she asks, lifting a brow. "Well, I know *you*. And there's no way you were spending your time and effort on someone who didn't deserve it. That fact alone makes me believe that he isn't as bad as you're trying to convince the both of us he is. I don't need to know him to know that."

My eyes bulge as I stare at my sister, a feeling of gratefulness swelling behind my chest bone. What happened to the thirteen-year-old girl who spent three hours on hold with the oven company because she couldn't figure out how to turn the oven on and *needed* to bake me a birthday cake? Or the seventeen-year-old who went to the drugstore in the middle of the night to buy me my own pack of pads when I got my first period because "every grown woman should have her own set of hygiene products."

I would do anything to go back and relive those moments.

"I always forget how old and wise you've gotten," I grumble.

She shrugs away my compliment. "Sometimes people surprise you, Sierra. You have to at least give him a chance to."

"Even if he did, it wouldn't matter. I would be setting myself up for an even worse heartbreak down the road. I want to get married someday, Clare. He doesn't believe in that sort of thing."

Clare surprises me by laughing.

"What's funny about that?" I narrow my eyes and tilt my head.

"You love him, right? And don't lie to me."

"I do," I reply softly. There's no doubt about it. If I didn't, losing him wouldn't feel like having my heart wrung out like a wet towel.

"Then don't be ridiculous. Men don't know what they want half the time. Not until they grow up and find the right person. How do you know that you aren't Braden's right person?"

"I don't know."

"It wouldn't be easy, but at the risk of sounding incredibly cheesy right now, nothing worth the risk is ever easy."

"That *was* cheesy," I agree. "But also very wise."

Lifting the wine bottle to my lips, I let her words marinate in my mind and the liquid slide down my throat. My immediate response is to tell her that she's right and promise to go see him. To make things right. But the fear of rejection is overwhelming. It looms over me like a rain cloud.

I hate that I've been wasting my last few days in Vancouver locked inside my apartment packing things that I don't even care to bring with me.

I should be with Braden.

I want to be with him, but does he care for me enough to want to try and make this work, knowing how complicated it could be? We both deserve closure, though. How am I supposed to move away, not knowing if we were ever really, really over? That there might have been a chance but I was too stubborn to take it?

Shit. Why is loving somebody so damn hard?

Braden

"HOLY FUCK!" I spit through a clenched jaw. My stiff body slides into the ice-chunk-filled bathtub and I start shivering instantly. Squeezing my eyes shut, I let my ass smack the bottom before unclenching my legs and pressing my heels to the metal sides.

"Did you expect it to be warm?"

I peel my right eye open and watch Tyler snort his reply from the row of lockers in front of me. He rips his locker door open and grabs his bag, tossing it to a bench before sitting down beside it.

"Hurry up and go home." I let my neck fall limp and my head sags forward, my eyes closing again.

"Someone's exceptionally touchy today."

"In case you haven't noticed, I'm a little sore," I grunt.

"That's what happens when you get your ass beat for the second time in two days by someone out of your weight class. I told you not to fight that guy."

The locker door slams shut and I clench my sore jaw. The last thing I want to hear right now is a fucking I told you so. Especially from my brother.

"Do you have anything useful to say or are you just going to continue to lecture me?"

"I'm not lecturing you. I just think there are better things that you can be doing with your time right now. Like trying to find a place to live in Toronto."

My eyes pop open instantly before narrowing on his shrugging shoulders. "Not going to happen."

"Was worth a shot," he sighs, leaning back against the metal locker with crossed arms.

"Was it?"

"It was. Not like it pulled your head out of your ass at all, though."

"Like I said. You can leave anytime now."

"You know that hurting yourself won't make you feel any better or bring her back, right? There's only one way to do that and you seem too stubborn to dump that damn pride of yours to do so."

I lift my right arm out of the ice water and place my palm on the edge of the tub, gripping it so tightly the cuts on my knuckle begin to pool with blood again. "I don't want her back. I was the one who ended things with her."

I'm not sure if I'm more upset with myself or Tyler for bringing her up right now, but in all honesty, it doesn't matter. I was thinking about her long before he brought her up. Like I have been every fucking day since I've last seen her.

It's been three days since I've touched her, kissed her, felt her body against mine. I haven't heard her laughter, or felt the lurch in my chest that comes along with each smile she gifts me. I'm pissed off at the world, just like I was when I was an angsty teen. It's ridiculous.

"Yeah, because you're an absolute idiot," he says and moves toward me. "It runs in the family, don't feel too embarrassed. It takes a lot of missed shots and sleepless nights alone, but it is possible to learn how women work."

I roll my eyes. "It took Dad a divorce to learn how."

"Your parents didn't get divorced just because Dad didn't know how to treat your mother, Braden. You know that." He flashes me a pointed look. "Plus, just because Dad was divorced, doesn't mean we're all doomed to the same fate. I've never been divorced, nor do I ever plan on it. You just have to realize what you have to lose and whether or not you're really willing to lose it. It took me far too long to come to that realization, brother."

"You and I are *very* different, Tyler Bateman."

"So what?" he asks stiffly, *aggressively*, like he doesn't like me calling him by his mother's surname.

I did it to put some distance between us, feeling too exposed under his expert stare. We've known each other too long for him not to be able to see right through me, but it still pisses me off.

"So, one of us is meant for a real relationship while the other is not. You, my dear brother, are the one that was destined to be a husband and father. You believe in the *happily ever after* bullshit. I don't. I don't want to have someone rely on me that heavily. I don't want that sort of pressure." I don't know if I would be able to stand beneath the weight of it.

"So, you plan on living the rest of your life in a different pussy every night? Give me a break."

"If that's what happens then sure. I could think of worse ways to live." Lifting my arms above my head, I stretch out the numbing ache in my shoulders. "Hand me a towel, would you?"

Tyler tosses me one, tenser than a stretched elastic band. "You can't fool me with this tough guy shit, Braden. You miss her and you're too stubborn to tell her that. You're going to regret letting her leave."

My teeth scrape the inside of my cheek as I get out of the tub and step onto the cement floor. I wrap the towel around my wet underwear, water pooling at my feet.

I don't just miss her. I'm way beyond that, and I'm sure the purple crescents of exhaustion beneath my eyes make that more than obvious. The bed doesn't feel the same without her warm, smooth skin or clumps of brown hair that almost always wind up in my face as I sleep.

"It doesn't matter what you think. I'm going to be fine—she's going to be fine, we're both going to be *fine*. We weren't even that serious."

Tyler bursts into a fit of laughter, gripping onto the side of the bench and keeling over dramatically. My anger begins to bubble under my skin the longer I watch him put on a show.

"Right," he chortles. "Let me ask you a question."

I blink, not trusting myself to speak.

"If you weren't serious, then I don't suppose it would upset you to think of her being swept off of her feet by some big-time successful hotshot in Toronto? It doesn't make you angry in the slightest to think of him bending her over their shiny kitchen countertops and having her scream his name, begging for more of his coc—"

His words stop short when I shove him against the lockers, my forearm pressed tight even against his throat that he feels the weight of it against his windpipe. With a tilt of his head, he grins, eyebrows dancing with amusement. "Exactly."

With a grunt, I release the pressure on his throat and place my palms on his chest to shove myself back. My nostrils flare as I shove my hands through my hair. "You have a fucking death wish."

"Call it whatever you want. But you know that I'm right.

You can't have it both ways. If you let her go because you refuse to stop letting the past live in the present, then you'll lose her. You can't live your life out of fear, Braden. You'll end up living it alone."

"Thanks for the advice." There's only a tiny note of appreciation in my tone. The reality of his words sits heavy on my chest, pressing down on top of me like a cement block.

I know that my parent's marriage screwed me up, I've never denied that. But my feelings toward relationships and marriage aren't going to change just because of one girl. It doesn't matter how much I care about her. There's no knowing if we would even be happy together somewhere that's not here. I would be risking my entire life in Vancouver over a pipe dream and a beautiful woman.

We could spend years together, but once it came to marriage, I would never be able to give her what she wants. I would only be delaying the inevitable heartbreak that we would be facing years down the road.

Staying away from her is the smart thing to do. And for once, I'm going to do the right thing, for both of us.

"Just think about it, Braden. She doesn't leave until tomorrow. You still have time."

Deciding to just give him what he wants, I nod my head, clearing my throat. "Okay."

Tyler grins and straightens his shoulders. "Okay? Like you'll actually think about it? You're not just saying that to get me to drop it?"

"Yeah. I'll think about it. Just for you."

"I'll take it." He laughs and tosses his bag over his shoulder. "Now get dressed so we can leave."

With a fake salute, I snicker, "Aye aye, captain."

33

Sierra

THE DESK DRAWER SLIDES SHUT SLOWLY, ALMOST AS IF I'M
trying to delay the inevitable. Which I totally am.

I wasn't in this office for very long. Definitely not for as
long as I had anticipated. But given that it was the very first
office I've ever had all to myself, I'm going to miss it. Even if it
was *way* too close to the men's washroom for my hearing
pleasure.

I never even had time to hang my degree on the wall. But
the Devil is in the details I suppose. From the pictures Cole
sent me of my new office in Toronto, I think it's safe to assume
that I'll have more than enough room to do so this time
around.

"You really pushed it to the last minute, I see."

Looking up from the sleek black desk, now completely
bare of anything but the medium sized box packed with my
few personal belongings, I see Cole leaning arms crossed in
the doorway. There's a typical teasing glimmer in his eyes, one
that pairs almost too well with his sinister grin. He smells like
trouble today, and that makes me nervous.

"I suppose I did," I reply tightly. I was hoping to make it

out of here without having to deal with him anymore than necessary. I'll already have far too much Cole time once we arrive in Toronto.

"Is everything else ready? Did you end up deciding on an apartment?"

"I did."

It only took a week and three Skype calls with the landlord, but I move into a new construction, two-bedroom condo the day after tomorrow. In a perfect world, I would be handed the keys as soon as I land in Toronto tomorrow afternoon, but with such short notice, I'm lucky to be moving in just a day late. Plus, who would say no to a free, company-paid hotel room for a night? Not me. I'm looking forward to spending far too long in the hotel spa. Maybe I'll even book an acupuncture appointment. There has to be a nerve that can be poked and prodded to clear Braden from my head.

"Excited?" Cole asks, dropping his arms and moving further into the room.

Of course, I am. But I would describe the cluster-fuck of emotion's inside of me as more so terrifying than anything else.

"It's going to be a big change," I say.

"One that I hope you're ready for?" The questioning edge in his words rub me the wrong way, but I shove my feelings to the side and bite my tongue, deciding to be the bigger person.

"If I wasn't ready, I wouldn't be going. You can trust me on that." Now please leave before I scratch your eyes out and feed them to a stray cat.

His smile is back as quickly as it had faded, and with an almost missable wink, he says, "See you tomorrow then, little worker bee."

I nearly puke.

———

"You want me to go to a club and get wasted with you the night before I hop on an early morning flight across the country?" I scoff, squeezing my phone between my shoulder and ear as I open my apartment door and drop the contents of my desk on the counter. "Is this payback for something?"

Re-adjusting the phone, I put the call on speaker and place it down beside the box so I can unbuckle my strappy heels.

"You so owe me this, Sierra. You're about to make a bunch of new fancy friends and forget about me while I eat cookie dough ice cream by myself and miss you," Sophie wines.

"I'm not going to forget about you, Sophie. You're my best friend," I promise her, hating that she's doubting that for even a second.

"Okay, well come anyway. It'll be our last hoorah. Don't miss out on our final girls night because you're scared of a tiny hangover."

I lean my elbows on the counter and let my head fall until my forehead touches it. I love Sophie to death but I was really hoping to just spend my last night here, curled up on the couch, eating my feelings in deep-dish pizza. But as hard as she tries to understand everything running through my mind these last few days, she really has no idea how I feel. I don't blame her for that, of course, but when she pushes these things on me it becomes more exhausting than helpful.

Besides, the only thing alcohol has done for me lately is make me unbelievably horny. Although, I do partially blame that on the fact that before this week, I wasn't going more than a single day without having sex. Braden is to blame for that. He completely ruined my single-girl routine.

"Fine. What time?" I rub my temples.

"I'll come get you at ten! Love you, gorgeous." She hangs up on me before I reply, leaving me confused and a little annoyed.

"Whatever," I whisper to myself and comb my fingers through my hair. Looking at the time on my phone, I'm grateful that I still have a few hours to relax before going to completely destroy my liver.

Now I just have to decide which one of my T.V boyfriends will keep my company until then.

———

MY HEAD BOBBLES as another hard chest pushes against my back. Sweaty hands cup the skin of my waist through the cut-outs in my uncomfortably tight dress. Sophie's choice, of course.

My thoughts are cloudy, tongue way too numb to tell whoever this guy is that I'm fine on my own. I let my eyelids slide shut as the neon lighting becomes too much for my throbbing head. In an attempt to collect myself, I lean against the body behind me, just for a second.

The man smells like cheap body spray and orange juice, a combo that makes my nose crinkle and my stomach to churn. Just a little bit longer, Sierra. Then you can hop in a cab, sleep for a couple of hours, and wake up, ready to start your new life.

Sophie and I got here about two hours ago, give or take an hour, but I haven't seen her for at least half of that time. My anger toward her lack of company probably explains why I drank so much so fast, and why the earth is doing the wave.

Hot breath crashes against my exposed neck, and I tilt my head to the side, as if on instinct. I'm too drunk to feel embarrassed for not pushing this guy away. And hopefully, tomorrow will just be a blur when I wake up.

I feel the stranger pull away from me and shrug my shoulders, muttering something unintelligible under my breath. Straightening my spine, I palm my thighs and start to walk off the dance floor, but stumble backward when another set of hands grab me. My skin sizzles where we touch, and I gasp.

The stranger's chest is hard but welcoming, and it molds against my back in a way that I can't comprehend. His jaw is rough and covered in stubble. He brushes it against my cheek, nudging my head to fall to the side to allow him to run his nose along my racing pulse.

"I saw you all the way from the bar. You're impossible to miss. Just like you were the first time we danced like this."

My eyes close when I hear his voice, my entire body becoming a burning ball of fire and melting away the ice I let build up inside my chest. Whatever was left of my guard is dropped as I turn around and reach for him. My palms lay flat on his rising chest and I swallow the boulder in my throat before raising my gaze to his, eager to see what's waiting for me behind those amber eyes.

"Braden," I choke.

The smell of whiskey is strong on his breath, reminding me that the sheen in his gaze probably matches the one in mine.

When he doesn't respond, I suck in a sharp breath and drop my gaze to the black t-shirt that looks as if it was painted on his model-worthy chest.

Jealousy—one of the most unwanted emotions—claws up my skin as I think of every one of the other girls in this club that probably caught his eye tonight. Did he look at them the way he's looking at me? Like he could take me right here, right now, and not care who watches?

"Why are you here, Sierra?" he slurs, voice rising to be heard over the bass thumping around us. "You shouldn't be here. Not dressed like that."

His possessiveness sends shock waves directly to my clit. "What should I be doing then?"

His bottom lip slides between his teeth. "Anything. You

prefer staying in, wearing those tiny little cookie monster pajamas and drinking all of my orange juice. Why not do that?" He sighs heavily and moves his hands up my body to cup my cheeks.

"I didn't want to come here either. But I'm starting to think it was a good decision." I lean into his touch and close my eyes, practically purring while attempting to think of my next words carefully. I don't want to scare him away.

"Stop thinking. Just let me kiss you before you leave. One last time." He's begging, not bothering to try and hide it. It makes my heart soar, knowing how desperately he needs me. Even if it's just for right now. Because I need him too. So much it fucking hurts.

I've barely nodded before his lips are on mine, pushing against them with an unspoken goodbye. A goodbye that makes my eyes burn with the fear that I've made a mistake. One that I'll never be able to come back from. He takes my mouth and owns it, pushing forward a million different emotions and feelings that have my entire body in a disarray.

He pulls back slowly, eyebrows scrunched with curiosity, eyes later-focused on my cheek. It's not until I focus on the wet feeling on my cheeks that I realize I've been crying, and that he's been brushing away every single tear with his thumbs.

"I love you," I whisper, unable to take the pain of holding back any longer. My voice is so quiet, so broken. The only thing that lets me know he's heard me is the instant look of fear that spreads across his handsome features.

Noise has never felt as silent as it does right now, as he drops his hands, almost as if my skin has burnt his fingertips. His head shakes, lips parting before meeting again, over and over until he jerks back, nearly tripping over his own feet.

"Fuck. *Fuck.* I'm sorry," he sputters, jaw tensing as his eyes harden to stone. "I need to go."

I stand frozen, my feet glued to the dancefloor of the place

I can never come back to. I watch him turn from me and walk away with an urgency that has my chest splitting wide open and my heart slipping to the ground, two severed pieces laying at my feet.

34

"WHO'S HANGING A FUCKING PICTURE?" I GRUMBLE, MY tongue dry as all shit.

The incessant knocking reverberates through the apartment, yanking me from my restless sleep. My hands press to my eyes until I see static.

When the knocking shows no signs of stopping, I grind my teeth together and slowly open my left eye, ignoring the blasting burn in my retina.

"Clayton!" I yell before a throb in my forehead scolds me. A tingle in my arm makes me attempt to shake it out from underneath my head, and I cringe at the pain that shoots through my shoulder at the movement.

It's not hard to tell the more I wake up that I'm not laying in my bed. And as my vision becomes less and less blurred, I make note of the bathtub and toilet. With a humourless, dark laugh, I drag a hand down my face.

I didn't even make it to my room last night. What a fucking accomplishment.

My short temper—my favourite side effect of drinking myself into a vomiting mess—begins sparking as the knocking continues. With a hiss, I push myself up off the floor and stand with a slight wobble, my jaw aching as I grip onto the counter for balance.

Ripping the bathroom door open, I shrink away at the brightly lit apartment with an immediate scowl. My attention moves to the front door when I realize the knocking is coming from behind it. With a huff, I look down to double-check to make sure I'm not stark naked and stalk to the door.

"Relax already! Jesus Christ," I grunt and unlock the door.

I don't even have the door pulled open an inch before a red-faced blonde is shouldering her way inside and pushing at my chest. She shoves me for a second time, and I take it, not lucky enough to have forgotten the reason that she's here.

Sierra. It's always Sierra.

I force myself to stand tall, even when I want to collapse to my knees and beg her to help me go get my girl. My head is pounding, and my thoughts look a lot like scrambled eggs, but the picture of Sierra, so broken and helpless, remains untouched, standing among the mess like a prized possession. It makes me sick, so beyond disgusted with myself.

Instead of doing what every fiber of my being wants and needs me to, I harden my features and with my tone like ice, say, "Get out of my house, Sophie."

My words seem to piss her off even more, just like I knew they would. With a look that probably could have tossed me six-feet under had I not already felt like death, she stabs a finger into my sternum. "You have some nerve, jackass."

"What the hell did I do to you?" I swallow past the bile in my throat and move away from her, closing the apartment door with more force than necessary. My fingers curl into fists that I want to throw through a wall, but I choose to bang them against my thighs instead.

"You did everything!" she spits, glaring so hard it wouldn't surprise me if she burst a blood vessel in her temple. "Do you have any idea the damage you've done? Or do you just not care?"

"How I feel isn't any of your concern. Now get out." I gesture to the door with as much arrogance as I can muster up through the growing knot in my stomach.

If only Sierra could see me now. She would have wished that she kept those pretty words inside her mouth and saved them for somebody deserving of them.

"Isn't any of my concern? Sierra is the only person I give a shit about in this world. And I was the one who took her home crying last night after you shattered her to pieces. I've never seen her that way before. So fucking lifeless, like the light was snatched right out of her soul."

I push back the wall of guilt rising in my chest before forcing myself to shrug. My insides are screaming for mercy as they're torn apart by the reality of what happened last night. Of what I *did*. My next words sound as weak as they feel. "Sierra is strong. She'll be fine."

Sophie barks out a humourless laugh and takes a brave step closer to me. "You're even dumber than I thought you were, you know that? I hoped you were more than just a pretty face, but turns out you're even less."

"I don't care what you think of me." I can't even keep eye-contact with her.

She wears her disgust for me with pride, and it carves into my back deep enough to scar. Sophie doesn't know me, and I don't know her, but we used to share something so fucking deep, something that made us connected on some weird, spiritual level.

We don't like each other—I'm pretty sure she would volunteer *my* name as Tribute if given the chance—but we did respect each other. Now, though? There's no respect there, not on her end. And I can't blame her for that.

"What kind of person walks away from someone when they tell them they love them? You can't honestly want me to believe that you don't love her too. I've seen it!" She ridicules me fearlessly, not backing down an inch. There's a warrior inside of this tiny girl. One that doesn't know how to tell when the battle has already been lost.

"I don't give a shit what you believe, trust me." I snort, crossing my arms across my bare chest and digging my nails into my biceps.

"You keep saying that but somehow, I don't believe you," she nearly sings, a cockiness flooding her confident tone that has the same effect on me as nails on a chalkboard. "We both know that you could have easily thrown me out by now if you didn't want to hear what I had to say somewhere very deep in that bitter, frozen chest of yours."

I narrow my sharp gaze. "Get out. This is the last time I'm going to say it."

"She's leaving in four hours. There's still time to tell her how you feel before she's gone."

My breath hitches before I shake my head shutting that hope right down. "She'll have fun in Toronto."

"You have got to be the most stubborn person I have ever met," she groans. "You're lucky I care enough about Sierra to even waste my time standing here arguing with you."

"Feel free to leave. I've only told you to do so a hundred damn times." I gesture to the door again with a pointed look.

"That's not what I'm trying to——" she cuts herself off by sucking in a dramatic breath and closing her eyes briefly. "You have one last chance, Braden. In four hours, you lose that chance. The chance to ever see her again. To ever hold her or see her smile again. Is that what you want? Because I know that's not what she wants."

The jaw-droppingly gorgeous white smile flashes in my mind, making my lungs tighten to the point of near suffocation. The urge to tear at my chest becomes overwhelming as I attempt to ignore the regret swarming my head with every flash of her tear-stained cheeks. The unmistakable taste of metal rings in my mouth as I clamp down on my tongue, her words playing over and over in my head like a broken record.

I love you.

Three words that turned every inch of me stone-cold without warning. The three words that I should have said back to her, but couldn't—*wouldn't*. Not when I knew they would have come with the plea of asking her to stay. To give up the chance of a lifetime, one that she deserves more than anything because I'm too much of a chicken to take the chance on her and me.

"It's too late. I can't drop my entire life on a pipe dream."

"Braden, if I had someone look at me the way that you look at Sierra, I wouldn't doubt love—real, passionate love—ever again. Don't give that up because you're afraid. We're all afraid. But sometimes it's worth the fear of the unknown. And I think you two *are* worth it. Don't you?"

"What would I even do? Stop her at the airport without a working plan as to what happens next?"

"You can figure that stuff out after you tell her how you feel. Don't let her leave thinking that all she was to you was a fuck buddy—a way to pass the time until you found something better. She deserves better than that."

"I know that, Sophie!" I curse, yanking on the messy hair flopping in my eyes just to feel the sharp pain. "This is too complicated."

"What's complicated?" Clayton asks, eyes droopy and bloodshot as he stumbles in through the front door, shirt hanging around his neck. I can feel my guard rising again as I straighten my back and shake my head, refusing to look at the hopeful glimmer in Sophie's eyes.

"You look like shit." I force myself to laugh.

"Ditto," he replies before turning to Sophie curiously. "What are you doing here? You two didn't . . ." There's something dark in his voice, something that he's attempting to hide.

"Hell no. You're disgusting," Sophie gags.

"Then what are you doing here?" He's too curious.

"She was picking up the rest of Sierra's shit before she

leaves town," I rush, nodding to the small collection of clothes piled up outside my bedroom.

Realization flashes across his face as he nods and breaks into a smile. "In that case, wanna join me for breakfast, gorgeous?"

"No thanks. I have to get those clothes to Sierra. She leaves in four hours." Her last sentence is shot toward me, and I hate that I'm going to pretend like I never heard this entire conversation as soon as she leaves.

My gaze drops to the floor when she bends down to grab the last remnants of Sierra, and I keep it there until she says goodbye to Clayton and leaves.

It isn't until I hear the front door click shut again that I look up and clench my fists until my knuckles are white.

Sierra

THE BACK of Clare's SUV sags as I place the last of my bags inside. I never thought I would find myself relating to an inanimate object, but I feel pretty saggy myself right about now.

I can almost feel the curiosity radiating off my sister as she remains eerily quiet and stands on the road behind me. When I step to the side, out of the way, she doesn't hesitate to reach out and close the trunk door with a forced smile.

"Is there something you want to say, Clare? You're creeping me out with the whole quiet thing. It's a bit out of character," I sigh, a ghost of a smile on my face that I know looks ridiculously fake.

"What? No." She laughs quickly. "I'm just excited for you.

It has nothing to do with the puffy eyes or the fake smiles that I've been getting since I saw you this morning."

Even though I pushed, it still sucks to hear that I have done a shit job at keeping my feelings hidden. I didn't need to be dealing with this on the day that I'm supposed to leave and start over.

"Do you want to talk about it? Liz tells me that I'm a good listener."

"Can we go first? I don't want to miss my flight," I mumble, playing with the uneven strings on my baggy hoodie.

"Of course!" She nods and moves quickly toward her door.

As she gets inside, I let out a slow breath and look back at the plain brick building that I called home for such a short time. I always thought that I would be here longer, that I would create memories here that I would carry around with me. But the only memories I have in the empty walls of my old apartment are ones that I never plan to revisit again.

The sting building in my eyes is enough to push my feet toward the passenger door. I open it and quickly crawl inside, almost as if I'm running away from something. Which, I guess I am. Or more so running toward something else. Something far from here.

Clare starts driving as soon as I buckle up.

"Thanks again for driving me. I could have called a cab."

"Of course. I wouldn't make you take a cab. Plus, it gives me a little more time with you."

My heart warms. "What am I going to do without you?"

"Honestly? I have no clue. Probably end up trapped somewhere or losing your mind because you can't find something that's been sitting in front of you the whole time," she teases.

"Wow!" I suck in a breath. "You're feeling ruthless today."

"It's true. You're a damn mess sometimes, S. But I love you anyway."

I give my head a shake and shove her arm. "I wish I could argue with you on that."

"It gives you spunk. Nobody can be as perfect as me." She winks.

"You wish."

She's quiet for a minute as she fiddles with the radio controls, browsing through them. I lift a brow when she ends up letting the original station play. "So, everything is taken care of here then? No unfinished business? I would hate for you to leave with any regrets."

"Regrets?" I ask, folding my arms across my chest. It's easy to realize where she's going with this. "Unfinished business?"

"You know what I mean," she hums.

"Do I?"

"Stop answering all of my questions with questions," she groans. "You know exactly what I'm talking about. Or *who*, I'm talking about."

"Nope. No idea."

"Braden? Super-hot, super buff guy who you've been spending every minute of every day with for a couple months now? I'm assuming it is him that's behind the puffy eyes and lost sparkle?"

"I'm just tired," I lie. "Sophie made me go out with her last night. I didn't get a lot of sleep."

"It looks like you didn't get any at all, S."

That's because I didn't. The only thing I saw every time I closed my eyes was the fear in Braden's eyes when I told him how I felt. I don't think I'll ever be able to sleep again.

"I got a few hours," I lie again.

"Come on. I know you better than that. I'm your big sister. And big sisters know everything."

"There's nothing else for me to take care of here. Trust me."

"Why not? Is he coming with you then?"

Her question makes a rough laugh rip up my throat and her eyes widen in shock. "I'm going to take that as a no?"

"Not in this lifetime, Clare. He doesn't feel the same way I do. That's all. Can we just leave it?"

"There's always more to it than that," she pushes, not dropping the subject. "Men just need a bit more of a shove than women do."

"I don't think that's the problem," I sigh.

"Then what is?" she asks. "I've never met the guy, but from what you've told me, he's just a hard shell to break. The typical fear of commitment and inability to open up type of guy."

"That's an understatement." A heavy one.

"He makes you happy though, right? I've seen it. It's been *nice* to see it. Really nice."

It's been nice to be happy. Refreshing, almost. But that's done, and I'm going to be happy again. Just in a different way. I don't need anyone to make me happy. Just myself.

"I can make myself happy," I reply confidently, nodding to myself and smiling slightly when I see the airport standing in front of the rising sun.

"I have no doubt about that. But maybe don't give up on him yet. He could always surprise you."

"Yeah, okay," I agree half-heartedly, my attention resting mostly on the excitement and nervousness I feel as we pull up to the drop-off lane in front of the airport. Butterflies swarm in my stomach, forcing me to swallow nervously. It's now or never.

As soon as the car comes to a stop in the drop off line, I'm hopping out and moving to the back. Pulling open the trunk, I collect my bags before dropping them on the pavement and turning to see Clare standing off to the side. My heart lurches when I see the unshed tears in her eyes, hiding behind the pride I see there as well.

"I'm so proud of you, Sierra. Don't forget that. And don't

forget to come visit us sometime. This will always be your home," she says, voice wavering.

I move to hug her quickly, wrapping her up tightly and nodding into her sweater. "I love you so much. I'll come back as soon as I can, and we'll Facetime every single day," I whisper, sucking back my sniffle.

She pushes me back but keeps a firm grip on my shoulders as she says, "I love you too. Now go get 'em!"

I nod quickly, smiling for real this time before grabbing bags and heading to the sliding doors, not daring to look back and risk changing my mind.

35

Braden

"THERE'S STILL TIME TO STAY HERE," I MUTTER, DROPPING A newspaper-covered plate into a small moving box.

Dad's scowl is immediate as he rolls his eyes and continues folding fuzzy pink towels before packing them away neatly. "You don't have to help me. Tyler and Gracie could have."

"And miss out on this amazing bonding time? Yeah right."

My attitude has only gotten worse the longer I've been at my father's house, but as much as I'm dying to get the hell out of here and drown my feelings in whiskey, I would regret not spending every chance I have left with him. God knows I only have a few chances left before he runs away with his child bride.

"Attitude like yours is meant for a teenager, Braden. Not a grown-ass man."

"Don't lecture me, Dad." My shoulders tense and I place the glass I'm holding inside the box harder than I probably should have. Lucky for me, it doesn't break.

"If you want to act like a kid then I'm going to treat you like one." He lifts a shoulder, sending me a fleeting look. "Can't you just drop it for a few hours?"

"Yeah," I grumble, leaving it at that. I don't have anything else to add. If he wants me to pretend that I'm okay with him leaving then he's being an even bigger idiot than usual. I'll never be okay with this.

"Do you want to talk about how you're feeling? Will that help? I'm ready to do just about anything so we can move forward. This is exhausting, Son," he sighs, shoulders sagging in defeat. "You don't have to like the idea, but I would appreciate it if you would just accept it and stop being such an ass about it so we can all move on. Lana isn't going anywhere."

"Right," I chortle.

"What?" he asks, brows lifted with an unspoken warning. "Spit it out."

I lean forward on the leather couch and grip my knees, meeting his pointed look with my own. "You expect me to believe that this marriage will be any different than your last one? You and Mom couldn't even make yours work and you had a little kid to think about. Not like that made a difference. You both dragged me into the middle of your gigantic shit storm instead of making it work."

The shock that crosses my dad's face nearly makes me proud, but I shrug away the feeling before it has a chance to fester.

"We never meant to drag you into anything," he whispers, eyes dropping to his sock-covered feet.

"Well, you did. Over and over again until Mom took off to travel the fucking world. Neither of you cared enough to hide your problems from me, and now you want me to believe that you'll be able to actually keep this one around?" I ignore the hurt in his eyes and continue, the built-up feelings crashing into me like a wave that I can't hold back. "I love you, Dad, but you both fucked up. And you fucked *me* up."

"If this is about Sierra, there's still ti—"

"No, there's not still time!" I'm shouting now, my skin burning under my fingertips when I rub my jaw and stand up. "She's gone and it's your fault! If my idea of love hadn't been so fucked up, maybe I wouldn't have let her leave me. Maybe I could have said it back instead of letting my fear destroy us! You should have seen her face. I *can't* stop seeing it."

"Braden," he chokes out, my name sounding muffled. "We never meant for you to carry our problems with you. If I could go back and change how we acted, I would have. You didn't deserve to witness that. Especially not at such a young age." .

"Well, there is no going back. It's too late. It's too late for everything."

My hands slide in my hair, yanking on it in an attempt to distract myself from the burning in my chest, a feeling I never used to be used to, but have quickly grown to hate. I've been sucking these words in for years, way too many years. They keep sliding out like my tongue is covered in soap, and as hard as I try to feel guilty for saying them, I'm not.

"Your mom and I weren't meant to be together, Braden. We were just too young and naïve to realize that. We ignored the red flags, and we paid the price—*you* paid the price. That doesn't mean that you and Sierra would have made the same mistakes we did. You can't let that ruin your happiness," he says gently, standing in front of me now, sunken eyes dull and glossy.

"The way you light up when you see each other and grin until your cheeks hurt, that's how you know you have some-thing special. Please don't give that up. Especially not because of your mother and me," he continues.

I squeeze my eyes shut and sigh heavily. "I love her, Dad. I love her more than I thought I could love anything or anyone and I hate it. I fucking hate knowing that to be with her, I have to give her the power to hurt me. How is that fair? How am I supposed to want to do that?"

"Nobody wants to give somebody else power over them. But we do it because we would rather have them for a short time than never at all. That's what you want, isn't it? To at least have the chance at real happiness with her? Even if it doesn't last forever?"

Is that what I want? Are a few more weeks, months, or even years with her worth the chance of it crashing down on top of us? By the way my stomach lurches as I ask myself that question, I think I know the answer already.

"What if she doesn't want me anymore? I wouldn't even be able to leave here for a few weeks. There's too much to do." I swallow, nerves starting to coat my skin.

"I don't think you have to worry about that," he chuckles. "As far as arrangements go, I know that Tyler wouldn't mind helping you. He acts like he owns the gym anyway. I'm sure he would love to be the real one in charge for a change. You can figure out the rest *after* you go tell her how you feel. The last thing you want is her boarding that plane thinking that your balls aren't in her carry-on."

A rough laugh tears up my throat before I look at the grandfather clock pushed to the corner of the living room and feel my mouth fall. Her plane leaves in an hour. She has to be at the airport already. "I'm not the guy that runs through an airport to make some intense, movie-worthy love confession, Dad."

He grips my shoulder in a tight grip and squeezes, staring at me with a look so intense my eyes widen. "Tough shit, Son. Today, that's exactly what you are."

My heart pounds against my rib cage, adrenaline beginning to burn beneath my skin. "Look," I say guardedly. "About what I said before—"

"Don't apologize," he cuts me off, voice heavy with authority. "You should never have had to feel like that in the first place. I'm sorry."

"I know. It's okay." I let my lips lift somewhat before I'm pulled into a rare hug. I know that the awkwardness I feel is shared between the two of us, but I try to ignore it and enjoy the moment.

"Okay." He clears his throat. "Now let me drive you to the airport so you can go get your girl."

My smile grows into a full-fledged grin as I nod twice and straighten my back with a new-found sense of confidence. It feels like I can breathe again, my head clear and body at the ready. There's a glimmer of hope in the horizon, one that I can almost taste.

It won't be easy, I know that. But I have to hope that she'll at least hear me out and understand where I was coming from. I still can't promise her forever, or that I'll be completely confident in handing her the reins and letting her lead me through the unknown, but she already owns me in a way that terrifies me the shit out of me. Why not offer her my heart on a silver fucking platter while I'm at it?

I look at my dad and say, "Let's go."

CAR HORNS BLARE and police lights reflect off the glass windows of the building beside us. My legs shake, my hands balled into fists on my lap. I try Sierra's cell phone again and get her voicemail. I hang up without leaving a message, not trusting myself not to blurt out that I love her. She's not going to find out how I feel through a voicemail, that's for fucking sure.

"Can you not get around them?" I snap at Dad, unable to keep my calm.

"No." He's frustrated, like me. The four-car pile-up ahead has the entire highway backed up. We haven't moved in twenty minutes.

With the car in park and the knowledge that there's no way of getting out of here anytime soon, I push open the passenger door and get out. I face the car and slam my palms on the roof hard enough for the sound to echo through the street.

"Fuck!" I shout, feeling the weight of the past week fall heavy on my shoulders, threatening to crush me like a bug under a boot. I welcome the feeling, knowing that all of this is my fault, my doing.

If I had just let the past go and focused on the future I could have had with Sierra, none of this would have ever fucking happened. We would be on that plane together right now, her head on my shoulder, my arm slung around her. I wouldn't be here, in the middle of the highway, banging my fists on the roof of a car and shouting like a maniac.

She left thinking I thought so little of her. Thinking that she was just some woman I chose at a bar to keep my bed warm until I found something better. But there is nobody better for me than my little fighter. The woman with all the answers all the time, a witty sense of humour that keeps my heart thumping and my dick hard, and a drive for success that has me wanting to do and *be* better.

She excites me, tortures me, and pisses me off like nobody I've ever met. We're such opposites that to most people, we don't look like we would work. But we do. We really do. Our chemistry is beyond anything that I've felt with anyone else. We fit together like we were made to do so, and just the thought of never having her in my arms again has my chest feeling so tight that every breath I take is like tiny razor blades tearing through my lungs.

I feel a hand on my back and flinch, tensing my body like I'm attempting to protect it from an outside invasion, as if the real monsters weren't already inside.

"You should call Sophie," Dad says behind me.

I nod, feeling too numb to do anything else. Sierra's gone, her plane already boarded and getting ready for takeoff. I only had an hour to get to her, and we've been stuck here for too long.

My cellphone is placed in my hand and I call Sierra's best

friend. She answers after the first ring, alarm evident in her voice.

"Braden? What's wrong?"

"I was too late."

The seconds pass slowly as she breathes heavily into the phone. When she finally speaks, I almost fall to my knees.

"No, you weren't. I'm going to help you fix this."

EPILOGUE
THREE WEEKS LATER

Sierra

"See you tomorrow, Sierra!"

Spinning on my heel, I stop and throw a wave at our sweet-as-honey receptionist, my lips forming a genuine smile.

"Have a good night, Gretchen," I reply, laughing lightly when she throws me a wink and nods, her tightly bound red curls bouncing around her head.

I've grown to care for the outgoing red-head over the past three weeks. It's been seriously hard not to. Her charismatic energy and warm smile always give me the warm and fuzzies. It's also been awesome having someone to talk about TV dramas with on slow days. It helps with how much I miss Sophie and my sister.

With a pep in my step, I pull my knee-length coat tighter across my chest and continue walking through the office building, giving the security guard a smile when he pushes open the door for me.

The smell of fresh garlic bread makes my mouth water the second my heels connect with the pavement, courtesy of the small Mom and Pop Italian restaurant a few buildings down. As if on a timer, my stomach growls, reminding me that I forgot to plan dinner tonight. I groan, fully aware of the extra weight I've packed on since moving to Toronto.

Pizza again it is. Or maybe Chinese. Eh, either work. *Stay focused, Sierra.*

There's still no snow on the ground yet and the temperature isn't too low, so I can still walk to and from work without getting too cold. I'm grateful for the moderate weather. I can't even imagine the nightmare it would be trying to find parking outside of our downtown office every morning. Plus, I really like walking to and from work. It gives me some much-needed time to relax after a busy day.

The only downside to walking everywhere every day is having the giant Toronto crowds of businessmen and women, bikers, and impatient teens all trying to do the same thing, pushing past you as if you're invisible. Which I guess to them, you are. It's not always so bad, but some days I think I might prefer the struggle of trying to find a parking stall. Emphasis on *some days.*

A grateful smile pulls on my slightly wind-bitten cheeks when I come up to the obscenely tall, forty-story condominium. I fiddle with the keyring in the pocket of my jacket, pulling out my fob and unlocking the doors before walking inside.

After greeting the concierge, I get into the empty elevator, and lean my head against the wall, closing my eyes as exhaustion washes over me. The ride up to my floor is a lengthy one, and I sometimes debate whether or not a power nap on the way could be warranted. The idea is quickly shot down when I imagine stopping to pick someone up on the way and being seen with drool running down my jaw.

My phone starts vibrating in my pocket, and my heart soars when I pull it out and see Sophie's name flashing across the screen.

"Hello, gorgeous," I sing. It's only been two days since I've spoken to my best friend, but in my opinion, that's two days too long. It's been hard adjusting to the distance, especially when I first moved here, but every day gets a bit easier.

"Hey, baby cakes. Did I catch you at an alright time? Are you on your way home?"

"Yep. I'm in the elevator. I'm surprised there's enough service here to talk, actually."

She laughs, the sound awfully nostalgic. "That's what you get when your rent is more than what I make in a month."

"How is work going? Have the kids driven you insane yet?"

A week after I left, Sophie got a job teaching kindergarten at her old elementary school. The previous teacher had quit midway through October, and they had been in the middle of looking for a replacement when Sophie's resume came up. This is the first steady job that she's had since we graduated, and I couldn't be happier for her.

"I had one kid throw a used Kleenex at me yesterday, but other than that it's been really great."

"Good, Soph. That's *really* good." I toy with the ends of my hair. "Have you seen Clayton lately?"

She sucks in a sharp breath. "Yeah. But what you really want to know is if I've seen his roommate, right?"

I chew on the inside of my cheek. Yeah, that's exactly what I want to know. But I don't ever ask directly. Just the sound of his name has tears welling in my eyes. Even after not seeing him for three weeks, his name remains branded in my soul.

"I haven't seen him in a week, S. Clay told me that he moved out of the apartment."

I stand still, frozen in time. I hate the way my heartbeat skyrockets, imagining all the reasons as to why he would have done that. But I shut down all of the what ifs before they grow into something too big and hopeful.

"Oh," I mutter, watching each floor the elevator passes light up in front of me.

Several voices are muffled through the phone before Sophie rambles, "I'm sorry to cut our convo short but I have to go! Call me soon! Love you." she hangs up before I answer her.

The dull sound of the dial tone leaves a bad taste in my mouth. Her swift dismissal after dropping such a bomb on me confuses and hurts me at the same time. It's not like Sophie to leave like that.

A few seconds later the familiar *ding* rings through the air and I hurry through the opening metal doors. The entire journey toward my condo is spent avoiding my thoughts and picking at the skin beside my nails to keep busy. It's a quick walk, but when I reach the door, it feels like I've been walking forever.

As soon as I slide my key into the lock on my door, I freeze, my mouth dry. A bright blue sticky note is stuck above the gold-plated numbers on the center of the door. My eyes remain scarily wide as I read the sloppy writing scrawled across the paper.

> *There's no me without you anymore baby. I'm sorry it took me so long to realize that. Meet me on the roof. I know that you know how to get there. Blame Sophie. I'll see you soon.*
> *P.S if you forgot about me in the past 3 weeks, I'll spank your ass so hard you won't be able to sit for another 3.*

I hadn't even realized that my hands had begun to shake until I lift one to my lips. Shock, fear, anger, and happiness are among the feelings racing through my veins as I re-read the note, not believing that he could be here. Especially not for me. Not after this long.

I knew that he tried calling me the day that I left, but when he didn't leave even a single message, I assumed they were an accident. He never called again, so neither did I. I learned to wake up every day and accept that we were over, as best as I could. I never thought that there was even the slightest chance that he was thinking about me, let alone planning on coming here.

I have no idea what to do. Do I go? Do I stay?

Shit, it shouldn't be this complicated. My chest is pounding and my stomach feels like it could fall to the carpet at any second. Oh, fuck it. I won't be able to forgive myself if I don't at least go and see what he has to say.

I pull the note from my door and slide it into my pocket before heading toward the maintenance door a few doors down. Yeah, it's kind of weird that I found myself compelled to open a maintenance room door one day, but I was bored and when I found out what it led to, I was happy that I did. If I hadn't snooped, I wouldn't have figured out that it was really only there to hide a stairwell that takes you up to the roof of the building.

The view is incredible. You can see the entire city. It's become my secret spot where I can go to simply hide from the world. But tonight, it's the place where I can finally get the closure that I've been needing.

I get to the door at that top of the stairs way faster than I expected. And now that I'm here, I want to puke, nerves unlike any I've ever known spearing through me. With a deep, shuddered breath, I grip the door handle and twist, half expecting it to be locked and for this to be some cruel prank.

I toy with the buttons on my jacket before opening the door and stepping outside. The wind nips my cheeks as I search for him, my knees threatening to buckle at what I find.

My lungs give out and I gasp for a lifeline, tears blurring my eyes. I stare at the several strings of fairy lights strung from the tall poles scattered along the roof, and the thick flannel blanket resting a few feet in front of me, covered in an array of pizza boxes and tin containers like they're the most beautiful things I've ever seen.

But then I see him—leaning back against the railing, hands shoved in the pockets of a tight pair of blue jeans, and that signature, cocky grin pulling at the dimples in his cheeks —and nearly jolt back at the pressure that builds in my chest.

My battered heart calls out for him, beating against my rib cage like maybe he'll be able to hear it and come running. Warmth flows through me like molasses, emotion clogging my throat.

I take a step forward, and then another, and when he opens his arms out in front of him, staring at me like he loves me, I'm running, colliding with his chest as the dam crumbles and the tears begin to fall.

"Hey there, my little fighter."

This is not The End.

TAMING THE PLAYER . . .

It was only supposed to be one night. But one night turned into two, and before they knew it, those two nights became every night.

Sierra thought that she had it all figured out. Back before Braden started throwing wrenches in her perfect plans and inserting himself into parts of her life that he had no business being involved in. With that familiar, arrogant grin, he dug himself under her skin too far to be pulled out. But that was before he let her go. Before he broke whatever they had spent months building together.

Braden wasn't expecting to fall in love with her. And he *definitely* wasn't expecting to sit back and let her move across the country without him, heartbroken and alone. Now she's gone, and Braden has some making up to do.

Three weeks later, Sierra has thrown herself back into her work, trying to forget about him. She didn't think that she would see him again, let alone find him waiting for her on the roof of her new apartment. But there he is, and he wants a second chance. He wants to *start over*.

Is it possible for a broken heart to ever fully heal? And if it can, will it ever grow to be as strong? With their future a giant question mark, can they make it work this time?

AVAILABLE NOW.

Thank you so much for reading Craving the Player!

If you enjoyed Braden and Sierra's story, please consider leaving a review on Amazon or goodreads. Reviews help authors more than you know!

Join my Facebook group, Hannah's Hottie's, and rant with all of my other amazing readers who also couldn't believe that I had the nerve to leave this book on a cliffhanger. Oops.

Interested to learn how Gracie and Tyler met and fell in love? Or want to get a glimpse at Braden back in his college days, playing hockey alongside the famous Oakley Hutton? Check out my new-adult, hockey romance series!

The Swift Hat-Trick Trilogy

Lucky Hit — Oakley and Ava
Between Periods
Blissful Hook — Tyler and Gracie
Vital Blindside — Adam and Scarlett

Acknowledgements

I don't even know where to start with this because there are far too many people that I need to thank. This is my third novel that I have written in the span of two years, which may not seem like a lot to some people, but it really does feel like such an accomplishment.

I am so blessed to have such an amazing team of people that I can rely on for each release, and who make my job that much better.

First and foremost, my fiancé, Mitch, thank you for being such a rock for me during the few intense months that it took for me to write this novel. I love you, and appreciate your never-ending fountain of support.

Mary, I don't even have the words to use to explain how much I appreciate you and everything you've done for my books. Thank you for creating such beauty.

My street team, beta team, and ARC readers, you might not think that your job is that important in the grand scheme of things, but there are truly no words for how much you help and for how happy I am to have y'all in my corner.

And to my readers, I LOVE YOU. Every book you buy, person you recommend me to, or personal message that you send to me makes all of this so worth it. I'm beyond grateful for each and every one of you.

About The Author

Hannah is a twenty-something-year-old indie author, mom, and wife from Canada. Obsessed with swoon-worthy romance, she decided to take a leap and try her hand at creating stories that will have you fanning your face and giggling in the most embarrassing way possible. Hopefully, that's exactly what her stories have done!

Hannah loves to hear from her readers, and can be reached on any of her social media accounts.

Facebook reader Group : Hannah's Hotties
Instagram : Hannahcowanauthor
Website: hannahcowanauthor.com

Made in the USA
Coppell, TX
03 September 2024

36754224R00174